A Perfect Souvenir

A Perfect Souvenir

STORIES ABOUT

FROM THE
FLANNERY O'CONNOR AWARD
FOR SHORT FICTION

EDITED BY
ETHAN LAUGHMAN

THE UNIVERSITY OF GEORGIA PRESS
ATHENS

Athens, Georgia 30602
www.ugapress.org

Designed by Kaelin Chappell Broaddus
Set in 9/13.5 Walbaum by Kaelin Chappell Broaddus

Most University of Georgia Press titles are
available from popular e-book vendors.

Printed digitally

Library of Congress Control Number: 2020940174
ISBN: 9780820358420 (pbk.: alk. paper)
ISBN: 9780820358437 (ebook)

CONTENTS

ACKNOWLEDGMENTS

The stories in this volume are from the following award-winning collections published by the University of Georgia Press:

Mary Hood, *How Far She Went* (1984)

Susan Neville, *The Invention of Flight* (1984)

Sandra Thompson, *Close-Ups* (1984)

Daniel Curley, *Living with Snakes* (1985)

Melissa Pritchard, *Spirit Seizures* (1987); "Disturbing No One" first appeared in the *Greensboro Review*

Gail Galloway Adams, *The Purchase of Order* (1988)

Philip F. Deaver, *Silent Retreats* (1988)

Dennis Hathaway, *The Consequences of Desire* (1992)

Dianne Nelson Oberhansly, *A Brief History of Male Nudes in America* (1993)

Peter LaSalle, *Tell Borges If You See Him* (2007); "The Cities He Would Never Be Sure Of" first appeared in *Euphony*

Margot Singer, *The Pale of Settlement* (2007); "Borderland" first appeared in the *Gettysburg Review*

Anne Panning, *Super America* (2007)

Geoffrey Becker, *Black Elvis* (2009); "Jimi Hendrix, Bluegrass Star" first appeared in *Prarie Schooner*

Lori Ostlund, *The Bigness of the World* (2009); "Idyllic Little Bali" first appeared in *Prarie Schooner*

E. J. Levy, *Love, in Theory* (2012); "Theory of the Leisure Class" first appeared in the *Paris Review*

Tom Kealey, *Thieves I've Known* (2013); "From Bremerton" first appeared in *Ascent*

A thank you also goes to the University of Georgia Main Library staff for technical support in preparing the stories for publication.

INTRODUCTION

The Flannery O'Connor Award for Short Fiction was established in 1981 by Paul Zimmer, then the director of the University of Georgia Press, and press acquisitions editor Charles East. East would serve as the first series editor, judging the competition and selecting two collections to publish each year. The inaugural volumes in the series, *Evening Out* by David Walton and *From the Bottom Up* by Leigh Allison Wilson, appeared in 1983 to critical acclaim. Nancy Zafris (herself a Flannery O'Connor Award winner for the 1990 collection *The People I Know*) was the second series editor, serving in the role from 2008 to 2015. Zafris was succeeded by Lee K. Abbott in 2016, and Roxane Gay then assumed the role, choosing award winners beginning in 2019. Competition for the award has become an important proving ground for writers, and the press has published seventy-four volumes to date, helping to showcase talent and sustain interest in the short story form. These volumes together feature approximately eight hundred stories by authors who are based in all regions of the country and even internationally. It has been my pleasure to have read each and every one.

The idea of undertaking a project that could honor the diversity of the series' stories but also present them in a unified way had been hanging around the press for a few years. What occurred to us first, and what remained the most appealing approach, was to pull the hundreds of stories out of their current packages—volumes of collected stories by individual authors—

and regroup them by common themes or subjects. After finishing my editorial internship at the press, I was brought on to the project and began to sort the stories into specific thematic categories. What followed was a deep dive into the award and its history and a gratifying acquaintance with the many authors whose works constitute the award's legacy.

Anthologies are not new to the series. A tenth-anniversary collection, published in 1993, showcased one story from each of the volumes published in the award's first decade. A similar collection appeared in 1998, the fifteenth year of the series. In 2013, the year of the series' thirtieth anniversary, the press published two volumes modeled after the tenth- and fifteenth-anniversary volumes. These anthologies together included one story from each of the fifty-five collections published up to that point. One of the 2013 volumes represented the series' early years, under the editorship of Charles East. The other showcased the editorship of Nancy Zafris. In a nod to the times, both thirtieth-anniversary anthologies appeared in e-book form only.

The present project is wholly different in both concept and scale. The press plans to republish more than five hundred stories in more than forty volumes, each focusing on a specific theme—from love to food to homecoming and homesickness. Each volume will aim to collect exemplary treatments of its theme, but with enough variety to give an overview of what the series is about. The stories inside paint a colorful picture that includes the varied perspectives multiple authors can have on a single theme.

Each volume, no matter its focus, includes the work of authors whose stories celebrate the variety of short fiction styles and subjects to be found across the history of the award. Just as Flannery O'Connor is more than just a southern writer, the University of Georgia Press, by any number of measures, has been more than a regional publisher for some time. As the first series editor, Charles East, happily reported in his anthology of the O'Connor Award stories, the award "managed to escape [the] pitfall" of becoming a regional stereotype. When Paul Zimmer established the award he named it after Flannery O'Connor as the writer who best embodied the possibilities of the short-story form. In addition, O'Connor, with her connections to the south and readership across the globe, spoke to the ambitions of the press at a time when it was poised to ramp up both the number and scope of its annual title output. The O'Connor name has always been a help in keeping the series a place where writers strive to be published and where readers and critics look for quality short fiction.

The award has indeed become an internationally recognized institution. The seventy-seven (and counting) Flannery O'Connor Award authors come from all parts of the United States and abroad. They have lived in Arizona, Arkansas, California, Colorado, Georgia, Indiana, Maryland, Massachusetts, Texas, Utah, Washington, Canada, Iran, England, and elsewhere. Some have written novels. Most have published stories in a variety of literary quarterlies and popular magazines. They have been awarded numerous fellowships and prizes. They are world-travelers, lecturers, poets, columnists, editors, and screenwriters.

There are risks in the thematic approach we are taking with these anthologies, and we hope that readers will not take our editorial approach as an attempt to draw a circle around certain aspects of a story or in any way close off possibilities for interpretation. Great stories don't have to resolve anything, be set any particular time nor place, or be written in any one way. Great stories don't have to *be* anything. Still, when a story resonates with enough readers in a certain way, it is safe to say that it has spoken to us meaningfully about, for instance, love, death, and certain concerns, issues, pleasures, or life events.

We at the press had our own ideas about how the stories might be gathered, but we were careful to get author input on the process. The process of categorizing their work was not easy for any of them. Some truly agonized. Having their input was invaluable; having their trust was humbling. The goal of this project is to faithfully represent these stories despite the fact that they have been pulled from their original collections and are now bedmates with stories from a range of authors taken from diverse contexts. Also, just because a single story is included in a particular volume does not mean that that volume is the only place that story could have comfortably been placed. For example, "Sawtelle," from Dennis Hathaway's *The Consequences of Desire*, tells the story of a subcontractor in duress when he finds out his partner is the victim of an extramarital affair. We have included it in the volume of stories about love, but it could have been included in those on work, friends, and immigration without seeming out of place.

In *Creating Flannery O'Connor*, Daniel Moran writes that O'Connor first mentioned her infatuation with peacocks in her essay "Living with a Peacock" (later republished as "King of the Birds"). Since the essay's appearance, O'Connor has been linked with imagery derived from the bird's distinctive feathers and silhouette by a proliferation of critics and admirers, and one can now hardly find an O'Connor publication that does not depict or refer to her "favorite fowl" and its association with immortality and layers of symbolic and personal meaning. As Moran notes, "Combining elements of her life on a farm, her religious themes, personal eccentricities, and outsider status, the peacock has proved the perfect icon for O'Connor's readers, critics, and biographers, a form of reputation-shorthand that has only grown more ubiquitous over time."

We are pleased to offer these anthologies as another way of continuing Flannery O'Connor's legacy. Since its conception, almost forty years' worth of enthralling, imaginative, and thought-provoking fiction has been published under the name of the Flannery O'Connor Award. The award is just one way that we hope to continue the conversation about O'Connor and her legacy while also circulating and sharing recent authors' work among readers throughout the world.

It is perhaps unprecedented for such a long-standing short fiction award series to republish its works in the manner we are going about it. The idea for the project may be unconventional, but it draws on an established institution—the horn-of-plenty that constitutes the Flannery O'Connor Award series backlist—that is still going strong at the threshold of its fortieth year. I am in equal parts intimidated and honored to present you with what I consider to be these exemplars of the Flannery O'Connor Award. Each story speaks to the theme uniquely. Some of these stories were chosen for their experimental nature, others for their unique take on the theme, and still others for exhibiting matchlessness in voice, character, place, time, plot, relevance, humor, timelessness, perspective, or any of the thousand other metrics by which one may measure a piece of literature.

But enough from me. Let the stories speak for themselves.

ETHAN LAUGHMAN

A Perfect Souvenir

The Cities He Would Never Be Sure Of

PETER LASALLE

From *Tell Borges If You See Him* (2007)

I. REBUILT LE HAVRE

It seemed that with Le Havre he had taken a long day trip there from Paris.

Sometimes all of that would be more than clear to Reynolds, and there was buying the ticket at Gare St-Lazare in the winter morning, after the weekday's rush, and there was the orange and white coach gliding out of the clutter of the city, the dingy factories and freight yards under a bulging purple sky that held just about as much the promise of rain as the promise of sunshine, not uncommon for that pocket of northern Europe. Reynolds had his seat in the coach to himself, and soon the train was winding along the rails as bright as liquid mercury in those low hills that were the valley of the Seine proper.

Then there were woods, and then there was that stretch of the automobile industry somehow nestled quietly amid the green hills, and as the train got closer to Rouen, there were genuine gold cliffs sparkling—the sunshine had scattered the dark clouds—even little islands in the wide river too. Reynolds, granting he was a businessman and a representative of the large New York investment bank he worked for, had always had a fondness for literature, ever since he had majored in that at the somewhat famous little liberal arts college in Ohio back in the sixties; why, while in Paris on a previous business stay he had made the pilgrimage to Rouen to retrace the steps of Emma Bovary there. And on this trip, concerning this one time he might have been to Le Havre, he looked down from the silver trestle that the train now crossed as it approached Rouen, and he wondered if nearby, possibly on one of those islands below, was where Flaubert had had the house, the family's country place that eventually became his residence. Reynolds remembered once reading in a biography that despite Flaubert's own noble pose as the recluse artist, he did for a while spend about half of his year in Paris, hobnobbing with high society indeed, and then half here; he was renowned enough in France that guides on Seine passenger boats would point out the house as a landmark, as Flaubert, in his robe, would do them the favor of waving back with an arm-arcing greeting if he happened to be out on the balcony. However, this time Reynolds didn't even get out of the train at Rouen.

He simply waited in the coach for the change of engines there, and, yes, it must have been a Wednesday, because the schoolkids were out early, and outside the city again the local train made several stops for them, a glorified school bus of sorts. Reynolds liked the noisy confusion of the kids with their rosy cheeks and their worn satchels, and when the last of them was gone into the streets of a tiny village of no particular consequence, it seemed that now he had the entire coach to himself, the two elderly women up front sitting far enough away from him to qualify as truly distant. (How Reynolds wished that his longtime lover and companion, Jimmy, were still alive, and with Jimmy somehow being the practical one—even in his lifelong gofer's job, really, there at the Museum of Modern Art—Reynolds could simply have said, "Jimmy, you're good at these things—I mean, I must have been in Le Havre, no?") The tracks were away from the river now, inland, and there was that ragged beauty to the tumble-down farmhouses, the absolutely too-green fields of winter alfalfa, the black-and-white Holsteins puffing their steamy breath into the afternoon's thin sunshine, all of it reminding Reynolds of ramshackle Vermont, another place of a beauty that was maybe amplified by the "hungriness" that seemed to define it.

The train arrived at Le Havre not long after two, and what Le Havre was—as opposed to what Le Havre had once been—struck him as soon as he stepped down the coach's steel steps and onto the platform of the station and its rails dead-ending there. Because, of course, Reynolds knew that Le Havre was a completely rebuilt city, reconstructed after the bombing by both the Nazis and Allies nearly a half century before, but now, on the other hand, he wasn't ready for the sheer impact of such rebuilding. Starting with the train terminal and right into the grid of streets of the relatively small city, it was all poured concrete gone to a lusterless dun in the weathering, with boxlike two- and three-story buildings designed by an architect more important to some than even Le Corbusier at the time, the Belgian Perret. Obviously, he believed in an utter Cartesian functionalism, as interrupted here and there by inlays in the concrete of little ceramic tile squares or stripes, orange or blue or very bright green; the inlays were chipped and crumbling, had also had a tough time of it in the gull-squealing oceanside air. The overall effect was bleak beyond anything that even a grim Belgian could have envisioned, but like that last stretch of farmland before arriving in the city, it offered a particular attraction in its shabbiness, here the hopefully futuristic that, well, didn't work out quite right over time. Which somehow made one notice more how the matching concrete central church—the cathedral?—at least still offered a towering symbolic steeple, and how along the docks of the protected harbor, the traditional café furniture out on the sidewalk (imitation wicker chairs and small frilled cast-iron tables topped with false marble) tried to make these concrete cafés in midafternoon look exactly like what they were—French cafés, almost quaint. No, there weren't many other people on the streets as Reynolds strolled around, just the occasional lump of a figure in a winter coat slow-moving along. The afternoon sunlight had intensified, now honeyish in the unexpected slight warmth, the seaweed aroma of the air itself was cut nicely by a tinge of the freighters' oily fuel; the gulls sighingly cried louder as they swooped, glided, and swooped some more, perhaps celebrating the good luck of a touch of weather like this when it should have been drizzling and cold, marveling about it to each other.

A strange city, all right, of so much dirty poured concrete and so much blue, blue sky, if, in fact, Reynolds had been there that afternoon. He seemed to remember walking down to the beach that was more gray stones than sand; he lingered in a café by the docks, had a *pain au chocolat* and a *double express*, overhearing two gruff stevedores, maybe, at an adjoining table talk about somebody's wronged sister-in-law.

He returned to the station at about four, and with the darkness coming early, Reynolds's gaze was soon but a reflection in the tinted glass of the deserted coach's window for the entire few hours back to Paris and Gare St-Lazare.

II. HYDERABAD BEFORE THE MONSOON SEASON

Because with Hyderabad, the other city he wasn't quite sure of, he thought that maybe that was exactly when he had gone there—in the true scorching of late May, before the monsoons, the time of such oppressive heat that even the bank he worked for had told him he could postpone whatever business that had to be done in Bombay and New Delhi until the following winter. Yes, on that one trip to India he had managed to take side trips to Agra, of course, and then to Mysore to see the nearby temples in the south, but the way he remembered Hyderabad it somehow wasn't a side trip at all. (Jimmy finally had to be moved to the hospice out in Queens. From the start, Reynolds had sworn to himself that he would never let Jimmy end up in a hospice, that he and Jimmy had been together too long for that, though he knew that he, Reynolds, was pressing it with the bank in Manhattan to take even the two months away from his job, as he had done at first after Jimmy himself could no longer work, and the following year there had been the continual nightmare of so-called assisted living caregivers from the various agencies, which seemed to almost screen applicants for what appeared to be the two important prerequisites for the job: unreliability and surliness. Not that Jimmy ever complained. And Reynolds would come into the room at the hospice to find Jimmy excitedly just having to show Reynolds something he had read in the current issue of *ArtForum*, or Jimmy saying that he was quite concerned, not about his own condition, but about that of some mustached skinny college-age boy suffering the illness in Room 21 or Room 23, so young, who had taken a turn for the worse; the boy had been coughing a kind of cough that Jimmy didn't like the sound of in the least—also, the boy's latest cell count tests, Jimmy had heard from an LPN, were more than horrible.) In Hyderabad Reynolds had met with the usual contingent of government finance types and too-happy engineers in what passed for private industry in India, India sometimes seeming like a massive repository for too-happy engineers, and there was the usual dinner after that in the freezingly air-conditioned restaurant of a hotel. But, again, that could have been somewhere else, because those restaurants in such hotels were inevitably the same, the Indians at the dinner joking with him about how Americans just had to have their purified mineral water, and assuring him, too, that he would indeed enjoy the show of traditional dancing to drums and sitar later in the hotel lounge—packaged tourist entertainment, in fact, that Reynolds never enjoyed. However, if he had been in Hyderabad—and sometimes he was very sure of it, in those moments when you drift toward velvet sleep and you catalog all the places where you have been, or when you wake up a couple of hours later in the darkness and say to yourself, whispering and half aloud, "Hyderabad, no, Hyderabad wasn't a dream at all, not at all"—if he had been there, he apparently took an extra day after the bank's business was finished. And in the heat that everybody had warned him about, the centigrade degrees that translated in Fahrenheit to a hundred and then some, he walked about the city on his own in the afternoon.

Actually, the heat didn't bother him, because before the onslaught of the bucketing monsoons, it was a dry heat, the fragrant desert something of Arizona, let's say, that couldn't be camouflaged even by the aroma of spicy Indian cooking everywhere, along with that of rank open sewage, the smell that was India and that you got used to, nearly appreciated, after a while. To be frank, he was often more than sure of having been there, as he pictured himself in his slacks and washing-softened plaid shirt, certainly his sturdy Adidas, wandering through the ancient market bazaar that felt like a medina, because Hyderabad, smack in the middle of Hindu India, was itself a decidedly Muslim city, ruled until quite recently by the powerful Nizams. And in this medina the black and yellow auto-rickshaws—just ordinary motorbikes with a passenger compartment rigged to the back—buzzed through the din of beggars and ox carts and businessmen in shirtsleeves shoving this way and that, and Reynolds explored the alleys and their cluttered shops; the jewelry for which the city had once been famous remained a staple, it seemed. And then he spotted the giant mosque, reportedly one of the very largest in the world, an imposing pale-pink stone rise right out of a dream as well, with spires and domes and a main minaret, plus—Reynolds pictured this clearly—some kind of complicated, sagging wire netting suspended on what looked like wooden telephone poles high above the tiled concourse leading to it, a blanketing against the city's ubiquitous big crows, possibly.

Men were removing their shoes, placing them in a little roped-off rectangle, then continuing on with the veritable trek of several hundred feet across the red tiles to the dim, onion-arched entrance to the mosque itself; the entrance was easily a few stories high. A ragged little boy, serious, was in charge of guarding the shoes, and Reynolds didn't even give it a second thought. The boy nodded to him, such liquid black eyes, very serious, and Reynolds nodded back.

Reynolds lifted the daypack from his shoulder; he jack-knifed his body to reach down and loosen the new white leather Adidas with their three green stripes on the side. Reynolds handed the boy the shoes. And Reynolds headed on the trek across the concourse himself, looking back once to try a smile on the boy who remained stone-faced as ever, now with a long pole in his hands for moving around and arranging the spread-out footwear—a suitable protector, all right, for the Shoes of the Faithful. True, it could have actually been a mosque he had visited in another city, and the whole idea of one of the largest mosques in the world being not in an absolutely Muslim country but in India was as strange a premise as finding perhaps the most architecturally ugly of all cities, Le Havre, in that most handsome of all countries, France. Nevertheless, Reynolds just walked in his stocking feet over the sun-warmed tiles along with the other men who were slowly heading that way, most in robes and embroidered caps (poor Jimmy, his beloved art books now forgotten), Reynolds just kept continuing on and on as if it were something that he was near programmed to do ("I still have no sense it happened to me," Jimmy once said from his cranked-up hospital bed in the last days, "despite all the percentages and the odds one way or another, everything they tell you, I still have no sense of it whatsoever"), Reynolds just adjusted the strap of the nylon backpack on his shoulder a bit, wiped his forehead with the flat of his hand, and entered through the front portal of the looming edifice, if, again, he had been there.

Reynolds just continued on into the cavernous, big-pillared darkness, so wonderfully cool. A mosque could always be so interesting, he told himself.

Disturbing No One

MELISSA PRITCHARD

From *Spirit Seizures* (1987)

Elsa Wagner navigated, leaving her feverish wake among the brightly preserved, gamy corpses of Rome, while her mother, a cloth laid over her eyes and ankles elevated, napped. She took a complicated series of buses to San Pietro in Vincoli to view *Moses* and the chains which had bound St. Peter. Elsa went in and out of dank, aphotic churches as quickly as if they were shops which did not carry the brand she insisted on.

Ingrid Toller was not unaware that her forty-two-year-old daughter, still handsome, and brainy in that unsensible way of aesthetes, was afflicted by a recurrent spiritual palsy, yet she had no clue as to the wild oscillations Elsa was beginning to make between the charged field of eroticism and the flat line of morbidity. While Mrs. Toller dozed in her silk slip, with instructions for the front desk to ring at four-thirty, her daughter dragged the stuff of her unlived selves like some bluish caul over the sundry, worn-down sights of Rome.

Ingrid and Elsa had toured what was mandatory: Vatican, Colosseum, Pantheon, Fountain of Trevi, Piazzas di Spagna, Navona. Elsa was patient as her mother bought up silk scarves, leather handbags, perfumes, glassware, giving over currency with the floppy ease that overlies deep wells of vaulted cash. At outdoor cafés they compressed enthusiasms upon the white backs of postcards, Elsa addressing the *Pietà* to her husband, and *Venus Rising from the Sea* to each of her two high-school-aged sons. Weakening to her own mischief at one point, Ingrid sent picture postcards of Pope Paul VI to her husband and friends, saying Rome's male escort service was an awful letdown.

Ingrid Toller gave off a ruddy, hot look of boiled crustacean. She wore Lilly Pulitzer skirts with turtles or whales or frogs all over them; her purses were varnished tackle baskets trimmed with lime or raspberry grosgrain. She had no eye for understating herself. When she spoke, her red, freckly arms waved about, segmented like a lobster's; in repose, her face resembled a balloon left behind the couch for a week. Her toes hurt; she could never find the perfect triple A, and she referred to her deadpan feet as drudgesome things, relations she could not shake off, literally, but owed something to.

As if in compensation, Elsa was tall, uncomplaining, subtly, classily pale, with blunt shoulder-length khaki hair. She ordered conservative pieces from the Talbot's catalogues, organized her wardrobe around taupe and wine, navy and camel. Elsa was visual understatement itself.

Their first afternoon in Rome, Elsa lay down, but her mother's stertorous bulk in the opposite bed was so vexing she put her low-heeled shoes back on, left a note, and exited their quiet hotel, her purse strapped across her chest to discourage thieves.

On her walk Elsa came upon the notorious ossuary of Capuchin monks. After paying a small fee, she was directed down a hall of gray stone with open chambers along its left flank. Each of the dozen or so chambers overflowed with a promiscuous jumble of bones. Skeletons of forty thousand Capuchin monks from the fourteenth to the nineteenth centuries, dismantled and re-set into primitive mosaics . . . jumbles and whorls of thigh bones, mushroom-cap skulls, hips like bruised gardenia petals, all this grim handiwork with monks' bones. And beneath glass, upon purple tasseled cushions, lodged the blackened clumps of human hearts.

"Excuse me. Is there more?" At her question, a monk whose oyster-colored face seemed pried from between its flanges of brown cowl, pointed to the wall opposite the souvenir shop. There was a large sign on its otherwise blank expanse, the words repeated in a dozen languages:

Once We Were Like You.
One Day You Will Be
Like Us.

Over dinner at La Rampa, Ingrid decided that Elsa had displayed something less than good taste, staying in such a grisly place, much less inquiring to see more.

"Religion, taken too far," she said, "turns people fanatic, Elsa. And fanatics have *no* aesthetic sense. It creates a vicious half-circle."

"Yes, Mother, but fanatics are the only ones not washed away by time. Excessive temperaments stand out in history. In order to hold the attention of future generations, you need to murder enormous numbers of people. Order a Colosseum made on the flayed backs of slaves. Be Michelangelo. Be a genius with ego and say no to the Pope. Be the Pope. Behave as if magnified a thousand times over."

"You are saying only the most flagrant action endures?"

"It's what interests us, isn't it? We carry guidebooks, buy maps which lead us to the results of excess. The distance of history morally numbs us to the acts of Caesar; he ends up impressing us."

Ingrid wasn't listening, she was over-paying a gypsy girl for two long-stem roses. She turned back brightly to Elsa.

"I'm going to have the penne alla vodka; our waiter recommends it. And for you, Elsa dear, two Roman roses . . . because I'm so pleased we could chuck our boys for a bit, have this adventure to ourselves."

Rome's buses were claustrophobic tumbrels whose passengers were stacked and flung like rendered sheep. Elsa, her hand gripping a chrome bar, was pressed against a variety of bodies, but determined to find her way, without taxi, to San Pietro in Vincoli. All at once she felt a subtle, deliberate push against her backside. Through the thin, expensive challis of her Talbot's skirt, she felt the bulgy gob of a penis nudge between her buttocks. She thought of a cigar, dropped between the raised lips of an ashtray. Then she thought, this must be a mistake, an absentmindedness on somebody's part. She could not bring herself to turn and look at her assailant, but at the next stop, as more people plunged onto the bus, Elsa shifted and repositioned herself. And though she had moved, she felt it again, the unmistakable plug of a half-erect penis. Such mean anonymity, when she was wedged in and could not possibly move. At the next stop, Elsa fought her way out, trembling, to the sidewalk. She hiked up a number of hills, narrowing like steep perspectives, until she reached the yellow church which held Michelangelo's Moses and St. Peter's chains.

Elsa did not pray in these churches she invaded. She tried in the first, but it was a costive, puny effort. When walking past the skeletons of monks, Elsa may have aimed for some form of spiritual reverie, but really, what she mourned was the slippage of her own life, the piecemeal loss of her looks. Women did not bother with her face anymore, though they glanced appraisingly at the expense and quality of her clothing. Older, fastidious men eyed her not with the lust she might have liked, but with admiration and guarded potency.

She walked, arriving late at their hotel. Ingrid, in a geranium-splashed dress, sat in a blue striped chair in the lobby, chatting with an attorney and his wife from Ohio. God, her mother could and did talk to anyone.

At dinner, as Elsa described her public assault, Ingrid's sympathy was curbed. "Money, Elsa, serves in part to elevate you above such experiences. It isn't sensible, risking insult in that way. Taking the public bus invites danger. It's nearly as bad as walking alone at night, for heaven's sake."

On their last full day in Rome, Mrs. Toller and her daughter returned to the Vatican. Elsa skimmed the artwork, keeping a distracted eye out for Mother Teresa, whom their concierge had claimed was in Rome. Going into a pink marble chapel, Elsa saw four nuns in pale blue saris. A sign said Service for World Peace. One of the shrouded figures praying aloud in Hindi was Mother Teresa, Elsa was convinced, yet the nuns' faces were swallowed in the fluted lips of saris. Was it a sign she should recognize, that she and Mother Teresa were here at the same time? Elsa tried diligently to pray for world peace.

Ingrid was not enamored of the Polish nun. Wasn't she, as a wife and mother, in involuntary servitude, a sad result of sexist distortions? Only now, with her children grown, her husband's fortune secure, could she pursue or identify her own interests. Mother Teresa, with her conservative exhortations to women, hardly seemed in step. It was saintly enough, this work with the dying, the poor. But, Ingrid complained, leave us modern, ordinary women alone.

As Elsa's religious self surfaced, nourished in the potent, etherous Catholicism of Rome, so did its surprise twin, lust. Hitting hardest, this free-floating lust, in hotel rooms. The sensuality of dimmed, vacated space, the dominant placement of beds where nothing personal existed, no familiar imprint to blunt the raw edge. The man on the bus, pressing himself against her, she wanted his sort of sex in the blank chilly caves of hotel rooms.

Of course, when her mother stepped into those places, all was immediately spoiled. Lights were flicked on, suitcases snapped open, the business of hanging clothing, placing out cosmetics, things strewn and piled about, banal conversation, all went into smashing Elsa's erotic, broody state of mind. It was in those purer moments, when she was given a key to inspect the room, or when her mother stepped out for something or took a long, quiet bath . . .

Throughout her adult life, Elsa had avoided scandal. Had never been sexually indiscreet. Had earned that worldly benefit of morality, an untarnished social prestige. Deliberately, she had undermined her interest in men, certainly in sex. Now, in Rome, and why she couldn't say, Elsa Wagner was being made physically weak by the sight of male bodies. She craved passing men the way her mother coveted expensive objects behind shop windows. Very young men drew her eye, which shamed her. Was it Rome, its decadent remnants, its lavish, undraped statuary? Its young men? (Repeatedly, she fixed on languid Raphael types, elongated feminine faces, greyhound leanness of limb, repelled by the bluntheaded types, who brought to mind bullish emperors stamped onto rough coins.)

Only in churches, among corpses of saints, among Americans earnestly examining history as it collapsed about them, and with so little discrimination that as a national group they looked exhausted and peevish (did they seek, with her, some common shelter?) . . . only in the dark sleep of churches could Elsa dodge her own alarming appetites.

On the train (because Elsa wanted this last-minute detour, hoping Assisi, clean, as a place of pilgrimage, might somehow help), Ingrid hardly bothered looking out the window of their first-class compartment. She circled her puffy ankles, leaned her head into moss velvet upholstery, shut her eyes.

"So, Elsa, what was your impression of the Eternal City?"

Picking my way across a sprawl of corpse, scuttling over its clefts of rot, feasting on its huge, graying bloat . . .

"It was more beautiful than I expected, Mother."

Elsa was looking at the countryside. Pink chips of houses, tiled roofs, ivy-green shutters. Vineyards, vegetable plots, chicken coops. Acres of blackened sunflowers, uncut, heads like scorched, bent spoons. She had no idea why they were like that.

She saw two big women, tamped down into heavy skirts, bursting from blouses, red kerchiefs on their ball-like heads, heaving things up from the soil. Roots, cabbages? She wanted to show these Brueghel-like creatures to her mother, but the drawback to rapid travel was everything slewing past before you could elaborate or confirm. You could say lamely, "I saw the most amazing thing just now," but it would be like a botched punch line.

By late afternoon they'd come to the walled hill town of Assisi. Ingrid settled at an outdoor café with her bar of chocolate and an English newspaper, scanning headlines about a second terrorist bombing on the train run from Rome to Florence. Elsa, starting with the two highest-rated hotels, worked her way down, finally finding a vacant room above a trattoria for eight dollars. Taking a key up the pinched, turning stairs, she unlocked the door and met with a room so frugal it physically pained her. A crucifix hung between thin, lumpy beds no better than cots. Her erotic impulses must have been some aberration of Rome, some side effect not uncommon to travelers temporarily unspoused.

She experienced little in this room but relief.

Elsa scrunched down so that she could lie in the high-shouldered, basin-sized tub and turn the waxy pages of a little booklet about St. Francis. Clammy, toadish water belled over her stomach. When she came out from the tiny bathroom, her mother was folded on her side as though she were an amulet carefully stored in a box. Elsa felt a chest-clot of affection for her mother. Shopkeepers adored her. So did hotel people. She lightened their monotonous work, was generous, garrulous with them. Unlike Elsa, embedded in peculiar solitude, the sort of tourist who gets under the skin of sales and hotel people. The type aching to understand humanity but buying nothing.

Ingrid had been resilient about their sparse room. "This will be good for us. Absolutely appropriate, to deprive ourselves in the village of a saint. A lovely idea, Elsa." She pronounced Assisi charming, naif, was already plotting which native potteries to buy. She would purchase a dozen at least of the smaller size rooster pitchers. Grand bridge and hostess gifts.

One night's self-denial had tested Ingrid and Elsa sufficiently. By early morning they were seated on an elegant terrace of the Subasio Hotel, paying twice what their night's lodging had cost for bread and pots of bitter coffee.

Elsa devised the day's excursion. Ingrid should see the Basilica of San Francisco, but briefly; overlong exposure to miracles, saints, blown-up virtue of any sort would make her mother restive, damp her enjoyment. Elsa would go on alone to the Church of Santa Chiara, walk the path down to the Convent of San Damiano. They would meet for lunch, pack, then catch the bus down to the station in Santa Maria degli Angeli. Leave on the four o'clock train for Venice.

At clipped pace they toured the Basilica, its upper and lower churches, the saint's crypt, the Sienese frescoes. The Giotto frescoes. They stood before Francis's sandals, his robe, a note he had scrawled to a close friend, Brother Elia. In this presence of saint's things, Elsa felt visceral shiftings, like the subtle swim of geographic plates. She believed the life of Francis, like that of Mother Teresa, was the truest life; her own, a job lot of overlapping loyalties, fickle intent, her convictions diluted by what surrounded and seemed to most need her. She lacked the will to act without compromise.

Elsa persisted, walking through the village, to the Church of Santa Chiara, climbing downstairs to the vault she had read about in the bathtub, to see the body of St. Claire, face upwards, hands stiffened in prayer, and, like Snow White, set into a crystal coffin. This grotesque, mummified remain, on its mattress of gold, had established the sister order to Francis's little brothers. Poor Claires, wasn't that it? In nun's habit, black netting propped over the carious black face as if to keep pieces from flying upwards . . . Elsa shuddered, went upstairs to a side chapel, looked at the painted cross that had spoken to Francis.

GO FRANCIS, AND REPAIR MY CHURCH,
WHICH, AS YOU SEE, IS FALLING INTO RUIN.

Elsa needed to repair herself, reduce her own selfishness, join a lay order of some sort, adopt a child from Nicaragua or Cambodia. Humanitarian intentions pelted through her. But her family, what would they think? Surely they would tease or object. Turning to leave, Elsa saw an area screened off by an elaborate grillwork. She went over to it, looked in, saw a woman's red cloak, a Bible, various personal articles on display. Seated on a diminutive chair, in the midst of these relics, a child-sized nun rose up fluid as air, came to stand before her. Will you hear the story of our Santa Chiara? Elsa nodded. The nun's voice was intimate and empty, her face veiled once by cloth and masked once again behind iron grillwork. She spoke in hypnotic, accented English about the merchant's daughter with golden hair, gesturing to a shank of saint's hair, pinned blatant and worldly to the otherwise bare wall. A young woman giving up wealth and social position to live out the ideals of her childhood companion, Francis. Elsa suspected the nun of rubbing the truth from this fairy tale. The stem of red-gold curling hair cried false from its wall. This tale of virtue was fabrication. Claire and Francis had obviously been in love. When Francis, swarmed upon by God, renounced earthly longings, including Claire, she said that if he would have God Alone, then so would she. So. The romance had been plucked from this story. Any fool could guess how Francis had kissed Claire, how they met by night in the olive groves . . . how Claire must have raised their illegitimate child within the cloister. Elsa was feeling giddy. The nun stopped, sat down until the next tourist appeared and she could float, wraithlike, up to the grill.

Elsa took the sloping footpath down through dusty olive orchards, hundreds of dwarfed knotty trees with coarse grass spiking around their bases. She toured Claire's convent, San Damiano. The rooms were shrunken, had the wet smell of unlit stone. The touted frugality seemed sensual to Elsa. Most rooms had tiny windows, and out those windows, like cut jewels, flashed gold fields, hillsides, deep sky, the dark scatter of birds.

. . . Droning at her, these gray humps of stone, the bulk and heft of timbers. The refrectory was cramped. She hiked back up the footpath, entered the cobbled village, out of breath, extremely hungry, light-headed.

And found her mother easily, spotted the bright whaleprint skirt. Standing with a pair of shopkeepers who had the look of people clobbered by good luck. She must have bought out their roosters.

Elsa stopped, bought postcards, then, strangely fascinated, watched Ingrid. Her mother took prescribed pills at mealtime. She grew short of breath. One day Ingrid Toller would be rived from her money, from the shops in which to spend it, would be moved quietly, with tasteful ceremony, onto the topmost layer of human history. A smear of topsoil upon fathoms of humus. Then it would be Elsa's turn. Both of them taken into the earth, breathed in, like billions before them.

One Day You Will Be
Like Us.

Elsa stood in the street, under the hot Italian sun, stripped, dizzied, thinking what she needed was food. Thinking how silly, this early grief.

She walked, wanting to catch up with her mother, unsure how to present this awkward, unchanged baggage, herself. Departing life bit by bit. Holding the pendulum's staff, death the steady swing. This person who would never define herself further than her own death. Still lovely, the flesh, thoughts, and instincts of Elsa Wagner, though in fewer and fewer lights could any of them sustain inspection.

Oh! What a source of cohesion and cowardice,
family bonds!

"Mother! My God, what have you bought now? I'm absolutely starved. I could eat a Roman cat. Where shall we go?"

"I just asked the darling people at the shop back there. They recommend this little place, out of the way, very untouristy. And we shouldn't miss the veal."

Mrs. Toller and her daughter asked directions and before long were conversing through a superb lunch, served in a walled garden, anticipating the next step of their trip through Italy. Venice.

Dutifully they wrote their postcards, Elsa with this doggish sense of betrayal (to that spectral self folding and unfolding out of darkened, tenebrous churches?), as she wrote:

> *Assisi a charming village, home of*
> *St. Francis . . . you remember, dears,*
> *the saint wearing birds on his shoulders*
> *and squirrels for slippers? Always my*
> *favorite saint. Grandma and I off to*
> *Venice. Home in ten days. Time flies.*
> *Miss you all. Love, Mother*

With trained, conscientious habit, Elsa thus bent her head to her task, at once tightening and submitting to the family bond.

Disturbing no one.

Rapture

SUSAN NEVILLE

From *The Invention of Flight* (1984)

All that Illinois winter she'd been afraid of a coming ice age and now here they were where the last one hadn't touched, where dinosaurs had fled and shrunk in the comfort, the ease of the life, to ruby-throated lizards which skittered across sidewalks, where prehistoric birds dove at the water for fish and plants looked like ancient and protective clusters of swords. She sits here now, in a fresh early-morning restaurant behind a glass wall looking out on the Gulf, on a small peninsula so she can watch the sun rising higher on the water as if she is in Mexico, not Florida. With clear lime water glasses on the tables, oranges in baskets and some on the ground outside rotting, dolphins arcing through the water, and white birds and sails both the transparency and lightness of communion wafers on the tongue, she feels something rising in her, an excitement, a joy in her that is almost difficult to contain. In Illinois the colors had been drab—wheat colors, dirt colors; here they are outrageous reds, greens, yellows. And here the warm air and moisture bathe her, close in around her like a pot so she feels, strangely, aware that she lives. (Her first memory involves water, warm air, and this same feeling. They're by a lake, her mother and father and she. The air that day was greenish-gold, mid-summer, a pleasant lake smell of rotting weeds, still water, and gasoline. Her mother had on a black one-piece suit and the legs cut into her thighs and her arms were round and her skin was blue-white. Her father stood in the water by a motorboat and tried to start the engine, but it kept dying. Later they would get it going and he would give her a ride around the lake, and that was exciting and full of action and she remembers the texture of her father's bare knees and the sticky smell of plastic seats and cool water, but that isn't her first memory, her first memory is the moment right before the engine starts, and it felt, and still feels, like before that she was unconscious and she chose that moment to wake up.)

When the waitress comes, her husband orders coffee, eggs, fresh-squeezed juice, a newspaper. She sees Eggs Benedict on the menu, something she's never had. When it comes and there's a slice of orange and a stalk of asparagus alongside, she feels dizzy from the happiness, as though the orange and the asparagus are signs, another symptom of the goodness here. She tries to explain this to the waitress and to her husband, and they smile at her, her husband turning slowly to his paper, the waitress no doubt thinking she's a tourist, giddy from the climate. She leans back in her chair, rubs her hands over her bare arms, and thinks no, I live here now, this is my home, cold weather will not touch me, nor the cold seasons of the heart. She drinks her coffee, watches a tree full of wild parakeets outside the window, the silver watch on her husband's left arm, his cheekbones tensing and relaxing as he reads. Last night they had gone outside, around midnight, and gone swimming in the warm water of the Gulf. They had gone far enough away from shore that it felt as though there were only water and sky, both the same shade of blue-black, and holding onto one another, treading water and looking up at the stars, both of them had the same sensation, as though they were swimming through space, like a dream of falling and there's no end to it, but a safe, euphoric falling, like flying. She reaches over now and touches his hand, asks him if it hadn't been wonderful, swimming in the Gulf at night, and he puts the paper down, apologizes for not paying enough attention to her. He says he'll be sorry when his job starts next week, that he might get too tired for a while to do anything like swimming at night, and she says she can't imagine that it could really be like any job he's been used to, not here. He laughs, and they begin to eat. My eggs taste like lemon, she says, sweet lemon. (Days before she had, automatically, tried to remember what she needed to be worrying about, a holdover from the way she used to feel, and she had found that there was nothing, nothing she was worried about. She'd even begun to forget old worries—the dreariness of Illinois, problems as a child—and could remember only the good times, the comfortable times, as though she had taken thread and made a stitch in every pleasant memory she had and drawn them together with the dark places hidden in folds, gone. And she herself is expanding, infinitely, a balloon that is not brittle, that will not break.)

As usual, he finishes eating before she does and sits drinking coffee and pointing out articles in the paper. There are new color photographs in here of Venus, he says. He shows them to her. The joy rises and settles in her chest like something tangible. She feels that she could run, climb mountains, and still it wouldn't be released. How amazing that those colors have been there all along, she says, and no one to see them. Yes, he says, amazing. He says that he might get a telescope, that he might make astronomy a hobby. He had never talked about hobbies in the North, had been so involved in his work there. She touches his hand again, knows she can't begin to explain how wonderful his saying that makes her feel. She turns to watch a dolphin, eats a piece of toast, and listens while he calmly talks about theories of the edge of space, the birth and eventual death of the sun, colliding galaxies, in between sips of coffee. Many scientists now think, he says, that the universe is expanding and will some day fall back into a cosmic egg and then explode again into a new one, will pulsate, which makes time stretch infinitely and allows cataclysmic things to happen, as they do biologically, which we can understand, but only so long in the future that it doesn't concern us and helps us feel less responsible. Some theories, he says, are more reassuring than others. She nods, smiles, thinks that sounds as logical as Superman and the planet Krypton and other science fiction, wonders if she plants a poinsettia now if it will bloom this Christmas, wonders when their grapefruit tree will bear fruit that she can pick in the mornings with a wicker cesta. She can find the Big Dipper and the North Star, and she saw them last night and she's seen them in Illinois, and the Indians saw them, and the Greeks saw them, and that's what she knows about stars. She reaches for her coffee, knocks over her water glass, the water darkening the cloth on the table. She takes the chipped ice in her hands, puts it in the glass, says just the same, tell me it isn't true, what you said, about galaxies colliding, the universe erased and redrawn. It isn't true, he says, laughing. Thank you, she says, I knew it couldn't be, and she looks out at the water, the palm trees, a blue heron walking like a cat. She wonders how he can so calmly think about such terrifying things when they're so happy here, and safe.

The waitress brings a basket of small pastries shaped like sand dollars, places it on their table, fills their cups with coffee. They both lean back in their chairs. Her husband looks calm, thoughtful. The cookies taste like anise. She breaks one in half to look for the doves that real sand dollars have in the center, but the baker hasn't put them in. She thinks that she would like to open a bakery herself and make sand dollar cookies with sugar doves in the center. People would bite into them, unsuspecting, and discover the candies, and in that way she could, possibly, begin to communicate the joy that she feels now. Her arms feel good to her, the soft cotton of her dress, the sandals on her feet, her hair, the way the edge of the tablecloth brushes her knees, the bitter taste of the coffee, the gritty texture of the cookie in her hand, the hardness of her husband's legs, his arms, the soft hollows at the base of his neck, beneath his cheekbones; all of these things are good. We'll swim or fish all afternoon, she thinks, watch the pelicans dive for fish while we eat dinner on the beach, and swim again at midnight.

The check comes and her husband pays it. I drank too much coffee, she says as they leave the restaurant, I feel like I've been drinking ether. Outside it is hot already, this early in the day. Everything shimmers. This is heaven, she says. I want to stop in the bait shop next door, he says, so we can fish this afternoon.

The bait shop is a shack, gray weathered wood, filled with plastic lures and the smell of shrimp and glass cases of fileting knives. Thousands of hooks tangle and gleam on the walls. She looks at her reflection in the glass cases, notices that she is smiling and that she doesn't stop. Two men come into the shop. They look alike—short unruly beards, sunbleached hair, leathery skin, sandals, cutoff shorts, T-shirts. They smell like gasoline, the smell of her father's outboard motor that day on the lake, her awakening, all her life, she thinks, comes to this slow awakening. She stares at the hooks on the wall while her husband buys shrimp. She holds onto his arm for balance. Water from his shrimp bucket sloshes onto her hand and she brings her hand to her nose, breathes deeply, to calm herself, the happiness becoming too great somehow, too large. Her husband takes her hand, but he's talking to one of the fishermen about the fishing that day, the good spots, the best type of bait. The other man shows her husband a shark's tooth on a chain around his neck, talks about shark fishing, how a shark had taken the leg of his brother when he was snorkeling in the Keys and how he and his brother try to kill as many of them as they can now, how they take the teeth and give them away as gifts. She looks at the tooth lying on his neck, bleached and white as milk glass. She tries to be frightened of it, to imagine it coming after her, after her husband, but she can't, doesn't believe in it. The man tells her husband that if he'd like to go shark fishing with them sometime to leave a message at the bait shop in the morning and her husband says yes, he'd like that, and asks what time they usually go out, and the man says at night of course, at midnight, that's when all the man-eating fish—the sharks, the smiling barracudas, but the sharks especially—come in near shore. They're hidden by the black water then, he says, but the water is thick with them. Wherever you throw in bait, he says, especially around here, you'll find a shark. Her husband thanks the man, holds onto her as they leave, tighter than he's ever held her, thinking no doubt of their swimming the night before, of the plans they'd had to swim again. She holds his waist as they walk to the car. He is pale but she is ecstatic, thinking only that they had made it through the danger, that last night they'd been swimming in sharks, swimming in them. That what she'd thought was the current brushing her legs could have been the smooth body of a shark, the smooth caress of a tooth, a fin. And her head back, her arm feeling the warmth of her husband, the world pulsing and glowing from the sun, something leaps up in her, finally, like a blind fish that rises and breaks through dark water for one, brief, clean taste of air.

The Purchase of Order

GAIL GALLOWAY ADAMS

From *The Purchase of Order* (1988)

Lou Maxey is hanging over the top of the seat, her behind a likely target. She's slipped her pink plastic shoes half off and they dangle like loose skin. There are rustling sounds from the back.

"What in the hell are you doing?" Marlon asks, pushing in the cigarette lighter, which he has to lean around her in order to do.

"I'm looking for that package of Cheese Nuggets I packed in here. I'm hungry."

"We just had breakfast less than an hour ago," he says around his light-up. "You had the Trencherman. You couldn't be hungry."

She looks back over her shoulder, tries to lift her foot up and sideways to jog his knee; it's impossible, so she bumps his shoulder with her rear. "How do you know? You're not me. And I'm hungry."

Lou is one of those little women who never look any older than about sixteen until you're close up. Her hair is crisp and close and dark and her eyes are the brown of spaniels'. She's had five kids, four in the first six years of marriage, and then a decade's wait before her baby Jason, now in the Navy on a ship anchored off Greece. Lou likes to think of her baby in the Mediterranean, near the place and the myth he was named for, and how apt the name she chose. Although there are lots of Jasons now, there weren't many then, and her boy, with his curly golden hair, thick and spongy as sheep wool on his arms and chest, was like a fleecy thing. "It looks like Santa's beard's on his legs," a little cousin said once at the beach.

You could never imagine your own children making love, Lou thought. She could never imagine anyone making love, but she could picture a dark Grecian girl with red ribbons in her hair cradling against Jason's chest. Marlon's body hair was different. It was rusty and tufty with a strange patch on the left chest. He had smooth upper arms that were furred like pelts from elbow to wrist. Everything about the man amazed her, and they'd been married almost thirty years.

Last night at the motel while she watched *The Sting* on TV, Marlon, feet crossed precisely one on top of the other in a wedge, read the local paper, which he always did wherever they stopped. "Guess who this sounds like," he said, reading a letter to the editor from a man who complained about the sewer lines, the garbage pick-up, and the planting of iris bulbs in front of City Hall. "'And in conclusion . . .'" Marlon pulled the sentence out. "'City Council should get going or get out.'"

Lou, who'd only half-listened from the second tirade on, said, "That's your mamma all over, Marlon."

He smiled, shook the paper back into creases, and settled in to reading the classifieds while she got up, one eye on the TV show, and wandered over to the window, which was oddly high, partly blocked by an air-conditioning unit.

"'Two bedroom house for $195,'" Marlon read. "That's not bad." She mmmed that she heard, but mainly was looking for something, anything previous guests might have left behind. Once she'd found a bookmark, navy leather stamped with gold designs, tucked into the Gideon. Another time a little girl's hairbow, fashioned into a rose with a frill of plastic lace. Lou collected such things as souvenirs. She liked to own matchbooks that she found under beds in which she and many others had slept.

Marlon had finished reading, was watching the movie with a bemused expression.

"What part's that?" She bent over him and without a word he flipped her over on her back and splattered his mouth against her stomach. She pushed at his head, saying, "Don't, no, stop, don't you dare," and then Marlon went from splatting to pink belly, and while she giggled and shoved him away, shouting for Robert Redford to save her, she was excited by the sound of his hands patting her stomach, moving fast up and down her flesh.

This summer's trip is following a pattern set ten years ago. The Maxeys hop into their van aiming to just go. That first day when Marlon drove it home, Lou walked around and around it, thinking it was as big as a bus. Marlon scraped off the manufacturer's name, KING OF THE ROAD, saying, "That makes me sick. I'll choose my own name." Then he left the space bare, tacky with a residue of stickiness that collects insects and dust. A decade later KI and RD still show like lines in the wax of a magic slate.

This summer, like all before, they'll travel anywhere and everywhere they want, not a plan in their heads, except to follow their own feelings. "What will be, will be" is the Maxeys' motto on these trips, but truth to tell, Lou does worry and marks the maps and schedules the stops so they can visit with all their kids and grandchildren. After Labor Day, when families leave the road to see to purchases of new notebooks and underwear, they turn back too, clean up their van, and park it to the side of the bungalow near Austin where they've decided to spend the rest of their lives.

Lou calls her friends, goes to the YWCA for her Jane Fonda exercise class, and twice weekly puts on her crinolines and she and Marlon go to the Square Dance Club. "No ties, not even string ones" was the deal before he'd go. She loves the way he looks standing across from her in the square, wearing his plaid blue shirt with pearl buttons, open at the collar, jeans turned up in a pale roll, and boots, cut-under heels marking up the gym floor. When the caller does his do-si-do, Marlon moves his nose sideways, lets his eyelids droop in a criminal manner, and swings circle-box-circle until she's his, caught at the waist. Even when these evenings make her ache and soak her feet, see them peel in a pan of Epsom salts, she loves it. She feels exactly as she did when she first met Marlon, then married him, against everybody's will.

Early in their marriage, when he'd lost his job, the one he quit high school for, a restlessness set in in him. She'd be at work, a half-day job her daddy got her at a plate glass company doing bills, and in the afternoons stuffing burgers into bags, when she'd look up to catch Marlon whisking out of sight. Sometimes, later in the day, he'd come to get a roast beef that had got cold. "Can't stick around," he'd say. "Got to see a man."

Sometimes he'd borrow a dollar, or pat her on the belly where the baby now was. They didn't talk much about the baby; somehow she knew it made Marlon too sad. Only at night in bed in the trailer, where the neighbors slammed their glass louvered doors so hard the foundation shook, Lou'd scoot up against him, feeling the swell of their baby between, and she knew how Marlon felt. "Wasn't supposed to be this way," he whispered, turning to embrace her. The baby's bulk pushed him to the wall as she felt the corners of her mouth tingling at the touch of his lips.

Near when the baby was due Lou began to worry about what would happen, how they'd work things out. She'd catch herself sitting at her desk at Mitchell's Glass having stapled the same bill twice. She found it harder and harder to force a smile for customers. The smell of onion and grease at her afternoon job seemed never to leave her. She was constantly figuring out schedules, adding sums in her head even as she sprinkled grated cheese on the taco special.

"I've got a job," Marlon told her when he popped up at the Burger 52 one day right after lunch and was persuaded to sit down and have a cherry coke and onion rings. Everyone liked Marlon. He was even-tempered, told good stories, and he worked hard: it's just there had to be work to do.

"Where is this job?" asked the other hop, whose boyfriend had got the boot a few weeks before Marlon. "In Alaska?"

Marlon looked up, winked, held an onion like a ring over his finger and said, "Yes." Everyone laughed but Lou; she knew Marlon never kidded about change. He ate that ring, finished his coke, and, pointing his finger at her like a gun, said, "Later."

That's how they ended up in a van with a three-week-old baby girl and some household goods, driving to this promised land where Marlon worked construction and Lou watched babies, her own among them, and all they made went for food and rent. The sunsets hung red for hours, it seemed, teasing them with the thought of dark, and Marlon wasn't happy. Evenings he'd sit in front of the television after the baby was in bed and hold his knees, shoving the heel of his hand like gunning a car, fast, faster, staring straight ahead and clenching his jaws.

One night when he came home Lou was nursing the baby, both curled up in a corner of the couch. He sat down on the coffee table facing her, clasping his hands like being good at school; then he leaned his chin against his steepled thumbs.

"Do you want me to rub your neck?" she asked.

He raised his head and his eyes looked swimmy, even though he was smiling. "I've got another job, babe. On the coast, doing something. Don't know what, but I'll guarantee you it'll be dirty and dangerous." He tapped Lou's chin with his fist, gently pulled the baby's hair. Lou was pregnant again, bigger this time, with things going strange. Her ankles swelled straight to her knees, turning white and crackly like old china plates. Marlon would pop her toes at night, rub warmth into her feet with his hands, which were small for a man's.

They never stopped making love, even when it seemed that everything they did or didn't do led to babies. Their second was born in Louisiana, then another boy in Tampa, then a baby girl born on their way from Arizona to Alabama, and Lou's chief memory of those years is of trying to keep her babies clean, keep them up off floors where who-knew-what had gone on. They lived on a live-in ship, in a one-room kitchenette on the third floor of a beach hotel, and once—she doesn't like to think of it—in the back part of a converted van. Some rainy days during that bad time she would gather her children around to sleep huddled like puppies. They saw a lot of places, and Marlon's excitement about them kept her going.

"Living in a place is not the same as visiting it," he'd said, "because while you get to know the towns better, you know them less." Lou thought that was true. Places were like relatives: somehow the longer you knew one, the less you valued it. Moving off and then coming back for visits let you see all the sweetnesses. She'd picked up Marlon's rhythm by this time and wondered as she wrapped her cups in the Sunday comics, readying for another move, if she could ever go back to one place. She'd met a woman who'd shopped at the same Piggly Wiggly all her life, and Lou marveled at that.

Sometimes the places where they had lived blended into each other, all seeming a dream that held these constants: a laundromat, a convenience store, and a drive-in on the edge of town where she and Marlon would get out to sit on a blanket spread in front of the grille while the children slept on in the back seat, the speakers turned low for their ears. Then sometimes Lou would be struck with a recall of a place so vivid that she thought, If I went back there now, I could find my way around. Sometimes at night, when she couldn't sleep, she played a game with herself. She picked a town they'd lived in and drove around in it in her head. When Marlon heard her muttering, "Turn left for the Dixie Pig," he'd sleepily ask, "Where are you?"

Getting used to change is easy for her now, but it wasn't always. She's happy to think she can adjust, move from place to place, seek out the stores, the banks, and the schools. She liked to get the family settled in and clear a place on the refrigerator for the kids' school work while Marlon went off to all the different jobs that he had.

Whenever she went back to the town Marlon came from she saw the same people walking down the same streets. They'd die in the same frame houses they lived in, she thought. Then she wanted to get in the car and go, drive away with Marlon and the kids to somewhere they'd never lived before.

Each year when they start their trip they have a purpose. It is one that has never been taken out and examined, one that is rarely discussed except in memories that come up—a purpose neither of them really knows how to explain. What moves these summers for the Maxeys is a search that has shaped their lives for the last decade: they are looking for a family they once knew, without whose presence everything in life has been more pale, a family they've continued to think about and talk about. Lamont and Jean Dillon and their kids—when they met them twenty-two years ago in Arkansas, it was one of those meetings between two families where everything hits right and it is forever and always. But in this case, the Maxeys don't know how, it fell away through not keeping in touch, both of them moving on too many times.

When Lou wants to make an event memorable, she ransacks her brain for recollections of the Dillons, especially Lamont in his boneless height. "How he keeps his pants up is a mystery, and I'm married to the man," Jean said, rolling her eyes, always in a laugh putting her left hand up to cover where a tooth was gone, another gone gray. Lamont's back seam fell flat between his thighs.

At various times over the years when Lou has helped her children learn to cut meat, do a chain stitch in crochet, or print between the lines, she's seen Lamont's hands as they shaped a little figure with his knife. Concentrating as solemnly as the child who stood waiting to see what would emerge from between the wood and the blade, he'd roll the scrap of pine in his fingers and seem surprised himself to see it become a donkey or a tiny dancing man. He'd lift up his head and his thick eyebrows, under which his eyes, so light a blue they were almost white, were innocent, and smile a fool's smile, the corners of his mouth pulling up into his cheeks.

"Now lookee here," he'd murmur, balancing the figure in the well of his outstretched hand. "Let me take my payment." The knife blade quickly cut the thinnest lock from the edge of the child's hair; the blade tip near their ears made the older ones shiver, the little ones giggle. "This here's magic hair," he'd say. "Have to add it to my pile."

"If he'd ever get money for those carvings we'd have a dozen pillows stuffed with duck fuzz down, if we wanted them," Jean would complain, then light a Tareyton, pulling in smoke, the cigarette moving from the center of her lip like a dowser's rod in the strength of her inhale. When she wanted to be funny she'd cross her eyes before blowing out the match.

That day in the laundromat Lou couldn't have known that Jean would be any other than the kind of friend you usually make there who helps you fold. Even though Marlon was good with the kids, Lou always took her brood with her; too many things can happen in a trailer court on an off-day when men, in work or out, are drinking beer and fixing cars. One guy with a saucer scar on his shoulder scared the kids by popping out his top three teeth and clanking them up and down. At the laundromat Lou would sit her four down, give them Chocolate Soldiers and Nabs, and buy each of them a comic book. Later, during Dry, Marlon would come to help fold. Sometimes he'd wrap himself like an Arab in a sheet, dancing a mummy's dance, and make everybody in the long linoleumed room laugh.

That's how they first met, Jean with her pile of threadbare

towels and striped Handi-Wipes she used for washrags—that's what she called them instead of washcloths—and all her kids, who made Lou's crazy. But she was such a good-natured lanky girl, so quick to smile at Marlon's silliness, so willing to let the children be lively in their romping around with peanut shell earrings clamped to their lobes, that Lou liked her right away.

Lou was folding diapers when all of a sudden this woman with hair yanked straight back and features looking forward began to help. "These sure are white," she said. "Why don't you use disposables?"

"Can't afford to," Lou answered, wanting to laugh and not knowing why, but knowing right then that this friendship, based from the beginning on knowing everything bad about each other's underwear, would last.

Where y'all staying?" she'd questioned Lou, having said she was Jean Dillon and with a wave of a hand, diaper flapping like a sailor's flag, pointed out her husband Lamont, who was loading a commercial machine with a jumble of goods from towels to blue jeans. Marlon was outside walking all the kids in formation on the parking lot, yelling made-up orders: "Walk on tippy-toes. Now stick out your tongues." The children collapsed on hot tar in giggling heaps.

"My bunch," Jean said, shooing them off, the other hand shaking out a Tareyton. "Maisie, Jasper, Gordon, Ceil, and Autumn Ann. Where'd you stay?" she asked again.

Lou had no choice but to tell her. "We're out at Doakes." She didn't like to be there. It was a rough place. Too many people slept in during the day, and they weren't on the night shifts either.

"Not so good for kids." Jean tongued her cigarette to the side of her mouth, squinted her eyes, and began to fold. "No place to let them run their spirits out."

"I try to get over to the park each day," Lou said.

"Come live by us," Jean offered. "Looks funny from the street—Clark's Courts—but inside it's just the place for kids. I manage there. It's not free, but no more than you're paying at Doakes."

Lou didn't know what to say, looked up at Jean, her lank brown hair wreathed with smoke, her bright blue eyes eager and hopeful. "I'll have to talk to my husband," she said, and right then Marlon burst through the door crying, "Save me. Save me! Please!" holding the plate glass shut against the force of all the sweaty screeching children, pushing and laughing and shoving and shouting out the different sweet treats they wanted. "Stay still!" He mashed a frog face on the glass. "Sit down like sombrero men with your knees drawed up and each and every one of you will get a Fudgsicle." Then he came and stood by Lou and asked, "Who's taking over my diaper duty?"

Jean laughed, then hailed Lamont, who'd been resting, back against the porthole of the big machine, head down, dreaming. "Lamont, come meet these people. I'm getting them to come and live by us."

When Lamont Dillon looked up and smiled, Lou's heart fled out of her and she, who'd never given love to any man but Marlon, knew she loved him; not in the way of Marlon, nor that of her brother who'd died in the war, and for whom she cried for years, waking sometimes in the night, face wet with tears from a dream that he was showing her how to hit a pitch, sock the tetherball and knock it back to him. No, somehow it was as though Lamont Dillon was her, or as if, had she been a man, she'd have been exactly like him. He sauntered toward them, tall, skinny with thick black hair and an eerie half-breed Indian look of dark skin and blue eyes, all of him moving bonelessly and gracefully as he slid his shower shoes along. Lou looked over at Marlon, standing even with Jean's height: both of them looked like lean alley cats, rusty and triangular, emitting energy as they stood. She felt a burning, as if had they joined hands in a ring they'd explode into flames.

"You're at the turpentine camp?" Lamont drawled. His voice was rumbling, deep, almost phony in its bass level.

Marlon was jazzed up; he was joking already as he answered yes.

They moved into Clark's Courts and Lou began to watch Jean Dillon closely for clues on how she lived; usually she let her kids go as wild as her house and the yard. Her kitchen was the kind where a brush filled with hair sits right next to a stick of melted butter; Lou always washed her own cups there. Once when Lou'd spilled a can of corn, Jean said, "Here, let me help you," then proceeded to kick the kernels under the shelf's overhang. She was always saying her kids were up to no good, even as she passed their school pictures around, and they loved her the same way, interrupting as she read her *True Romance*. "What do you want, you dirty bum?" With a long arm she'd grab a boy and kiss him as he squirmed, protested, "Mamma, no." They asked for Nutty Buddy money or a dime for the picture show. Jean always gave it.

They couldn't scare her either. "See here—spiders," said Ceil, a bony-chested ten-year-old with harlequin glasses that were pearl-tipped. "Bet you'd be afraid to touch them," she challenged Jean, who pulled her face all to the center and said, "Oh yeah?" then mounted them on her fingers and displayed them like rings. "Here, kids, Popsicles," she'd shout, or "Root beer floats, everyone." Her children had cavities and scabbed elbows and greasy hair and grayed knees and were totally secure in their parents' love.

Autumn Ann was a foster baby who'd been given them by a cousin to keep for a weekend, then left for a lifetime. Jean lugged her three-year-old weight around, fat diaper perched on a hip, Autumn sagging back like a Siamese twin joined at the waist. "Autumn Ann's like an extra pair of hands, aren't you, honey?" she said, and the little girl reached out for the bananas that were collecting flies in the fruit bowl. That year they'd taken in a little boy named Traveling Apple, born and raised in a veggie commune; he'd turned orange from being fed too many carrots. "Look at this sweet Seville," Jean said, kissing his apricot face.

"He's got a suntan all right," Lamont said and cradled the baby on his chest, the man's neck showing red in a V, the rest of his torso wiry with each muscle as defined as a drawing under his skivvy shirt. "Sleep, little fellow, sleep," he crooned in that deep voice that hummed the air.

One night they danced out on the cracked concrete patio of the courts. Jean tucked her hands into Lamont's back pocket and he wrapped both arms around her shoulders and all the children came running up to hang from their waists and trouble them; they looked like a whirligig that spins, ribbons floating in a circle. Wedged between was Autumn Ann, fat face pressed against their thighs, baby foot on each of their insteps, making them stiff-legged as they box-stepped to "In the Still of the Night." "Sho do, sha debe do," Lamont sang, and Lou, holding her littlest on her lap, legs dangling into the pool, felt the baby's feet kick splashes on her shins. She felt like crying as she watched them dance to Lamont's music. All the kids were giggling, Lou's and Marlon's trying to get in. They insinuated their arms into the circling couple, dragging their feet, acting like flour sacks instead of kids. Lamont and Jean pretended not to notice, kept their eyes closed and looked extra gooey as they staggered this hoopskirt of children around. Marlon sat down beside Lou, put his arm around her, and rubbed the baby's foot. "Why is it," he said, "life makes people so good and treats them so bad?" Lou buried her head in his neck, smelling chlorine on him, loving him as she felt the baby squirm and wiggle to get free.

So on this trip, like all the others since they began their quest, Lou and Marlon followed the fairs and flea markets and asked in each town where it was that people might raise goats or lots of kids, and always got a laugh. They'd gone to each town in a Louisiana parish Lamont once mentioned he lived in, asking if anyone knew them, knew a fine mechanic, a wood-carver named Dillon, and got no answer but no.

On the third week out they decided to lift their spirits by looking for barbecue. Here on the edge of a Louisiana town they saw a place that was exactly what you looked for when you were hungry for good barbecue: a wood shack, discolored by smoke and redolence rising out of the wood, the sky perfumed with the odor of wood chips and vinegar and crisp roasting, and in the yard off to the side, a lean-to with tables and little children climbing on them.

"Let's stop here," Marlon said, pulling in. When they got out, Lou looked down the slight hill and saw a small frame house with a square dirt yard. A woman about her age in a faded blue housedress and slippers down at the back, a coffee-colored woman with fried hair tucked under at the ends, was sweeping down the yard. On the porch sat a tin watering can and at the side a rake.

"I want a chipped pork," Lou said. Then, "I'm going down there." As she half slid down the slope she could see the other woman looking at her. "I'm Lou Maxey, and excuse me, do. It's only I saw this dirt yard and I simply could not go past it, don't you know?" Lou was talking fast to cover up her nervousness and embarrassment, but she knew she couldn't go back. The woman was husky but her face was kind, with a long, full mouth. "I haven't seen a dirt yard in I don't know how long."

"I'm Lacey," the woman said, nodding toward Lou. Her voice was warm.

"Would you? I mean, this is probably going to sound crazy to you—but would you let me rake a little bit with you? I had a friend once . . ." She found herself unable to stop. "Jean Dillon—her Granny in Greensboro, North Carolina, had to have a dirt yard or go crazy."

The woman listened. A smile crimpled her cheeks; she held out the broom, walked back to get the rake.

"It's the oddest thing. Here we are—we're looking for them—the Dillons, trying to figure out where in the world they went to. And I saw this yard. How do folks lose track of things?" Lou's scratching the earth now; it is mostly weeded out and very dry. Lacey sprinkles it to keep the dust down and even, to try and set the pattern.

"Are you putting the arches here?" Lou asks, then feels compelled to explain, "One time—one time we lived together when we were young in this old crummy motel with kitchenettes and cabins," the woman nods, "with all our kids. You notice now how no one has lots of kids anymore? I had four and that was nothing to my grandma. My fifth was too far apart—like an only baby."

"I had six," says Lacey. "Six and one boy killed in the war, four girls."

"Any of them around here?"

"My youngest girl—up there. She runs the barbecue. A good girl. A fine husband. Three grandkids."

"That's nice," Lou says. "So nice to have the kids near. This time I'm telling you about—the time we made us a dirt yard. We made it from scratch. That sounds funny, doesn't it?"

"It does. It does. Usually you just clears them away."

The two women are moving shoulder to shoulder now, walking backward. Lou sweeps the dirt clear and then Lacey pulls in the design, slightly wavy lines that curve around the cement stepping-stones.

One late August day Lou and Jean sat in plastic strap chairs, fannies hitting the ground, watching the kids run dirty circles around the motel compound. Clark's Courts was marked by a line of soot-covered plaster ducks advancing on a three-legged concrete deer; his left antler was a single metal spike. Rocks, painted alternately blue and white, rimmed the swimming pool, which was choked with leaves and olive algae etched on its sides and circular stairs.

"What you need, Lou, to calm your nerves," Jean said, "is a dirt yard." Lou had had a crying jag that morning as a result of the heat and the baby pressing on her spine and peepee sheets and a three-year-old who bit. "My granny in Greensboro once told me she'd have gone crazy if she hadn't had her dirt yard to rake. Kids love them too." Then she yelled, "Hey kids!" They stopped their wild running to stand sweating as dirt puffed over their feet, then turned to face Jean in a band—Lou's in sunsuits and clean pinafores and roman sandals, Jean's in torn shorts and aprons tied like capes. One wore a nylon bridesmaid's hat.

"I've got a game!" Jean called. They leaped into the air, all in a bunch, mud daubers rising to cluster near the two women. Lou's timid son, tagging at the rear of the group, rested his hand on her bare shoulder. Ceil and Maisie pushed up to the front, Ceil's eyeglass frames balanced on the end of her nose, Maisie's braids fuzzy and coming undone. Autumn Ann clambered up into Jean's lap.

"Get down. It's too hot. And listen to this." Autumn Ann curled closer. Jean huddled them and Lou saw how Gordon and Jasper bent over just like Lamont, as though they had no bones but were willows being arched. "We're going to make us a dirt yard—no more mowing the lawn for us." And all those little children, some not over two years old, never having heard the words "dirt yard" before, knew exactly what she meant. You could see it in their shiny eyes as they looked around the compound to size up the destruction that could be wrought. Autumn Ann picked up a handful of pebbles and licked them. Lou was getting tickled and the baby inside her kicked out—hard. "Ouch!"

"What, Mamma? Mamma, what?" all of hers shrilled, even as their hands ached to pull up clumps of grass.

"Nothing," Lou laughed. "I guess we better start pulling."

"From here . . ." Jean stood up, unfolding her long arm like a measuring rod. "From here to that deer's broke foot, I want down to the dirt by suppertime. Now run get some things to dig with," she said.

"Can we use combs?" Gordon asked.

"Why not?" she shrugged. "Combs, spoons, sticks, anything that'll dig'll do. We need to lay this lawn bare, get it back down to the basics. Now go on and get."

Now, on this day twenty-two years later, as Lou sweats next to Lacey, using a borrowed broom, waiting for her turn at the rake, she tries to tell the story and why, whenever she is feeling low, she'll bring up that afternoon.

"There we were," she says, gesturing with the broom, bringing it down to make half-circles in the dust. "Jean in Lamont's skivvy shirt knotted at the shoulders, cut-offs, and her stringy hair plastered to her head—it must have been 95 degrees—and me, p.g. with a summer top and shorts with that hole cut in the middle for space, feeling air cool against my belly and the sweat running right across my navel, both of us hunkering in the grass, pulling weeds and clover and everything that grew. All those kids—Jean's five, my four, who knows how many others and where they came from, and everybody with a spoon, a stick, a pointed thing. Autumn Ann used the prong of her barrette to scratch the dirt back."

And every one of them, she can't explain, with a purpose, as they unearthed old bottle caps, rusty nails, cigarette butts, a pile of treasure put to one side for when the digging was done. Lou can still see clearly her son squatting, both hands dug deep into the grass, tugging at a clump, straining back on his heels to lift it by its tufted roots, pulling hard to break the sod away; can see him fall back, clod against stomach to cry out in triumph just as a grasshopper leaped free, the movement of its wings no more than the shimmer of heat.

"We did it too," she says to Lacey. "We did. By six o'clock that evening, before Marlon and Lamont got home, we had a perfect circle of dirt, so sweet smelling. Too thick to really rake, but the children went and stuck the edges with forks as if it was a big patty pie."

"Lord, Lord." Lacey shakes her head and smiles. She's stopped raking in order to hear this story and she leans on the end of her rake, using it like a cane. How can Lou tell her of the great grass hummock to the side of the yard that got thrown and sat and climbed upon? Jasper mounted to the top of it, put a dirt clod on his head, shouted, "Lookee here! See my false hair?" then blew back dribbles of dirt that peppered his cheeks. All felt the taste of mud melting in their mouths, gritting their teeth, and the thickness of soil caking under their fingernails. As the day deepened into night the sky paled and shadowed the trees while the streetlights outside the Courts sneaked light over the wall. Then the children lay down in that cool damp dirt to push roly-poly bugs around and swim their arms and legs in those dark elements.

"Later," Lou says, "I later lost the baby I carried then, but I've never lost a second of that day." She can still feel life turning inside her as she dug her fingers knuckle-deep into the earth.

Lacey reaches out her hand and lays it on Lou's arm, and as Lou slows her sweeping, her tears spatter the dirt. "Thank you," she says. "Thank you for letting me help you with this yard." Then Lou is confused. She is standing on the edge of the intricate design and she doesn't want to spoil it. Lacey takes her arm and leads her up to the porch and over to the side. "Right here," she motions. There are three steps down to the grass. Lou sees the clothes flapping on the line and up on the hill sees Marlon leaning against a car talking to a man who must be Lacey's son-in-law. Children and a dog circle the car in a running game. Lou realizes she is still holding the broom in her hand and turns back. "Here."

"Wait," the woman says, going quickly through her belled-out screen door; it slams behind. Lou stares at the smooth dirt yard, so different from the one she remembers—this one dry and designed but still powerful enough to move her. The screen door opens again; Lacey is at the steps. "Here." She holds out a navel orange—deep russet and glowing. Lou can already taste the sweet tang of its flesh. They smile at each other, each old enough to remember when an orange was a gift you hoped for, hoped to get tucked into the toe of a stocking, or icy cold from lying on a block of ice when you were sick, sweet pulp sipped over ice chips. The color of carrots, or persimmons, of the baby Lamont cradled on his chest.

"Here's for your traveling," Lacey says and puts the orange into Lou's hand.

"Thank you. Thank you again." Lou, holding the orange tight to her chest, climbs the hill.

Sometimes on these trips, when she's tired, Lou despairs and wonders aloud to Marlon if they will ever find the Dillons. If maybe they should quit, break down and take out ads before it's too late. Maybe Jean and Lamont are dead. He always pats her on the hip, leans close to kiss between the point where her shoulder meets her neck, and says, "You know we'll find them. Now, don't give up. But we'll take out an ad if you want to. Hell, let's buy a banner. Buy a blimp. I can afford it."

She is cheered holding him and being held by him, her face mashed sideways against his shirt buttons, an errant wire of hair pushing from his neck-V. She feels his heart thrumming through her hands as she fits her palm around his shoulder blades. "I love you, honey," she mouths against his buttons. He murmurs back, rocking her in a silent dance.

Two days later Lou can still feel the broom in her hands, the scritch of the dirt, the powder of it as it moved away in patterns, and how it puffed up when Lacey sprinkled it. She fancies that if she holds her right hand cupped over her nose she can still smell the yard, smell again the end of the broomstick stuck into stiff straw, the wood split with paint flecks filling the creases in her hands. She's happy to recall that Lacey leaned on her rake, tucking the end under her breast to stand like a tripod and listen, shake her head, and smile at Lou's telling. The orange she gave her is in the cooler case at this very minute.

When she'd joined Marlon at the hill, looking back to wave, grinning until she thought her face would split, Lou felt mixed up. Once in the van, she turned to Marlon. He was looking straight ahead, left leg bent at the knee and propped up on the seat in a way that was dangerous and drove her crazy. She didn't even know how to begin to tell him what she'd done, and said, or why. She wanted him to already know it.

"That reminded me of Mamma," he said, shifting his position, making the van speed up, slow down.

I could kill you, she thought. She was nothing like that. Marlon's mother was not a thing like that. Never was.

"Reminded me too of the time y'all dug that whole yard up," he added. Then, alarmed, "Lou, what's the matter? Lou? Why are you bawling?"

She could only shake her head. Then she lowered her face into her hands and cried while Marlon kept changing the stations, swiveling the dial to find some music to comfort her.

That night in bed at the Promo Motel, where everything was harvest gold or green shag and scarred with cigarettes, she tried to tell him what had happened to her in Lacey's yard. He held her, patting, saying, "Hmmm," or "Yeah," or "Oh, honey," gentle interruptions. "It'll be all right, sweetheart." Then he stroked her thigh in a way she always remembered. She moved to him, marveling at the wonder of knowing Marlon all these years, and so long ago, that other Marlon who'd first pulled her away from her safe home and life. She almost thought she could feel that young Marlon, so skinny, so eager, so crazy to get up and go, as he moved in her now.

A few mornings later they are driving along when Lou is alerted by the blue van ahead of them. "Catch up with them," she says. "Hurry, Marlon. That's exactly like the kind of thing they'd drive. Look at all the stickers on it."

The van is plastered with *Knotts Berry Farm* and *Save the Whales* and *Luray Caverns* and *Disneyworld* and the whole back window is covered twice, once with drawn-down green shades that filter light, then with stickers of mountain ranges and other natural wonders in this hemisphere. *Wash me! Quick!* is fingered out in the bumper dust.

Marlon, revved up by Lou's excitement, guns the motor, catches up to cruise side by side with the van. It is muraled on the side with great tongues of flame pointing to the headlights, a map of the United States with stars in every state and a tribute to the Baltimore Orioles. All the side windows are shaded in green too, and the rushing sunlight makes it seem to be traveling underwater.

"That mother's going fast," Marlon says, lowering and twisting his head to see the van off which Lou is reading signs.

"*White Sands Proving Grounds?* They never would go there, would they?"

"Hell, I don't know," Marlon says. "People change."

Lou looks at him. "This seems too new a van for them."

"Look at us, damnit," he says. "We've got a Saab at home. You think Lamont and Jean ever expected to see us in anything but an old Pontiac?" He speeds up even with the driver as Lou pokes her head up and out. The front window of the van is copper glazed with a reflective sheen.

"Speed up some more, Marlon, so I can get the angle." Then she sees, as though through fire, a young man, bearded and bespectacled, singing at the top of his lungs. Marlon pulls ahead, blinkers right, and pulls in front.

"Not them?"

"No." Lou falls back in the seat and adjusts her seat belt. "But it looks like the kind of van they'd be driving." Marlon is looking out the rearview mirror at the van; its great coppery windshield glints, shooting silvery lights off its convexity.

"That guy was singing with his head thrown back—singing at the top of his lungs—just like you do," Lou says, and she puts her hand on Marlon's knee.

He breaks into a tuneless but buoyant "Home, home on the range" as Lou says, "I'm gonna wave anyway. I bet there's little kids in there." She scrambles up and over to the back, undoing her seat belt and standing bent-kneed in the back seat, leans until her upper body is wedged into the back window. She begins to wag her head and wave back and forth, looking like one of those bobbing backview beagles that are so popular. In the rushing of the light made by the two vehicles, Lou's face looks back at her from the other van's copper windshield. In this strange trick of light for a moment it seems that she is sitting beside the young singing driver. She sees herself bronze, smiling, waving back at herself.

"Hold on, honey, I'm pulling out," Marlon says as he steps on the gas and moves them away.

Revenge

DANIEL CURLEY

From *Living with Snakes* (1985)

When Peter Dillon got off the bus at his hotel near the Angel in Mexico City, he took two steps and felt for his billfold. It was gone. He smiled. He was content. But as he approached his hotel he became aware of a man running toward him, waving his arms and cursing violently—at least Dillon assumed he was cursing. He had lived long enough in cities to know that there are crazies everywhere, many of them given to waving their arms and cursing if not often to running. He moved to one side to allow the man to pass, but the man veered toward him. Dillon moved aside. The man veered.

Then Dillon was on the ground. He was contemplating shoes. Mexicans in the city do not wear sandals, he acutely observed. He also translated without difficulty the words *gringo* and *borracho*. He rolled an indignant eye and picked out a policeman wearing the familiar badge that showed he spoke English.

"I am indeed an American," he said, "but I am not drunk. I have been robbed and beaten in the middle of the Reforma under the very eye of the Angel." He rolled his eye further to take in the rest of the crowd and noted that the man who had beaten him had become an interested bystander with no one appearing to be the wiser. The man smiled. Dillon managed a smile of his own. "*Claro*," he said, his third and perhaps his last Spanish word.

He saw the man's face darken. He saw his lips move as he repeated "*Claro*," his face full of dark confusion as he struggled to grasp whatever further outrageous but obscure insult Dillon had intended by simply agreeing, *yes, clearly, to be sure.*

"*Loco*," the policeman explained to the crowd. It turned out that Dillon had four Spanish words.

In the hospital Dillon had time to review his success—there was no doubt it was a success. That man would have beaten him again if the policeman had not been standing in the way. As it was, he could only rage and glower as Dillon was placed in an ambulance and carried away out of his reach. Decidedly the whole affair had been a triumph for Dillon. He rested well. He had had his revenge. It had been a long time coming, but he had had it.

In the beginning, twenty years and more before, he had had his pocket picked in the classic manner on the Route 100 bus, the very bus everyone is warned about, that and Mariachi Square where he had wandered safely the night before. He had assumed that if he could make his way among those throngs of unemployed musicians he must be invulnerable. Of course he was not invulnerable. He was only a challenge.

He had just swung to the ground and the bus had only just begun to roll away from him when he knew what had happened. He ran after the bus and beat on it with his hands, but it accelerated and left him hopelessly behind. It was rage that he felt. Indignation. He had been invaded. It wasn't the money—or at least it wasn't the money to any serious extent. To be sure, he had lost more than he cared to lose, but then he didn't care to lose anything. It wasn't as if he had lost it at the fronton, although he never bet. It wasn't as if he had spent it on foolish things—he never shopped. It wasn't as if he had shot his wad on some unimaginable orgy—he was the most abstemious man he knew. No, he had had nothing for it. He had not had the excitement of a losing game, of tourist booty, not even of a hangover and regrets. On top of that, he had suffered indignities such as he had never known.

As he sat that night on his balcony overlooking the Reforma—and the Route 100 buses—he drank his usual two carefully measured bourbons mixed with purified water and cooled with certified ice. He preferred not to remember that he had once seen an iceman scooping spilled ice cubes off the ground and dumping them into a plastic bag of exactly the sort he had at other times seen delivered to the hotel. It was impossible to control everything.

It was impossible to go back to that moment just before he got off the bus when the man ahead of him, the man waiting in the back stairwell of the bus, had dropped a handful of coins about his feet. Careful reflection had enabled him to isolate this moment as the one when his hand should have gone automatically to his pocket. He knew there was no going back. He hadn't noticed even the decoy except as a pair of hands scrabbling about his feet. Still, he ached for revenge.

He fantasied the moment. He caught the hand of the pickpocket in a steely grip and brought him to his knees with a jujitsu twist—Dillon's fantasies, he was quick to admit, were somewhat antiquated and hadn't yet incorporated the more innovative arts of karate and kung fu. On the other hand, when he imagined shouting "Thief" on the crowded bus, the other passengers righteously turned on him and he found himself in a Mexican jail. Even his fantasies often betrayed him and offered nothing but dampening views. Still, in spite of this and in spite of the fact that there was only a nameless, faceless enemy, he contemplated revenge.

The revenge had to wait, however. The next day he retrieved his traveler's checks from the hotel safe and set out for home as scheduled. He traveled fast and without rest. It was his constant fear that he would arrive too late, that someone with all his identity would have arrived at his house and established himself securely. Not only that, but he was sure that this person, this small Mexican with a small mustache, would be better liked by his wife, his children, his neighbors, and his employer and that he himself would be turned away, nameless, and perhaps even deported to Mexico.

The fact that none of this turned out to be true reassured him—but only a little. The person could still appear, flash his impeccable credentials, and turn him out. "I always thought so," his wife would say. His employer would rub his hands in relief and graciously not bring in the police, frowning the while as if doubting his own wisdom and questioning the folly of his own good nature.

Meanwhile, Dillon continued to contemplate revenge. He perfected a hundred plans of highly romantic and impractical natures. He saw himself—almost in mask and cape—becoming the scourge of Route 100 pickpockets, destroying the ring, exposing the complicity of the drivers, bringing to light the corruption of the police. Hi ho, 100, away.

But gradually he settled on a scheme less romantic but still satisfying and apparently without danger to himself. He would ride the buses with a dummy billfold in his pocket and invite the pickpockets to do their worst. In the early versions of this scheme, the billfold was attached to his belt by a stout chain. He would run the chain through a hole in his pocket and, thoroughly concealed, up to his belt. For a while he even added an alarm to the chain and tried to work out a handcuff that would automatically clamp onto the thief's wrist. Then the scheme reversed itself, and he eliminated handcuff, alarm, and chain and introduced instead a simple slip of paper bearing a simple message.

The message, however, was not easy to decide on. It had, if not to express his own rage, to generate a comparable rage in the thief, any thief. "April Fool" would not do. And his own rage was too vast for any catch phrase or slogan. He was very much at a loss until his Spanish phrase book came to his rescue. He was looking under Insults, Invective, and Imprecations when he chanced upon "*Chinga tu madre*" which the book chastely translated as "Rape your mother" and assured him was the one unforgivable insult. He was somewhat disappointed. He had expected Spanish to be more fertile of invention than that, but he was willing to accept the editor's authority and many editions. What had happened to him was unforgivable and he wanted only to reply in kind.

The next time he was sent to Mexico he carried his carefully prepared billfold, a cheap one but new. After his appointments he rode the bus between his hotel and the anthropological museum until he was exhausted. Disappointed, he returned to his room, poured the first of his drinks, and sat down to inspect his bait for any flaws. To his astonishment the paper on which he had carefully printed his message to the world had been reversed, and he now read: "So's your old man."

He was depressed. He was up against a more formidable adversary than he had believed. Further, his faith in his message was shaken. "So's your old man" was doubtless out of an English phrase book, and as a result the credibility of all phrase books came into question in spite of any assumed authority and any number of editions. However, there was no one he could ask about his little phrase. It wasn't exactly the sort of thing he liked to mention to the Mexican clients of his firm, nor did he care to try it on, say, a cabdriver or shoe-shine man. He felt no doubt that he could say it right, but he had no confidence that he could explain his interest before he had a knife run into him, if indeed it should turn out to be more potent than "So's your old man." That night he lost track of things and actually drank three drinks.

The next day, the last of his stay, he struck pay dirt at once. The first time he got off the bus at the Museo de Antropologia he had the sensation of having started a chain reaction. Behind him was a man with his hand stuck to the dummy billfold, and behind that man was another man in the very act of slapping a handcuff onto the first man's other wrist. It was so like Dillon's fantasy that he could only stare.

The policeman snatched the billfold and waved it about. "Evidence," he said in perfect English. "How much money?"

"No money," Dillon said in no less perfect English—he was on his mettle.

"No money?" the policeman said. He clearly felt there was a failure of communication, because he looked into the billfold. Immediately his face darkened. He whirled the pickpocket about like a lasso, and Dillon found himself chained fast by the other handcuff. Unfortunately in his haste and anger the policeman had chained them right hand to right hand so that they looked as if they were in the act of bungling a simple handshake, and when they moved to the patrol wagon it was Dillon who had to walk backwards.

The visit to the police station was not edifying. First, Dillon was charged with insulting a police officer in the performance of his duty. "Your mother wears army boots," the offended policeman said when the charge was recorded. At least his phrase book seemed to be some forty years closer to being in date. The only comfort Dillon could find was the assurance that his insult did, in fact, seem to be a bona fide insult of the first water.

However, the real trouble began when he was searched and his actual billfold came to light in his special secret inner pocket. The policemen passed it from hand to hand and checked his IDs. They nodded wisely and made very Mexican sounds which Dillon tentatively interpreted as "Aha!"

The charges now became theft and misuse of credit cards. There was a long account to settle. He had evidently led the Mexican police a merry chase. It was their turn now and they were going to make the most of it. "I'm being accused," he told the company lawyer when he finally was allowed a telephone call, "of stealing and misusing my own credit cards." But he was still not in the clear. He remained in jail for three days, and only the direct intervention of the Embassy brought about his release.

"You'll have to be more careful," the Embassy told him.

"This puts us in a very bad light," the company said.

"It was in all the papers," his wife said.

He thought he would lose his job or at the very least never be sent to Mexico again, but as it turned out, the Mexican clients took to asking specifically for that so-amusing Senor Dillon, and he became, in spite of himself, almost indispensable. His job was secure but his revenge eluded him as much as ever.

His next two visits to Mexico were fruitless. He rode the buses religiously, but the plainclothesmen glowered at him, known pickpockets gave him the Mexican finger, and bus drivers threw his change on the floor. Once, indeed, he thought he had scored, but the bus, which had started, stopped abruptly. The back door opened, and a plainclothes policeman hurled his billfold at his head. He was discouraged and began to see himself as a kind of Flying Dutchman self-condemned to ride the 100 line forever or an Ancient Mariner forever deprived of a Wedding Guest to ease his pain.

Then, strangely, his fame seemed to have faded. New generations of police and pickpockets knew him not. New generations of bus drivers accepted his exact change without a sneer. He felt almost abandoned, almost as if he were starting all over again, older, tireder, and with little hope of ever achieving a goal he had almost forgotten.

The message in his billfold was faded now, the paper dirty and crumbling at the edges. He was afraid that "*Chinga tu madre*" would no longer pass current, but he hadn't the interest to check it in any of the newer phrase books. He was simply riding the buses now because that was what he did when he came to Mexico. Even he knew he had become a harmless eccentric, a man with one very odd spot in his makeup.

It happened, then, when he was no longer paying attention, that he got back to his hotel one night to find his dummy billfold missing. He felt at first that he had been deprived of something, something important, that something that really mattered had been wrenched out of the fabric of his life. Then as the sweat-stained billfold, the tattered message came back to him, he remembered his revenge.

He tried to feel elation but he felt nothing. He tried to understand that he had completed a lifelong quest, but nothing at all seemed to have ended. He went back to the beginning, to that day his pocket had been picked, and there he found anger. He beat once more on the back of the bus with his fists. He shouted, "Thief." His heart raced. He broke into a sweat. One more tiny twist would break the thief's arm like a matchstick. He had been wrong all those years thinking it would be enough to know that the thief had taken the bait, was reading the message, was wanting to break his limbs one by one, to slice him with a dull knife, to roast him over a slow fire, and all without having any idea who he was or where to find him, he, Dillon, having been until that moment at best merely a professional problem involving a pocket and a billfold.

Deprived now of his revenge just when he thought he had achieved it, deprived even of his old familiar lure, Dillon could only go blindly back into the old pattern. Without hope now, he bought a new billfold. He wrote a new message without even caring if it was still in a language used by living men.

And then, once again, and the very next day, he was standing on the sidewalk looking after a bus. He watched it all the way to the next stop, feeling the vacancy in his hip pocket, the emptiness in his heart. He watched the people boil out of the bus and one man detach himself from the group and begin to run back along the route of the bus. The man was stumbling in his haste, churning his arms and legs as if in a mad attempt at a takeoff, a heavy water bird slow to rise from the surface, dabbling the pavement with his tiptoes. As he came close, Dillon could hear his shouts.

Dillon knew the cities were full of crazies, mostly harmless, so he effaced himself, but the man clearly had him in mind and only him. They maneuvered on the sidewalk as if actually they were trying to avoid each other with the best will in the world. And such was Dillon's well-practiced skill in avoiding that the man nearly did run past him, but just at the crucial moment he threw an object into Dillon's face—the new billfold, the ancient message. Stopped in the midst of his most skillful maneuver, Dillon was run down, trampled, bloodied, and pulped.

Ah, he said to himself. This was rage. This was what he himself had felt and what he had wanted all these years in return, rage so enormous that no violence could assuage it, no mountain of heaped indignities reduce an atom of its monstrous debt. His fall to earth was gentle. The pain of being moved to the ambulance was a recognition in every bone that his revenge was complete. His bones would mend, his blood restore itself. He had now only to contemplate a placid age, a contented death.

Frog Boy

DIANNE NELSON OBERHANSLY

From *A Brief History of Male Nudes in America* (1993)

Rocky Davis is all hands and eyes. Big hands—state of Texas hands. Shoulders broad enough to suggest his first good sport coat. He is already wearing size 10 men's shoes, and since last Thursday, Rocky has been on fire. It started as a hot, hopeless weight in his chest and then suddenly blew wide open, his hair smoldering, his arms and face so flushed that twice his father, Wade, gently reaches over to him, puts a cool square hand on his son's shoulder, and tells Rocky to go shower.

"Christ, the kid just can't stand this heat," Wade says, shaking his head. Rocky is his best son, his only son, the big sleepy kid who doesn't look a thing like him.

It is late August in Tucson and each day the temperature slowly bulldozes upward to 107 or 108. Everywhere in the city, people have lost their patience for summer, for the flies littering windowsills like shiny black tacks, for the steaming sidewalks, and the small patchy Bermuda lawns turned brown, the gardenia and palm leaves limp as day-old sandwich makings. Some of the small restaurants have even closed for the month and put signs in their windows: *Too hot to cook.*

Rocky just stands there a few moments, as if his father's words take that long to unspiral and plant themselves. Finally, he heads for the shower, taking his time, dragging those Texas hands of his along the dresser until they encounter his father's credit card there. One flick of his wrist and the shiny red plastic is gone.

Rocky doesn't like being told what to do. He'd rather choose. He'd rather live in a free universe, he says.

"Rocko, my boy," his father tells him, "this is about as free as it gets."

Wade resumes eating his Baby Ruth, which is breakfast that morning. Three fingers on his right hand wear the delicate brown signature of chocolate, until he licks them and begins to look for the opened sack of Cheetos which he knows is somewhere nearby, and probably under some clothes there's a mini-bag of Oreos. Usually Rocky and his father don't eat like this, but they're on vacation and whatever rules composed their former life in Denver have been erased.

In the big white tiled bathroom of the El Conquistador Hotel where they are staying, under a stinging spray of water, Rocky stands still and counts to three hundred, which is longer than he has ever stayed in a shower before. It's dangerous in there, he thinks—a bad place to be in an earthquake, the plumbing folding permanently up around him like a tiled coffin.

Steam billows around him and the plastic shower curtain rustles in a warm synthetic breeze. He crosses his arms and buries his hands in the smooth, slick pockets of his armpits. He tucks his head and lets the water pour down over him—a rain, a flood taking off his first skin and leaving him the raw thirteen-year-old that he is: long thin legs interrupted by knees the size of salad plates and, recently, tufts of dark jungled hair down there.

He knows beyond a doubt, there in the shower with his hands safely put away, that he loves her: Ellen Castillo—his father's girlfriend—the woman in the adjoining hotel room who has touring maps of Tucson spread around her, blue *X*s marking the sites that they will probably visit: the air museum, the desert zoo, the mission. A tortilla factory. A designer underwear outlet.

Rocky doesn't care where they go as long as it's with her. Africa. Iceland. He and his father were backpacking in the rainy mountains of Tennessee two years ago and he thinks he could probably even stand that again, if she were there, despite the grenade-sized mosquitoes and the sloppy one-pot meals cooked over a campfire.

In a few minutes, his father is there knocking on the bathroom door, telling him that they're waiting. "Hey, buddy, let's get going," he says.

Wade Davis's voice dulls as it passes through the door and into the steam where Rocky, now standing with a soft white towel around him, hears only a low frequency disturbance—a bug, a bee, something mildly whining out there on the landscape of the tan carpet. He reaches for his T-shirt and shorts and smells them before he dresses: wind, fading fabric softener, and the steely edge of that morning's earlier sweat—the second since he has awakened.

Last year in August on their annual vacation they had flown to Seattle where he didn't sweat at all, he and his father and Eve Resnick—the woman back then, someone who had insisted on high heels, though she couldn't walk in them. She teetered down Pike Street. Packed into Spandex pedal pushers, she wobbled up the long sidewalk leading to the Space Needle. Rocky looked the other way or tried to make it seem he was with another family. He crowded up behind two dark beanpole brothers, hoping to make it look like three. Down on the wooden wharf, as a rusted tugboat pulled up to dock, Eve had finally caught a heel and fallen, and for the rest of the trip she wore scabbed-over knees and consoled herself with tall gin and tonics. Mai tais. Red table wine.

Rocky notices that Ellen Castillo wears blue tennis shoes or sandals with lots of tiny straps across the toes. On the first day of their vacation, which was last Thursday, at a Denny's where they were eating lunch, Rocky discovered Ellen's feet, and the match was lit; the fire in him began, though his understanding of that fire was elementary still: heat, dizziness, a pulse hammering in his ears—he was not even sure it was his own. Back in Denver, he had only briefly seen Ellen, but now, in the long sunblasted days of what seemed like the other side of the world, he was getting to know her, or at least beginning to become attuned to her every move.

That day at Denny's, wayward and without cares and lugging big tote bags, they all ordered just what their hearts told them. Wade ordered a shrimp cocktail and a hot brownie sundae, which he intended to eat in reverse order. Ellen ordered the peach melba plate. Rocky opted for just an order of French fries, but when they finally arrived he found that he had no appetite. Food seemed boring, a waste of time when Ellen was sitting there in what smelled like a cloud of orange or sweet lemon.

"Gotta keep your strength up on this trip," Wade reminded his son when he saw him fidgeting and the fries untouched. "We're going to be in high gear," he said. "We're going to be seeing everything there is to see in this town."

Wade arrives in a new place—Tucson, Tennessee, wherever—with all the spirit of an invading general. He carries guidebooks and maps and has a hit list of places to definitely see. For months before his vacation, he falls asleep on the sofa each night with a Fodor's travel book opened on his chest, and it is as if, during those naps, he absorbs the intricacies of a given place—falls in love with the names of unseen streets and rivers and mountains.

During lunch at Denny's, Ellen had her legs crossed, her right foot sticking out from under the table. Rocky had never really noticed a foot before, let alone fallen in love with one. Her painted toenails made him feel inexplainably happy. Across each, she had pasted a glittery gold zig-zag so that every toe ended in a tiny bolt of lightning. A sizzle. A pop. He noticed that her foot was clean and tanned, that her toes curled or pointed up when she laughed or leaned forward to make some teasing remark to Wade. The arch was high and white, a secret place. Her small bare ankle bone pushing up under the skin made him sigh, which in turn caused Wade and Ellen to look up from their plates at him.

"What?" his father asked him.

Uncomfortable, Rocky shrugged and scratched his ear.

In what seemed like a minute to Rocky, Ellen's melba plate was gone and there was only a smoky green lettuce leaf left on the thick white china. She looked at her watch and tapped its face. "Hey guys," she said, "are we going to spend all day eating lunch?"

While she waited for Wade and Rocky to finish, she reached up and behind her and examined a heavy woven valance hanging in the window. Ellen is a drapery consultant and says she is in love with the feel of things—burlap, sateen, canvas. A good brocade makes her dizzy. Silk—good silk—she says you won't find in this country. Wherever they go, she has her hand out in front of her and opened, like a blind person who is searching a path, but instead she is registering the thread weight and gauge of chairs and curtains, anything covered in fabric that comes her way.

Rocky is not at the point where he can actually look at Ellen's face and listen to her. Looking at the door to the Denny's restroom, however, was safe. Looking out the window was momentarily calming. The windows were tinted, but even so, he had never seen sunlight that savage.

When the three of them were almost out the restaurant door, Rocky had a flash, did a quick backtrack to their table, snagged the lettuce leaf from Ellen's plate, and put it in his pocket.

In a sky-blue rented Mustang with the top down, Rocky's father drives faster than he probably should. Rocky sees cactus and palo verde zip by, long adobe walls, and the vast brown plate of the desert. In the wind that hits his face and batters his hair, he smells sun and exhaust and the brown coyote smell of dirt. He can't see the speedometer from where he's sitting in the back seat—slumped in the left corner, sitting on one crushed leg, leaning into the plush upholstery for strength.

In the front seat, Wade has placed one hand casually on Ellen's neck. Slowly his index finger moves up and down across the skin just below her ear, making a tiny but suggestive path. Rocky homes in on the hand and can't let go. His shoulders tighten and he can clearly taste the spicy composition of last night's food.

The three of them are headed for a movie set west of Tucson. Wade leans his head to the right and half-yells back at Rocky. "Isn't this great? Getting to see a movie being made and everything?"

Ellen swivels toward the stick shift. "Yeah," she says into the wind. "We're just too lucky, aren't we?"

Rocky can't quite make out what either of them is saying. It's not just the speed and rushing air that distort their voices, but the fact that Rocky's ears are half-plugged. He sees their mouths move. He hears a droning. Every few seconds, an understandable word flies, comet-like, at him: "everything," "lucky." Like a foreigner, he scrambles to patch together the conversation.

For the first time in his whole life, his father's hand bothers Rocky, actually repulses him. Up until now, it has mostly been a good hand—generous, caring, luminous in the dark. Now, it seems to Rocky, the knuckles are too big; the nails, squared-off and thick and almost yellow. He wishes Ellen would say something about it, would complain that the hand is too hot and heavy, would squirm in her bucket seat until she cast his father off and he had two hands on the steering wheel again. Rocky thinks that for once his father should be concerned with safety.

About ten miles out of town where a graveled road takes off from the highway, Wade makes the turn to the movie set a little too sharp and the three of them lurch toward the right. Ellen and Wade laugh as if a car and a roller coaster are supposed to have something in common. Rocky, irritated, hunkers down lower in his corner, trying to keep from sliding across the seat.

When the car finally stops in the dusty parking lot and Rocky tries to stand, he finds that the folded leg he has sat on is numb. Ellen and Wade hurry across the dirt lot and into a huge, abandoned machine shop where the movie is being made. Rocky follows more slowly, slightly limping, trying to shake the pins and needles loose.

The film is not yet titled. In it, an alien of unknown origin—masterminded by two special effects men—confronts a woman at an old rundown desert motel. On the set, there's a bright pink neon sign rigged up—Tumble Inn—buzzing and half-lit. Portable lights are set up everywhere, creating a sharp blue-white halo that appears thick as cigarette smoke. A man wearing a cap with horns sprouting out the sides is being raised up above the set on a noisy black crane. He is obviously unhappy—yelling and pointing and shaking his head. "Fuck you, Louie, just fuck you," he hollers from about twelve feet up.

Ellen can't believe how skinny the actress is. "You can't tell me that's attractive," she says quietly, standing on her toes for a better view. She turns to Wade. "Is that attractive?"

Wade shakes his head no and puts his arm around her shoulder. Ellen smiles and settles herself into the tan muscled groove of his bicep. At home in Denver, he and Rocky share a Joe Weider weight set, and Wade has been making good progress, though Rocky finds the weights boring. He'd rather lift one of the wrought-iron kitchen chairs over his head, spin it like the people from the Moscow Circus who could make a whole ladder of spinning chairs, or he'd rather see, with just one leg, how far he can push the bulky gray sofa. Besides, Rocky lately finds his muscles ungovernable. Right in the midst of flag football, for instance, or a neighborhood game of catch, a leg cramp rivets him to the ground where he clutches the grass embarrassingly.

At the movie set Rocky watches the show of affection between his father and Ellen—pats and rubs and long full-body presses, the quick birdlike kisses of the newly in love—and at the same time he somehow watches the filming. He can see both up and down, far left and far right. It is as if his field of vision has quadrupled. His brown eyes flick and rotate, finding both the obvious and the hidden: a star-shaped mole on a woman's neck, a hole in the sleeve of a cameraman's shirt. When Rocky can't stand it anymore—the lights, the swirling movement, the actress's face being dabbed with sponges, his father pulling Ellen closer and closer—he heads for a portable Coke stand back by the entrance.

He gets in line and starts to dig in his pockets for change. His left hand comes up and in it is shredded paper, a button, a few twists of lettuce and orange peel. He stares at the contents of his pocket, confused. The line keeps shortening until there is only one man in front of him. Rocky hurriedly feels for coins in his right pocket, but everything there is vague and unfamiliar, the warm dark terrain of someone else's clothes. The man in front of him is reaching up onto the counter now for a red and white paper cup. The girl selling Cokes brushes hair from her eyes and starts to look back in the line.

Rocky feels the pressure of the moment as a huge bubble that works its way up from the bottom of his stomach and lodges in his throat, threatening as a chicken bone. Even if he had the money resting coolly in his hand, he knows he couldn't say a word. The Coke girl, tired and bored, would lean forward, waiting for his order, the mounds of her small earthy breasts rejoicing momentarily from the top of her halter.

Rocky slips out of line and shoulders his way to the restroom. The one sink in there has been torn inches away from the wall and a chipped green welder's tank temporarily props it up. A silvery stream of water snakes down the wall from a joint in the plumbing. Rocky pulls the water lever on and dunks his head, and when he finally straightens back up the water runs down his neck and soaks the top of his shirt. Drowns him. Saves him. In four days, he hasn't felt this good.

Wade is browsing at the souvenir stand—a wooden cart loaded with T-shirts and cactus highball glasses—and when he sees Rocky standing over by the extras, wet almost to the waist with his dark woolly hair slicked back, he stops and looks again. "Criminy," he says when he's standing at Rocky's side, "I almost didn't know you. What happened?"

Rocky doesn't know how to explain much of anything. Ellen strolls up behind Wade, and Rocky certainly doesn't know how to explain this feeling he gets when she's near: his arms and legs become weighted, his throat tightens to the width of a string. The bare blue heat intensifies between his legs. Yesterday his shoes would not stay tied in her presence, and if it had not been for the egg-frying heat of the concrete, he would have thrown them away.

Ellen looks sleepily around the movie set and says that, all in all, she's disappointed. "To tell you the truth," she says, "I'd rather go to a theater and watch a movie than see it being made."

Wade raises his hand in agreement, votes yes for Ellen.

They look at Rocky, but his answer has darted completely away from him, slippery and unreliable, and when his lips open, when he tries to coax it out, a small low-pitched belch is all he can muster.

Ellen giggles and Rocky thinks it's the sound of glass and silver and sunlight falling.

Wade rubs Rocky's head and smiles, and instantly, with a fierce and nauseating instinct he's never felt before, Rocky's hand closes tight at his side, as if he were grabbing onto and then raising a two-by-four against his father.

Just before they leave for the Sonora Desert Museum, Wade discovers his credit card gone. He hits the side of his head a couple of times like he's just come out of a swimming pool and needs to empty an ear. "Now where in the hell would I have left that?" he asks himself. He's mad and worried, which Rocky finds a strangely satisfying combination.

Ellen starts to work their way backwards for him. "Let's see. We were in the hotel café for breakfast this morning. And last night . . ."

In Rocky's room, behind the swivel stand of a 21-inch color TV, back where no right-minded maid would ever clean, there is a collection of valuables. Wade's sunglasses and electric razor. Now the credit card. Rocky knows that he should feel ashamed, but that's a feeling he can't get inside of and wear anymore. It's like last year's T-shirts—too small, too tight at the neck.

Wade calls and puts a stop on the credit card, and then, not to be deterred, they drive to the desert museum.

Ellen is dressed in green—green shorts, green top. If she were any more green or beautiful, Rocky knows that it would drive him mad, that he would climb the thick cyclone fence and join the pack of gray wire-haired javelinas they are watching. Actually, there's not that much to watch. The javelinas are woven among the boulders of a gray concrete wall. They are facedown in cool dirt, sleeping in deep ovals of shade.

"They've got the right idea," Ellen says.

"Yup," Rocky adds, and it's only a small word, but he soars with confidence. He feels himself smile, his back arch a little. He bites at his thumb and looks down to make sure his fly is zipped.

They move on toward the porcupines. Ellen leads the way. She carries the map and easily decides everyone's destiny. Neither he nor Ellen nor his father can find the porcupines within their enclosure. The three of them lean their faces up to the fence and scour the trees and around the rocks, but can't sight any of the dark barrel bodies.

Warm and frustrated, Wade volunteers to run for snacks, and then it's just Ellen and Rocky walking along a dirt path toward whatever animal comes next. Marsupial. Primate.

It is only midmorning, but already the air is thick and dry as rope, leaden to the taste. People stroll by in clothes that have been cut up for the weather—sleeves and legs and shirttails are raggedly cut off. Parents stop to swathe babies in sun block, then turn and dot each other's shoulders.

Rocky wears a black and white striped legionnaire's hat that his father bought for him the day before in a surfers shop. "Keep the sun off your head," he told Rocky, and for a while Rocky was irked—more instructions—but actually Rocky likes the way the long flaps off the back of the hat flutter against his neck.

He looks up and the cloud-streaked sky is bone pale and beneath it Ellen's hair is streaming with sunlight and the sweet powdery smell of shampoo. She turns the map sideways and reads the fine print that details the petting zoo. Rocky is engrossed with her every move. It seems that he is seeing the small, everyday movements of a human for the first time. She pushes her sunglasses up onto her hair and then squints at the map. She cocks her head to the right and studies.

Then, in the distance where a group of shaggy cigar-colored camels are bunched together, Rocky spots his father holding a big cardboard snack tray, and he makes a split-second decision. He guides Ellen to the right, just nudges with his shoulder, and amazingly she doesn't even look up from the map. She veers softly right, and they weave strategically among other zoo-goers, then head toward the big cats and the elephant. Rocky doesn't remember what all they see on this loop, but Ellen reads to him and points and makes the morning alive. His skin crackles. His heart tentatively climbs back into his chest where it rustles and whirrs.

Rocky doesn't wear a watch, so he doesn't know how long it is before Wade, sweaty and winded, finally meets up with them in the Reptile House. The ice in the drinks that Wade is carrying has completely melted. Cheese nachos tumble one by one off the cardboard tray and the orangey topping oozes over his thumb.

"Hey, Rocko," he says, "didn't you see me back there? Where in the heck have you guys been?"

"Everywhere," Ellen says, waving the map. "Give me a Coke. I'm dying."

There is a strong sour odor in the Reptile House and the first thing Rocky does is drop back from Wade and Ellen, lift his arm, and smell to see if it's him. Rocky doesn't know what to expect out of himself anymore—what strange pink appendages might protrude, what swampy smell might emanate. When he checks out all right, he lowers his arm and hurries ahead.

Ellen practically has her face against the glass of a chamber where a long bright-green snake is wrapped next to an almost perfect replica of itself—a dark recently shed skin. She puts her finger against the glass and taps lightly. The snake is frozen and only the thread of its tongue flicks the stagnant air. Rocky doesn't like watching the snake. He chooses a bark-skinned lizard in a tree doing what looks like push-ups. Wade shakes his head and moves toward the exit. He says he has a bad case of heebie-jeebies.

That's the way that Rocky ends up alone with Ellen in the Reptile House, going from glass to glass, hardly breathing at all, staying the whole time within a foot of her shoulder.

There are huge propeller-sized fans blowing everywhere around the tortilla factory. The deep, sorrowful smell of grease spreads through the whirring air of the fans, though Josephina, the factory tour guide and a former masa-maker herself, does not refer to it as grease. "Shortening," she says, her accent hardening the *t* and *n*'s, making the word sound like some exotic ingredient. All of the workers wear nets on their heads, spidery black webs that flatten their hair similarly. The edges of their oversized white cotton aprons wave slightly from the fans, and to Rocky these people look like ghosts as they stand solemnly here or there to catch a breeze.

Ellen must feel the tortillas, of course. Josephina says yes, by all means. Ellen picks one up and holds the soft gold and brown specked treasure up to the light and it becomes a round opaque window. Soon there is flour on her fingertips and a white iridescent smudge on her face. Wade walks up to her, licks his finger, and rubs it over the spot on her cheek. In an instant Rocky knows how it feels to have his chest crushed, though he realizes it isn't much of a chest yet—bony, hairless, white.

Rocky pushes ahead to the sales office where the tour will end. He sits in a brown molded plastic chair and stews while he waits for the rest of the group. With one foot, he kicks the sole of his other shoe until that foot throbs, but it is a disconnected pain—just a steady chain of blips on a machine somewhere.

The tour group arrives sampling bits of rolled tortillas, powdered sugar and honey on their hands. Wade saves some for Rocky, but he doesn't want any. He shakes his head and moves next to the air-conditioning unit set in the wall. The icy air pours over his arm and even whispers to him.

Wade wants one evening alone in Tucson with Ellen. "You don't mind, do you, Rocko?" his father asks him when they're back at the hotel. Wade has stopped and bought himself a disposable razor; he thinks his electric razor will show up when they have more time to look. He is at the mirror, already shaving for the evening. He flicks white lather into the sink and stretches his mouth to one side for a clear smooth run of the razor. He wants to take Ellen somewhere special to eat, he says. "What do you think?" he asks Rocky. "Seafood or French?"

Wade splashes after-shave on his face and the sweet layers of pine hit Rocky like a gut punch. "French," he tells his father, not even really knowing the word in that moment or why he says it.

As Wade and Ellen hurry to get ready, Rocky glides once through their room, and the car keys are there on the nightstand waiting for him—flashing, metallic, calling to him in the way that jewelry or a lighter calls to the solitary shoplifter. When he drops the keys quietly into his pocket, he feels nothing. He tells his father and Ellen he's going to his room to look at TV.

Instead, he goes down the elevator and out the side door of the hotel. He walks down the sidewalk and feels his skin shrinking, the keys pressing his leg each time he moves. The sun will dip behind the long, purple belt of mountains soon, though it is still unbearably hot outside. A group of older women in stretchy floral swimming suits at a nearby cocktail table wave bright Chinese fans before their faces, which send their blue-gray hair fluttering.

No real plan opens itself to Rocky. Instead, it is the dense oleanders and privets decorating the outside wall of the hotel that open to him—a large shadowy parting between branches. He bends quickly and crawls forward. Close to the ground and with the greenery shrouding him, he is surprised at how comfortable and right this place feels. The leaves turn to him and kindle tiny bursts of the last bits of sunlight. Slowly, the noise of the bushes takes over—the locusts, the lizards, the low pulsing of sap. Rocky stretches out and rubs his cheek in the cool soothing dirt. One of his hands closes over damp leaves and the other takes hold of a ball of dried roots.

Finally, in the thin mauve twilight, out on the sidewalk that stretches big as a runway from where he is hidden, Rocky spots his father's shoes—a worried pair of white canvas topsiders pacing back and forth, then halting, then moving into the grass.

Rocky reaches down and checks to see that the keys are still in his pocket, curls up, tucks a foot under the opposite thigh, then closes his eyes. He listens to his name being called again and again—a frantic singsong message that drifts away toward the pool and then farther: to rocks and weeds and moonlight and beyond—but in the darkness of a summer's night, there is no boy left to answer.

Theory of the Leisure Class

E. J. LEVY

From *Love, in Theory* (2012)

I. CONSPICUOUS LEISURE

The Scottish Brewer and his wife have not joined us this afternoon for our trek through the forest of Tapantí. They are protesting the mud. Boycotting the birds. Outraged by the sloppiness, the untidiness of nature. How they conceived of an ornithological tour that did not require hiking through muck, I cannot conceive, but the Scottish Brewer seems to have imagined that the birds would come to us. Regrettably, the Duck Man and his wife are undeterred; they come up the path behind us, talking loudly. Manuel, our guide, has shushed them repeatedly but to no effect. Our only hope now is to outdistance them, but every so often, through the canopy of green, from amidst the vines and leaves, I hear a distant quack and know that they are out there still, the Duck Man and his wife, somewhere in the jungle, gaining on us.

We are fourteen: six married couples, the General, who has come alone, and Manuel. There are the wealthy Scottish Brewer and his wife, serious birders who seem to feel they are lowering themselves to be traveling in the company of Americans. There are the Sandersons, the very nice couple from Illinois (he was a state legislator for many years and a professor of political science; his wife, Geneen, heads up her local League). There is the Duck Man and his young wife. I call him the Duck Man because he quacks when he wants to screw (pardon my French). These are the things you learn about people on a tour such as this: all the phobias and quirks come out, as if inhibition were taking a vacation too.

In the course of our ten-day tour, we have slogged through mud, mosquitoes, wet, and rain; where possible we have stayed in good hotels. Ours is a domesticated adventure, organized by the American Museum of Natural History. Our guides have been very knowledgeable, very good, and we've traveled a great deal to remote wildlife preserves for which Costa Rica is known.

Most days I've made it a policy to walk at the front of the group with Manuel, where the bird watching is best, but on this, our last day, my husband, Milt, and I have remained back with the General, who lags behind, watching the path for snakes and roots. I point out liana and bromeliads for him to see, but he is too upset to notice. He's been sullen ever since we saw the spiders copulating.

The General was the first to spot them on the philodendron leaf, a mile or so back. He has keen eyes—he was a pilot in the war—and he enjoys holding forth on entomology. He takes pleasure in pointing out a butterfly or spider that the rest of us have missed. He seemed particularly excited by his discovery today. He pulled out his thick British pocket guide to identify the pair. Then he called me over to watch, and then the others came, and together we watched as the male courted then mounted the female. We were all quite moved by the tiny drama—the miracle of creation taking place before our eyes—right up until the moment the female turned and began to eat her mate. His tiny legs quivered, kicking air.

It was not a surprise, of course. We all know about the birds and the bees and that spiders devour their mates. But we are aging—most of us are in our seventies, the General must be eighty, at least—and we are a little sentimental about sex.

Only the Duck Man—who is in his forties (his wife is younger still)—seemed unperturbed. He leaned over the quivering pair on the leaf, shook his head, and said, "Dying for a fuck. Now that's the way to go." Then he laughed and clapped the General on the back.

The General was quiet for a long time after that. He is recently divorced, the General is. His third, I think, though I wouldn't dream of asking.

II. FORMS OF SACRIFICE

This trip was my idea and Milton is being patient in a way that makes it clear that it was my idea. That he is being a good sport. That he is a good and loving husband, evidence to the contrary. He is always doing things like that—making me look foolish and demanding by pretending he is neither.

Milton would have preferred to lie on a beach somewhere in Florida or the Caribbean, but his doctor recommended moderate exercise after his bypass surgery a year ago. The heart is a muscle after all. And so, because it has always been an ambition of mine to see the Resplendent Quetzal of Costa Rica, and because he owes me now that I know the truth about him, about her, we came here.

"It is possibly inauthentic," Manuel says of the Temple of Quetzal by which we now stand, in a small clearing. He holds a flashlight in one hand and points it into the darkness and raps on the stone wall with his knuckles. "Possibly," he says, "it is a fraud."

This temple is not mentioned in my little yellow guide book, *Inside Costa Rica*, a fact that does not surprise me. Costa Rica is not known for its archaeology. We have come here to look at birds, not ruins, but ruins, it seems, are everywhere. Ruin appears to be inescapable.

The temple, Manuel explains, is likely of Olmec origin, if authentic.

"Despite the practice of human sacrifice," Manuel says, "the pre-Columbian peoples of this region were highly sophisticated. They were arguably no more barbarous than we."

Perhaps Manuel expects to shock us, his post-Columbian tour group, but James Sanderson, the dapper gentleman from Illinois, says, "It's not so very different from the sacrament, is it? The old wafer and wine."

Judging by his comment, Sanderson isn't Catholic.

Judging by his expression, Manuel is.

"The pope might disagree," I say.

"Indeed," says Sanderson's wife, Geneen, "he would."

She and I exchange a complicit smile and ascend into the cool musty interior of what might once have been a temple. Milton waits with the General on the steps. In truth, I think we have not changed that much in five hundred years. We still pluck the heart from the body. Only now we call it a procedure not a ceremony. There are no prayers. The only difference is that we haven't a prayer.

Manuel leads us toward the back of the low, dank room, and shows us with his flashlight the points and pot sherds they have discovered, the bones and seeds. I have heard that one can sometimes feel the presence of the past lingering in a place like this. But I feel nothing—only the cool dead still air, laid against my face like a cloth. The past haunts me these days, but not here.

We stand in darkness, smelling age.

A friend of Milt's and mine, a psychologist who leads trips into the wilderness, says that when she hikes the canyons of Grand Gulch, Utah, where the Anasazi lived a thousand years ago and where their ruins still stand, she sometimes feels someone walking behind her on the path. And once, sleeping amid Anasazi ruins, she dreamed of tea cups and woke to find she was lying on pot sherds.

Recalling this, I feel a presence close behind me, the sense of breath on my neck, a faint heat, and then hands on my waist. I jump and suck in air.

"Quack, quack."

There is some laughter around us. Brief and uncomfortable.

"I'm over here, honey," a woman's voice says from across the room.

"Oops," the Duck Man breathes into my ear. "Wrong bird."

"Pity it's not duck season," James Sanderson says.

When I step out into the light after the others, Milton is surrounded by the group. He has his arms spread wide, like a vaudeville comedian concluding his act. He shoots his eyes right, then left, in a comic imitation of a search for danger, and says, "It's a *jungle* out here."

Everyone else laughs.

III. SURVIVALS OF THE NON-INVIDIOUS INTERESTS

Ahead of me, Milton puffs, each step a pant. His chest canted forward, he takes slow steps. Stops. His hands braced on his hips, he tilts his chin up, his face to the jungle canopy, and squints into the uneven light and the leaves. As if this were the reason for his stopping, to look closer, when really it is merely that he is tired. Fat. But he doesn't fool me. His heart is not strong. Better since the operation, but not strong.

There is a purple scar across his sternum where they went in to fix his heart. It looks like a zipper into the body. I imagine opening it, separating the sides, peeling back the keloidal skin, and lifting out the heart to examine it. I once saw a peasant farmer do this in a film on PBS; the man tethered his goat to a post and, cradling the animal's neck in his arms, his cheek pressed to the goat's foreflank, he drew the sharp tip of his knife in a line from the goat's clavicle to its groin, reached his hand in through the slit to hold the heart, and stopped it. I believe this footage was filmed in Greece. Though it could, I suppose, have been Turkey. What I remember is the worn-out citron of the hills. The startled goat. The beating heart. Stopped.

Funny what you remember, what you forget.

Milton doesn't remember the details. He says it was all a long time ago. But I remember vividly that day in the hospital, the yellow elm leaves scattered like coins across the sidewalk outside, how I cried thinking I might lose him, and how he told me about the woman he almost left me for. I've thought of leaving. Our children are settled in their own lives; they're no reason to stay. But I do.

Ahead of me, Milt waits, his lower lip thrust out as if in contemplation, his habitual sensual frown. His mouth was the first thing that caught my attention that day on campus fifty-two years ago, his mouth and his pink pants, his white cotton T-shirt, his canvas shoes; I took him for Italian. This was just after the war and there were many foreign scholars at the university then; American universities were like tiny European cities in those days. Milton looked exotic; he looked like a movie star; he looked like that actor in *Love Affair*. Charles Boyer, was it? I studied his mouth as we played chess by the lake on our first date that spring in Milwaukee. I loved that frown, his handsome suntanned face, his deliberation, how he watched me when it was my turn to move. I was winning and was about to take his queen, when he first kissed me. I used to joke that he kissed me just so that he wouldn't have to lose.

As we walk back to the bus, mud squashing beneath my tennis shoes, I worry about the camera that dangles from the nylon strap around my neck. There is a fungus that can get inside and fog the lens. Manuel has warned us of this, as he has warned us to watch for the fer-de-lance, but today we have seen no snakes in this Edenic forest.

At times the branches and ropey vines above us obtain a human aspect, in the half-light filtered through the leaves, and I cannot help but see them as limbs of that other sort, dangling above us as we slog this muddied track, their dissevered arms providing an amputated audience to our travail. I used to know the names by heart, the names of the bones and the muscles, like our children's names, which Milton, not I, mistakes; once upon a time—when I was a medical student before I married and gave it up—I could name those structures of the body as if we were on intimate terms: the long muscles that embrace the tibia, the fibula. But I am getting old. Now I have to look them up in *Gray's Anatomy*. The tiny bones of the hand.

IV. MODERN SURVIVALS OF PROWESS

At two, we board our tour bus to return to the hacienda for a siesta before the final evening's dinner and festivities. We have spent a good deal of time getting from here to there—on planes and buses—and to pass the time, to keep my mind occupied, I read about what it is we're seeing. It's important to me to know these things; Milton prefers to rely on intuition and impressions, to feel his way through a place, but I like to know the details. It seems all we have, sometimes.

On the bus, we are packed in like sardines and jostle. I read aloud from the guidebook, hoping to cheer the General, who mopes across the aisle, hoping to amuse the Sandersons, and to drown out the Duck, who moans about his aching feet. Milton dozes and wakes, dozes and wakes. But I read on.

"Snakes make up half the nation's reptiles," I say.

The Sandersons murmur admiringly.

"Tourism has replaced coffee and banana exports as Costa Rica's primary source of foreign currency."

Milton opens his eyes wide with mock alarm. "Y'mean," he says, "we're the latest cash crop?" He is mugging for the others. Several of them laugh. Milt squeezes my knee. I move it.

When the bus stops in Orosi, Milton leans out the window and jokes with the locals who try to sell us trinkets. They hold up woven baskets, rattle gourds. He asks if they'll wrap it, or if he can eat it here. They do not understand, they miss the joke, but he laughs, so they laugh. The roads are dusty, sun bleached, empty. Sometimes I feel a terrible fear that they lead nowhere.

As we drive on, trucks pass us on their way to San José, huge semis loaded with tree trunks stripped of branches, stacked six high, held in place by heavy chains. Their fronds wave like hands, hair. Manuel identifies the different species: yolillo, palmetto. "Palmitero," he says, speaking of the local woodsmen, "cut out the hearts of palm, a delicacy."

The bark of the guanacaste trees we pass is covered with yellow flowers. It's the same bright yellow of elm leaves in autumn, the yellow of the leaves I saw on the sidewalk outside the hospital the day they took out Milton's heart. I had read up on the procedure. But some things you cannot prepare for. A man cooled to the point of death. His heart stopped. Then they warm him again, bring him back to life. But is it the same man? The same man I married forty-seven years ago? The same man who pressed my hand, looked at me, his eyes wet with fear, before they wheeled him into the operating theater. I watched from above with the medical students. "Amazing," one young man kept saying, tapping his pen on a clipboard.

When we reach the lodge, our group lingers in the air-conditioned bus to discuss the evening's plans. Only the General retires directly to his room. The Duck Man lies supine across two seats, still moaning about his sunburn and his feet, while his wife murmurs consolation.

Manuel stands in the aisle and explains the schedule: there will be a two-hour siesta before dinner and, as this is our last night, dinner will be a traditional banquet followed by a *grupo folclorico*.

"Put on your dancing shoes," Manuel says smiling, clearly pleased to have mastered cliché.

At the mention of shoes, the Duck Man moans. "My feet are killing me," he says. "God damn. Why did you let me get these shoes?" he says to his wife.

"Honey, I wasn't there," she says.

"Of course, you were there. You're always there. I can't get a goddamn minute alone."

The rest of us fall silent. But Manuel presses on: He tells us that the folkloric group is famous in the region, that the bus for the airport tomorrow will arrive early, so it is best if we pack tonight.

"Goddamn corns," the Duck Man says.

There is a rush of questions as we try to pretend we aren't listening to the Duck.

"Do you want a pad?" the Duck Wife asks. "I'll get you a pad, hon."

"Unnnhhh," the Duck Man groans, as if he might die of a corn. "Unnnhhh."

"Oh, honey," she says. "I'll get you a pad, okay? You just stay put."

She steps out into the aisle and we stare.

"Excuse me," she says, then hurries off the bus. We linger in the air-conditioned bus, making small talk, making plans for the evening and the next day, loathe to leave the cooled air.

When the Duck Wife returns a few minutes later, she is flushed. Her dress is damp and clings.

"Hang on, honey," she says. "Let me help you." She is sweaty and her dress has slipped off her shoulder, revealing a beige bra strap, a fleshy, freckled, sunburned curve of shoulder. She bends over and takes hold of his shoe in the aisle. Her dress gaps. The sheen of perspiration across her chest makes her skin look swollen, puffy.

We look, then look away.

From the corner of my eye, I see her struggle to peel off the backing from a moleskin pad with her long shellacked nails. The Duck Man grabs it from her, strips the adhesive, and slaps the pad on.

He gives a deep appreciative groan, a guttural moan.

Relieved, we begin to discuss tonight's cocktails, tomorrow's final sunrise walk.

The Duck Man sits up. His feet drop to the floor with a slap. He puts a palm on his wife's plump shoulder and steps out into the aisle. He stands, leaning on her a moment, testing his feet, then he turns to us and winks.

"See you at dinner," he says. Then he gives his wife a firm slap on the rump. "Quack quack."

The Duck Wife giggles and flushes deeper pink.

He follows her off the bus, quacking as he goes.

V. THE HIGHER LEARNING AS AN EXPRESSION OF THE PECUNIARY CULTURE

While Milt naps before dinner, I sit in the library, French doors open to the veranda, looking out onto the garden of this hacienda, and write in a little notebook I've bought for the trip. The library adjoins the dining room and one can relax here in the late afternoons and read or hear lectures on botany and natural history. Large Zapotec rugs in red and black spread across its floor.

I am keeping a list of what we see. Not like the life list that the Scottish Brewer keeps or the nice couple from Illinois, the Sandersons. I am not a serious birder, as they say. I make lists to keep things straight—lists of what we see and eat—to help me remember these details, to keep things in their place, past separate from present, to keep unbidden memory out.

We have seen the plumes of smoke from Arenal. We have seen the yellow-bibbed toucan with its florid beak. We have seen the Blue Morpho, the iguanas and the basilisk, the world-weary heron, its long neck thrust forward and held, the image of patient, unrewarded hope. We have seen the Nikon and the Nikes and the bared and hairy legs, the sunglasses and embarrassed tippers.

Nine degrees above the equator, summer and winter are not much different and it's easy to lose track of days. The way, in age, one's days begin to blur. One's memories bleed like watercolor, staining the present, leaving me confused. At the kitchen counter, in the house we've shared for forty years in Iowa, I can be making coffee when suddenly I'll be flooded by a memory of Milton in the hospital, confessing as if forgiveness were mine to give.

Since Milt retired ten years ago, we have been taking classes together at the local university. Milt was a law professor before he turned to business, and learning is a thing we love. Last term we took one in Women Writing Life: Woolf, Duras, McCarthy, Nin, Hong Kingston, and Kincaid. The instructor encouraged each of us to keep a journal, and I have kept one ever since. Milt always wants to know what's in mine, to read over my shoulder. Cheating even in autobiography.

This semester we are taking a course in the sociology of the middle class. We are missing three lectures to come here, but it's worth it. In class we have talked about the construction of taste as a means of distinguishing the emergent middle classes in eighteenth-century England. We have discussed the American myth of classlessness. We have debated whether the derision heaped on liberals these days is a proxy for a corporate assault on the middle class. We are the accused. We, the beleaguered, much-mocked, middle classes.

Our professor claims that we have outlived our glory. The disdain heaped on liberals is a stand-in—he maintains—for a general disdain of the bourgeoisie. The League of Women Voters. The PTA. The Rotarians. Members of NPR, PBS, the ACLU—the names alone sound like a punchline to a joke.

But in our defense I say that we are the ones who are neither so poor nor so rich as to be indifferent. We have the leisure to sympathize and mourn, and the good sense to be ashamed of ourselves. My psychotherapist friend maintains that shame differs from guilt. Guilt, she says, is the consequence of a disruption of the social order, while shame results from a disruption of the natural order, the order of things. Guilt can be made right by an apology, a bread-and-butter note, but shame requires penance, the righting of a wrong; it requires sacrifice.

The professor says we are a dying breed, the middle classes. Even in this country that gave rise to Veblen's theory of the leisure class. Even here, we are going the way of the dodo. Our professor has documented our decline. The United States is, he says, coming more and more to resemble a Latin American country, with the mass of underpaid workers serving a small, self-perpetuating oligarchic class. You see it everywhere, in the cuts to public education, the shift to temporary workers, the lay-offs, the assaults on unions and workers' rights. His thesis is essentially that the culture wars are a distraction from the corporate assault on the citizenry. As the middle class is squeezed out by downsizing and globalization, we have no one to hate but ourselves: Jews against blacks, blacks against Koreans, everyone against the feminists and the intellectuals and the young and the homosexuals, a free-for-all of loathing.

Those of us who believed in the Great Society are dying out. I can hardly stand to go to the opera any more. All the heads are gray. And what will happen when we are gone?

Après nous, le déluge. Après nous, le canard.

It is too depressing to contemplate, so I put aside my journal and pull out Veblen, to read for class; reading before dinner has always felt like a great luxury, a private vice.

"What are you reading?"

It is Sanderson. I am startled by a voice outside my head, but glad to see him.

"*The Theory of the Leisure Class.*"

"Veblen. It's been years."

I tell him about our class and how we're missing three lectures to come on this tour.

"It's worth it," Sanderson says.

"Yes," I say, "it is."

Sanderson is on the board of a local museum and symphony, as I recall.

"What's it about?" the Duck Man asks, appearing in the doorway.

"Us," says Sanderson, expansively, and laughs.

I explain that Veblen was a nineteenth-century economist and sociologist who applied Darwin's theories to the American bourgeoisie to examine which traits survived in the modern industrial age.

"He coined the term 'conspicuous consumption,'" I say.

"I've heard of that," the Duck Man says, then he wanders over to look at a vase.

"Your son's a political scientist, isn't he?" Geneen Sanderson asks.

"Our daughter, yes. She's finishing her PhD at Chicago."

The Sandersons nod and smile. They are from Oak Park. Nice people.

"That's a good school," James Sanderson says.

"You must be very proud of her," says Geneen.

"We are."

When Milt arrives, we four go in, leaving the Duck Man to wait for his wife. Often we take a table for four to avoid the Duck Man and the Scottish Brewer, but tonight it is banquet style. There is no helping it. The Duck Man lands across the table. He leans toward me and says, "Gee, you clean up nice."

VI. PECUNIARY CANONS OF TASTE

This is not a proper hotel restaurant or night club. We are too far out in the countryside for that. It is an old converted hacienda. I wonder if the smooth dirt floors are mixed with goat blood, the old way. They are dark brown, solid as stone. Flecked with bits of hay. Flecks of straw can be seen in the thick walls where the white wash has chipped away. Each spring they plaster the exterior with micaceous clay against the year's rains, shoring up against the relentless process of erosion. This afternoon, it rained and the dining room smells of dust, moist earth.

The table where we dine is covered with a heavy linen cloth, the former owner's table perhaps. It has the length and general dimensions of the table you see in paintings of the Last Supper.

I take the liberty of rapping discreetly on its surface to test the density of the wood and find the tops are plastic, metal fold-out tables set end to end. They wobble slightly when the large ceramic platters are placed on them, heaped with stewed beef in chili sauce, rice, chicken fried in oil and spices, cooked pumpkin, potato, carrots, onion, with a small glass bottle of oil, limes, peppers, fried plantains, a platter of limp lettuce leaves smelling of chlorine, sliced tomatoes, cilantro, hearts of palm, cold beer.

I am pleased to know the names in Spanish; my accent, Manuel tells me, is quite good. Milton, however, insists on speaking to the waiters in Italian, which he learned in the army during the war, as if any foreign tongue would do. He likes this pretense of ignorance, likes pretending he does not know what he does. But he does, I know. As if he were an innocent abroad, a charming bungler, but I know better.

Marion, the Duck Man's wife, holds an ice cube in her plump

fingers, which are pink and swollen as tropical slugs. There is perspiration on her upper lip, glistening above her coral lipstick. She runs the tip of her tongue over her lips, darts at the sweat, glancing around the table to see if anyone has noticed. I pretend not to. When she catches my eye, I do not smile. Earlier, she wedged three fingers into her water glass to extract the ice she holds in her hand. She'd glanced up midway through her procedure and smiled deprecatingly, as she extracted the chunk of ice and palmed it in an effort at discretion. She rubs the ice cube along the sides of her long, plump throat.

"Failure is the family business," the Duck Man said on our first day out, flashing a broad salesman's smile. But he didn't need to tell us. Milt had already heard of him from men he knows in Omaha. The Duck Man has a reputation: Like the smell of a slaughter house, it carries distances. He is known for buying scrap metal that was once the basis of a productive business. He has made a fortune in scrap, in destroying what others built.

At dinner, his wife holds forth on the eating habits of parrots. They have not been able to have children. She keeps one as a pet in Detroit, where they live, and dotes on it.

When Geneen points out that the exotic animal trade is ruthless and often cruel, that parrots are usually tortured during capture, illegally transported in trunks, often dying en route, the Duck Wife looks uncomfortable, then distressed. She tears her napkin, shreds it.

"I never heard that," she said. "Honey, d'you think it's true?"

The Duck Man shrugs and chews.

They talk about the ballroom-dancing lessons they take each week, about their boat; they seem to signify some unhappy truth about the dying century. Perhaps it is unfair to judge them, but they seem to be all that is tawdry and sad and commercial. They confirm my worst fears, that we are slipping in some significant way, that we are losing ground, *après nous, le canard.*

"Failure is the family business," he says proudly, repeating what is clearly his motto.

"Oh, you," the Duck Wife says. "He's always saying that. You can just ignore him if you want."

Would it were true.

They remind me of our neighbors in Iowa, who are in a state of perpetual tan. The Herberts smile hugely at us from across the hedge. They stopped inviting us to dinner years ago, but they continue to wave at us from the driveway as if it were a great and remarkable pleasure to see us again. They always look as if they were about to set sail, when the fact of the matter is they are going up the street to the Olive Garden at the mall for a bite to eat. It is worst in summer. Then they are in tennis whites, baring their aggressively good teeth. Huge, athletic, unreflective people. Even in winter they are tanned. As if they could defy the season we are in.

VII. THE BELIEF IN GRACE

After dinner, young women collect the plates and ask if we would like coffee. Milton excuses himself and retires to the room, too tired to wait for the folkloric dancers. Since his operation, he is careful not to overexert himself. Procedures that would have killed us twenty years ago now are routine. Like Darwin's creatures on the Galapagos, we are still evolving. The phrases sound so innocuous—bypass, double bypass, triple bypass, quadruple bypass—more like highway construction, like urban planning, than a matter of the human heart.

The young women bring out bouquets of flowers to fill the empty places at the centers of the tables. One of the dancers invites the General out onto the floor. Soon, the others, even Manuel, even the Sandersons, go watch.

I am alone at the table, when I see the bird of paradise and remember the hospital room. The bouquet by the bed. It was after the operation. We were holding hands and I asked Milt how he was feeling and he said, "I had an affair." For a moment I thought he meant that he was having a ball, a fair, a riot, in the hospital, that he was being ironic. "It ended ten years ago," he said.

That was the first I heard about the woman he had almost left me for years ago. The hospital room reminded him; she'd died in one, he said. If she hadn't died, he would have left me. He was sixty at the time; she was forty-four. He'd been involved with her for twenty years, half our marriage. Those are the numbers, the details I cannot get out of my head. Specifics I do not want to know.

The hospital room was private, thank God. There was no one else to hear his confession. An ugly room. Blank as the heart of God, with all the charm of a dentist's office. White linens. White walls. The only color came from the flowers I'd brought. A vase of orange tiger lilies, a sunflower, a bird of paradise, a spray of greens, a branch of yellow elm. I don't know why he had to mention it, after all these years, after three mortgages and seven cars and all the loneliness and compromises.

He reached for my hand and I jerked away and knocked over the vase.

"Damn it," I said. "Goddamn it." I crouched to get the pieces. The bird of paradise had snapped its stem. Water seeped across the linoleum tiles.

"I'll tell you whatever you want to know," he said.

"I didn't want to know."

"I want things to be clean between us."

"How dare you," I said. "How dare you tell me this now."

Later, I will say, we have done worse things to each other, we have survived much worse, but I'm not sure. Is there worse than this: to make of someone's life a lie?

I don't ask for details. I don't want to know. But Milt tells me when he feels like it. What he remembers. Which isn't much. An amnesiac about his own indiscretions.

Leaves. That is what I remember. Funny the things you remember and don't. Yellow elm leaves. The shadows left on the sidewalk after the leaves had been swept away, their silhouettes like shadows of bodies after a nuclear detonation. The aura remains. Even after the body is gone.

I cannot see what all the commotion is about. The others have formed a ragged circle at the far edge of the room, and they stand together on the dance floor, smiling and clapping to the music. I finish my coffee and stand to leave, and then I see them: the ridiculous couple, waltzing. The Duck Man and his wife. The music is all wrong for a waltz, but they are undeterred. The folkloric dancers have cleared the floor, and, like the others, they watch the Duck Man and his wife, moving around the room in one another's arms. I stop and stare. The couple bobs and glides and turns; they bob and glide and turn. And all the while between them there is a gap—between their thighs and hips and chests. And I understand suddenly that this is how waltzing works, this is what gives it grace, what creates the tension and the poignant beauty of the dance. This empty space. What moves us is not the dancers' proximity but the careful distance they maintain: it is amazing that two people can be so close and still not touch.

And despite myself, I have to say it, they are lovely.

When I get back to the room, the moon is up and bright enough to see by. I make my way to the bed, undress, and slip beneath the covers. Lying there, I am filled with what I'd felt that day in the hospital, just after the moment when I knew that Milton wouldn't live, when they started the dead man's heart again: the unexpected relief that I'd been wrong. And I think of the couple on the dance floor, moving around the room in one another's arms and of that empty space between them. You'd never have guessed they had it in them, that couple, so unlike what I had imagined we'd become. And I cannot help but ask myself, Who'd have believed they had beauty in them, who would have guessed they were capable of grace?

Hindsight

MARY HOOD

From *How Far She Went* (1984)

They met after a rock concert. She had lost sight of the friends she had come with, and her rabbity glance, seeking a landmark face in the multitude, encountered his, a stranger's, then moved on, still seeking. Then found him again. He stood alone on the periphery of the flowing crowd that propelled her toward him. He reached for her, pulled her toward him by the small silver cross at her throat, drew her close enough to be heard. She shook her head and giggled, "I'll miss my ride."

"D'you ever go ninety miles per, with nothing between you and your fears but black wind?"

She laughed as though she understood.

It was her first motorcycle ride. To hear her squeal, he shut off the headlamp and drove blind on the causeway. He laid the machine almost over on its pegs as he rounded the last corner and drove across the lawn and up the walk to deliver her into the circle of her mother's porch light. He didn't stay. She could hear him ripping back down G Street; he must have made all the lights; he didn't stop. She trembled up the stairs to bed, still smiling. He had her phone number written on the thigh of his jeans. During study hall she wrote *I love Steve, I love Steve, I love Steve* on the soles of her tennis shoes. A summer's beachcombing erased it heel and toe, and his motorcycle pegs wore it off under the arches. By Labor Day they were engaged.

When they had satisfied the Church that they were prepared for the sacrament of holy matrimony, they married. She was eighteen. After not quite a year she gave birth to a daughter who coughed, gurgled a moment only, then died. The priest infiltrated her twilight sleep to break the news and to tell her that it was all right, God did not mind, she had not entirely failed for she had fulfilled her obligation to try, and no doubt would have another chance soon. Her husband, nervous, silent, chain-smoking at the waiting-room window, watched cars as they went by, going elsewhere. Thereafter, occasionally, with increasing frequency, he too was elsewhere.

The child was never mentioned. It had its fate, no reality. She never got to hold it. No one could understand her lingering depression, which was her only remaining defense, for it seemed to her that every vulnerability in herself had been found out, examined in the merciless committee work of priestly counsel. To all complaints and sighs came the exhortation: try again, try harder. She confessed her suspicions about her husband: her sisters and their husbands, with their sharp eyes and vantages and biases, reported his drinking, his late evenings spent in the company of rowdy bikers and potheads. This too, the priest said, was her fault. She had driven him away with her coldness; she should examine herself and determine how, then try harder.

She was to win him back; she was to want him back. But he didn't see it that way. When she most sincerely and valiantly tried, he abused her. Once he knocked her down. She asked the priest to forgive her for provoking him, for she had learned, had finally learned, the rules of the game. And of course she tried again.

Despite all chances for disillusion she remained an innocent, a dreamwalker. When would she wake? Her best friend from school asked her to stand with her when she married and confided later how her husband's clan demanded the "cloth of proof" after the wedding night. She did not understand; she went to her sisters and asked, her sisters with their crammed houses stinking of boiled dinners and damp wash and poxy children. They teased her into retreat. She walked home in the rain, blushes (How could I be so stupid?) steaming on her cheeks. All her life it had been like that; being the youngest by half a dozen years, everyone got the joke before she did, understood everything before she did, years ahead, so she must hasten to catch up, or fake it, laughing along in ignorance. They knew it all before she did, from long division to menarche. Their competency awed her, silenced her, and her silence had been her shield against ridicule . . . All the way home she was saying, "Why am I such a fool?" and when she got home, her husband was entertaining someone in their bed. She turned and fled into the rain again, finally taking refuge in the Church. Incoherent, she humbly confessed her total failure as a wife and prayed for death. At nineteen.

The priest and his seniors, rung by diocesan rung to the highest, consulted. The marriage (so the decision filtered down) was not to be set aside; it was a sacrament and had left its certain indelible mark on their souls.

They went for counseling. Her husband, in an ugly scene, boasted that he had married to avoid the draft and the child had been meant to make that avoidance absolute. But the war ended, and with it, all necessity. He didn't need her; he'd be glad to be rid of her . . . She fainted (shock and anemia). The priest looked a little pale himself. The Church tried again. Up and up went the petition.

Meanwhile she went to live with her mother, holing up in the attic room from whose diamond pane she had watched as a child to see her father, roaring drunk, back the truck down the alley with its latest load of illogical firewood—perhaps a canted chicken coop, perhaps a piano. All to be axed into submission while he caroled at the top of his Irish lungs. Dead now, from complications. So the empty house had plenty of room, but she retreated to the attic, lying on her maiden bed, listening to the season pass. She slept hours at a time, days at a time, weeks. Her mother brought her meals (mostly uneaten), gossip from the street (it rolled off the wax of her alienation like rain), a priest (she excommunicated him), nieces (she held them on her gaunt lap and wept into their hair), Christmas cards (not many), birthday cards (she turned twenty), and finally a phone number (a lawyer's).

She had no savings. Her husband had cleaned it all out and wasn't to be found. She sold her rings for what she could get (not enough) and her sisters and her mother took up a collection among themselves, shaving grocery money and tithes, keeping their own counsel, going without, so that she could go . . . to El Paso on the day coach, all arranged, one fee covered all, everything arranged. She was met at the airport by the *abogado* and his wife. They made all the explanations as they crossed the bridge into Juárez over the shining river. The customs officials made only a cursory examination. She had never been even one hundred miles from home, and now this, another country, accompanied by strangers whose purchased kindness might fail at any time. They drove to the hotel where her residency requirements would be accomplished; they drove away and left her, saying they would pick her up in the morning for some sightseeing, and paperwork, at their offices in a nearby street. That would be fine? Yes, yes, she nodded, pretending poise: her life's work.

The hotel clerk jangled the keys and she followed him to her room. He called her *señorita* and said, "Any little thing?" and when he left she locked the door behind him. She felt the whole building tremble (she feared at first it was an earthquake) as the elevator whirred and plunged back down to earth, and she made up her mind that she would take the stairs when she went back down for supper, included in the blanket fee.

Her eyes watered and stung from the glare of the ride into

Mexico, from the shimmer of the whitewashed buildings and tin roofs. She set her overnight case on the stained, cigarette-scarred dresser and avoided her reflection in the wavery mirror. She yawned. She threw back the lank coverlet and lay, clothed and shod, on the jaded mattress. Down in the street in the day's heat, life raged on, like the song of cicadas. She was tired but not sleepy. The noise and heat oppressed her. With the window open, she felt vulnerable. With it shut, she suffocated. Her head ached. She had not brought aspirin.

It had sounded so easy when they explained it: fly down, cross the border, spend the night, cross back home, fly north again, freed. Free.

She picked up the phone.

¿Sí, señorita? (Insolent perhaps? Knowing? Sly?)

"Aspirin. Do you have anything for headache? Aspirin tablets?" She spoke in broken syllables to make herself understood. Was she understood? Would he bring her aspirin?

¡Sí señorita!

But an hour passed and nothing happened. She unlocked the door and went down, by the stairs, avoiding the cranky, dark elevator. The clerk looked up. She did not know if he was the same one who checked her in. Was he the one who took her call?

"Aspirin," she enunciated.

Ah, sí, sí, duele la cabeza, sí, he agreed. Was he going to help her? Uncomprehending, she advanced across the lobby with its palms, once venerable, now in a season of molt and despair. A man slept behind his newspaper at the window with its trapped flies. The fake leather of the chairs caught the afternoon's light in old impressions of anonymous waiting flesh. The fan, overhead, was still. People, place, furnishings had come down in the world so gradually that they still had their pride.

The clerk, when she came to the desk, put out his hand and insinuated, *Señorita is lonely?* in English good enough. She fled back upstairs, ran the chain in its channel, and turned the lock.

She had left the window open and her purse in plain sight. She hurried to it and checked—everything was there. Relieved, she secured the window. As she stood there a man in the street, looking up, caught her eye and made a gesture in whatever language comprehensible. She drew the shade.

She had a growing horror of everything in the room, of its probable past, its likely uncleanliness, its unrighteousness. This was her Purgatory; she had cast herself into it; she must bide here a while. She splashed water from the reluctant tap onto her hands, her face, careful not to let any drop of it pass her lips.

The phone rang. Was it the lawyer and his wife? She answered on an outrush of grateful breath, "Yes?"

The clerk? Someone else? A man. The one sleeping in the lobby? The one in the street? A stranger, accented: "May I come up?" She hung up.

Later, within the hour, another call. The lawyer's wife. "You all well and happy? All okay?"

What could she say? "All okay," she hoped.

"Tomorrow we pick up, ready on the time early?"

"Yes oh yes."

Night came, the same stars shining there that shine down on all the flags of the world, but the sky looked alien to her. In the street, past midnight, the same loud living: talk, arguments, parting, arrivals, jokes, despairs, threats, and barking of dogs, as though the town ran on a twenty-four hour clock. In the corridors beyond her bolted door, perpetual footsteps, whisperings, bargainings. She lay unblinking on the bed and wondered if she should pray. For what? For her immortal soul with its certain indelible marks? For her daughter who breathed only twice? For her failures? For her success? The Church had left her; she had left the Church. Suppose within two years they granted her an official annulment; by then it would be worth what to her? Who would she be? It wasn't anger she felt; it was a quietness, as though there had been a final argument and things had been said that couldn't be unsaid, things that outweighed love. The priest had said . . .

The phone waked her from confusion, not sleep. From her terror of waiting. "Yes?"

A long silence, then a man's rough offer. In Spanish? In German? In Latin? She did not know. She flung down the phone and paced, then moved the dresser, inched it over the cracked linoleum to bar the door, to fortify her position. She trembled from the effort, from the necessity, from hunger. She had not dared go down to the lobby and into the restaurant to eat. She chewed her last stick of gum and checked the time. Her watch was gone! Fallen as she moved the dresser. She crawled on hands and knees, patting into shadows, listening to its tick, finding it. It had suffered. Its hands stood still. It began to lie. She buckled it on anyway and from hour to hour sought its opinion, however incredible, out of old habit. She lay down again, waiting. Songs and laughter from the street below. Traffic and heat unabated. The monotonous barking of dogs. Church bells.

Morning came. She stood ready. At the *señora*'s knock and voice, she moved the dresser back in place and unlocked. They went downstairs, out past the clerk (same one? new one?) and into the morning with its scant freshness on the stale dust, nothing so virginal as dew . . . Perhaps spit, perhaps tears.

They rode in the car to the *abogado*'s where, in the small glassed cubicle, she signed papers. She had already signed papers. She would sign more papers. She listened again to the explanations and then handed over the check, her eyes resting themselves in that distant place on her mother's countersignature. After the business was accomplished, they rode around, just around, killing time.

No, she wasn't hungry. (Everywhere the rancid smell of cooking oil.)

Here and there, over a crumbling wall, flowers on strange, unkind stems, daring her to near with swords drawn. Traffic paused to honor the slow pedestrian file of patient mourners trailing an infant's shouldered coffin. She lay back, eyes closed, till the procession passed and they drove on. They put in the necessary hours. She drank a Coke. She was resident that legalizing while, then on the exact hour they headed for the bridge, her papers in order. They opened her little green overnight case with its cargo of pink nylon to the sky, like a melon. The officer snapped it shut with a smile and a salute. Welcome home. There on the far bank, the American flag. Seeing it, she burst into tears. The same flag that stood in the corner of the dark stage between assemblies all through high school. The same flag that sagged on its rusty pole over the post office in her hometown. She noticed it for the first time. She said she would remember.

Back home she handed the papers to the American lawyer, and eventually they went through. She was free. The Church, after a time, granted the annulment. Her Bulova, when it returned from the shop, was again in step. There was only that little scratch on its face, indelible, a scar. Resetting it, she made new appointments. She saw her husband (now legally and in the eyes of the Church a stranger) on the shore road, on his motorcycle, going fast. Going, it turned out, away. She only recognized him in the rearview mirror, after he had passed. When it was too late.

Borderland

MARGOT SINGER

From *The Pale of Settlement* (2007)

Susan could spot an Israeli anywhere. Among the tourists in the Thamel Backpacker's Café—the familiar crowd of Germans and Australians, rangy kids and rugged types who looked ready to head up Everest at a sprint—he stood out right away: the ropy muscles, the jiggling knee, the ashtray full of cigarettes smoked down to the filter or stubbed out half-done. He had broad sideburns, an Adam's apple as sharp as a stone. He was wearing a Nirvana T-shirt and baggy Bedouin pants. He was writing in a notebook. Not left to right.

Two tables over, he looked up. His left eye twitched, then widened—a tic, not a wink. She could walk over and say Shalom, but then she'd be stuck explaining that she didn't really speak Hebrew after all. She could ask him for a cigarette, but she didn't smoke. She could say, My parents are Israeli, too.

From here in the center of town, you couldn't see the mountains, just the white disk of the sun burning through the morning haze. There was a musky scent of incense and donkey dung, a chaos of passing motorbikes and rickshaws, bicycles and beat-up cars, bells and horns and shouts. Across the road, a little girl peeked around the doorway of a child-sized shrine. A dog lay panting in the shade of a stand stacked with bins of mangoes, persimmons, apples, packages of crackers, chocolate bars, wooden flutes, garlands of orange marigolds, bright pink sweets. An old woman squatted by the shop, spat on the dusty ground.

Susan touched the face of her grandmother's watch and counted back. It was nine hours and forty-five minutes earlier back home—still the day before: October 19, 1998. The extra fifteen minutes off New Delhi time were Nepal's little hat-tip of independence from its big neighbors to the north and south—an interval intended, Susan supposed, solely to annoy, or to make you stop and think. She fingered the watch's gold bracelet, its delicate safety chain. She should have left it at home.

In Gaza, the Arabs lined up at dawn. They waited at the checkpoint in taxis, crammed four across the back, in cars and trucks. The heat swirled in a yellow haze. Everywhere, there was sand. The soldiers—Dubi, Ofer, Sergei, Assaf, and the rest of the unit—stood by the concrete barriers and sandbags and razor wire and checked identity cards and waved a metal detector wand. The Arabs were laborers, field hands, merchants, factory workers, students, fishermen. They were on their way to Khan Yunis or Gaza City or across the border to Israel. They carried their belongings in plastic sacks. The women wore loose dresses, scarves wrapped around their heads. They smelled of sweat and cigarettes; their speech tumbled from their throats—glottal ayins, rolling *r*s. The sea was less than half a mile away. At night, you could hear it breathe.

Go take a hike, Susan's brothers used to say. After a while, her mother started saying it, too, although coming from her, like many English idioms, it never sounded right. She had a way of making everything seem literal. Go take a hike, she'd say, as if she really expected you to jump up, grab your rucksack and alpenstock and march down eight flights of stairs, out into Van Cortlandt Park and across the Bronx.

Susan's grandparents had been the hikers, the lovers of Alpine forests, wildflower glades. Her own parents preferred the beach. What Susan remembered, though, about their summers in Haifa or at the Jersey shore, was that the beach was the place her parents fought. They fought at night, after Susan and her brothers were in bed. They argued in Hebrew, an escalation of harsh whispers breaking through to shouts. Then the screen door would rasp and slam, and Susan would lie awake, anxiety fluttering in her chest, waiting for whoever had gone out to return, but all she ever heard, before she fell asleep, was the hissing of the waves along the shore.

In the morning, of course, she'd find her mother in the kitchen making breakfast as usual, a kibbutznik's bucket cap atop her head, her father drinking his coffee, rustling the newspaper, as he always did, as if nothing at all had happened between them the night before.

It's good to have a short memory, her mother always said, flicking her hands.

But Susan didn't have a short memory. She had a fickle, sticky memory, an inability to let go. She accumulated arguments, misunderstandings, fallings-out and fights, storing them away like the stacks of old letters and photographs she kept in shoe boxes underneath her bed, like her closets full of poorly fitting clothes. Her mother couldn't understand why Susan wouldn't throw things out. Leah was always shedding her own belongings, passing them along—*here, take this Suzi, this is for you.* As a result, nothing got thrown away at all, but piled up at Susan's place instead.

Susan's mother would have liked it here in Kathmandu. She had an enthusiasm for spicy food, exotic scenery, the romance of the East. She loved bargaining for trinkets, the whole charade of feigning outrage and pretending to walk away over the equivalent of fifty cents. She would have made a pilgrimage to every temple, drank the yak butter tea. Susan had actually considered inviting her mother to come along. But when she'd mentioned the trek, Leah had tapped her temple with one finger and said: *At meshuga?* Are you insane? For what do you want to sleep on the ground in the freezing cold? To see some mountains? Go to Switzerland if you want mountains! There at least you can sleep in a bed like a civilized person!

Civilization had its limits, in her mother's mind.

Gaza was a cesspool, and Dubi was the operator of the valve. He turned the spigot on and off. Green light on. Red light off. When the light turned red, the Arabs in their trucks and cars and yellow taxis stopped and sat and waited for the road to open again. They rolled down their windows and fanned themselves with sheets of cardboard or a scarf. They stepped out into the sun or squatted in the shade of the trucks and smoked. Pallets of dahlias wilted in the heat. There was a smell of rotting fish. Cell phones bleeped, babies wailed, chickens clucked, arguments broke out. Khalas! the Arabs yelled, waving their fists. Enough.

In the heat of the day, Dubi draped a shirt over the back of his helmet to shade his neck. His M16 rocked against his side like an extra limb, his flak vest heavy and far too hot. He scanned exit permits and searched the trunks of cars. From time to time, he'd pull aside a suspicious man or boy, force him to the ground, and hold him there beneath his pointed gun until a jeep arrived to take him off to jail. But the mid-1990s were not a time of war; from Rabin's assassination in 1995 until the second intifada began, things were relatively quiet there. Quietly, the shit flowed out at dawn, and at dusk it flowed back in again.

The group that Susan had signed up with for the Everest Base Camp trek included a truck driver, a retired shrink, a mining engineer from the Yukon, a neurosurgeon and his wife, a hairdresser from Redondo Beach, and four other single women, all from New York. They stood around the lobby of their hotel, looking, with their baseball caps and fanny packs and camera gear, just like the American tourists that they were. They shook hands and said, Hey, how's it going. Susan wished she had the nerve to travel on her own.

Susan was assigned to share a tent with one of the other single women, who, it turned out, lived only three blocks away from her on the Upper West Side. Joyce was a talkative woman in her mid-thirties with ash-blond hair and a pale, moist face. She'd come on the trip, she told Susan, in hopes of meeting a man, but had already ruled out the immediate possibilities: the truck driver, the hair-dresser, the mining engineer. She should have been born a Hindu, she said. An arranged marriage wouldn't be so bad.

Clipboard in hand, the group leader circled around, inspecting their duffel bags and gear. He checked off the essential items, fingered their mummy bags, their water bottles, their stashes of granola bars. When it was Susan's turn, he shook his head. He told her to go rent some fleece pants and a warmer jacket in the Kathmandu bazaar.

Susan skipped the bus tour of Patan and Bhaktapur and headed out to Durbar Square alone. She felt sealed inside her body, her limbs unnaturally light. It might have been the jet lag, although she'd never felt more wide-awake. It was festival time, and the city streets were hung with strings of flowers and prayer flags and tiny lights. Groups of children passed playing flutes and drums, chanting Tihar songs. A girl who could be no more than eleven or twelve carried an infant in a sling across her back, her eyes rimmed in black, her mouth and cheeks smeared red with rouge. Shop windows were stacked with Nikes and Nintendo cartridges, bootleg Chinese CDs and videotapes. In front of the Kathmandu Tours and Travel Agency stood a ribby, sway-backed cow.

In the maze of stalls in the bazaar, Susan found a pair of Russian army-issue fleece pants and a puffy blue down parka that looked as if it had survived its share of Everest expeditions. Feathers flew out of the seams when she pressed on it; it would certainly be warm. She hoped she'd have time to wash the pants before they left for the mountains in the morning. She didn't even want to think about some soldier's unwashed groin.

She was on her way back to the hotel when she noticed him, crouching in the shadow of a courtyard, pointing a video camera at a balcony above. There could be no mistaking those Bedouin pants, that close-cropped hair. Three young monks were leaning over the rail, shiny-headed and bare-shouldered in their saffron robes, jostling each other and waving down to passersby. Susan wondered if this was the Temple of the Living Goddess, the Kumari Devi, the little girl selected by augury, whose feet must never touch the ground. She'd read that the girl sometimes came out onto her balcony, but if this was in fact her home, there was no sign of her now. Susan watched the monks, wondering if they knew they were being videotaped. Didn't they care? She turned around, but the Israeli guy had disappeared.

The army was what everybody did. After high school, you went to the army, and when you got out you did your *miluim* for a couple of weeks a year until you got too old. The army was the melting pot. The army was where you made your closest friends. The army was there for you, for life.

As a child, the only thing Dubi could really imagine about being a soldier was the uniform. He pictured himself in the lace-up boots, the olive-green fatigues, an Uzi underneath his arm. He saw himself hitchhiking at the bus stops, his arm held out, his index finger pointing down. Later, he imagined himself carrying out daring raids on the arms-smuggling tunnels in Rafah, or Syrian positions in the Golan. He'd leap through the gun turret of a tank, crawl on his belly through the burning Negev sand. The army made you strong.

Dubi wasn't even born until the mid-1970s, was just a kid during the Lebanon campaign. He remembered the Gulf War, though. He'd never forget waiting with his mother in their apartment building's basement shelter, their gas masks on. They sat on the edge of a cot, listening for the whistle of an approaching SCUD, the tremor of explosion, the wail of ambulances speeding to the scene. He remembered the metallic taste of adrenaline, the expansion inside his chest as he put his arm around his mother, cupped her shoulder in his hand.

Dubi's father had slipped in his military service—a desk job in Tel Aviv, on account of his bad back—between '68 and '71, when everything was quiet. He was killed in a car accident in Hadera when Dubi was five years old. Dubi often told people that his father had died in a burning tank in Sinai during the Yom Kippur War. He told the lie so often that it seemed that it was true.

The nineteen-seat Royal Nepal Airways Twin Otter took off at 7:28 a.m., banked sharply to the northwest, and rose out over the terraced fields and knobby green hills of the Terai. Susan pressed her forehead to the window, feeling the vibration of the engines inside her head. In the seat next to her, the truck driver was droning on about the engineering qualities of short-landing-strip aircraft, the high standards of the Nepalese Air Force, the good fortune of a cloudless sky, but Susan wasn't listening. She was watching the shadow of their plane flitting across the valley floor. It was ridiculously small, as insubstantial as a fleck of ash.

A murmur ran through the cabin as the Himalayas appeared in the cockpit windscreen, beyond the pilots' upraised hands. The 26,000-foot snowcapped peaks floated across the horizon, looking just like any other mountains, the Rockies or the Alps, until you remembered that the ground they rested on was over 15,000 feet above sea level to begin with, and that they went up from there. Everything was out of scale.

And then they rounded a crenellated ridge, green and steep, and they were there, the Lukla landing strip rising suddenly in front of them, an uphill dirt runway cut into the mountainside.

The plane roared, bounced twice, and skidded to a stop just short of a stone wall. They climbed down underneath the wing, ducking their heads, taking deep breaths of the sun-warmed air that smelled of smoke and mud and ice and pine, 9,200 feet high.

Transported, Susan thought, as they pointed out their duffel bags to the Sherpa porters who had gathered to meet them there. Transported, carried off. It was glorious to be plucked up and carried off like Thumbelina on a swallow's wings. To be raised into the air, like the Kumari Devi back in Kathmandu. What a comedown for her, at puberty, to be sent back to the ground.

The trail to Phakding, their first stop, wound past lowland fields of beans, potatoes, radishes and peas, smoky teahouses, children playing in the sun. The dirt path was broad and flat, more a road than a mountain trail. Susan walked alongside Joyce, her daypack bouncing against her shoulders, her hiking boots rubbing a little on her heel. A Nepali girl passed them, whistling, barefoot, two gigantic duffel bags tied onto her back with a rope looped across her forehead. Outside a teahouse, a sign read COKES $1.50, HOT APPLE PAE. A man passed herding a procession of *dzokyos* and yaks. The air rang with the sound of tumbling water. The sun turned red, lost heat, fell behind the ridge. Susan looked up, light-headed, and wondered if it was possible to get motion sickness solely from the spinning of the earth. A vulture wheeled across the sky.

After dark, they sat inside the Phakding trekkers' lodge and Susan played gin rummy in the light of an oil lamp with Ross, the hairdresser from Redondo Beach. A group of children trouped through the smoke-filled room, giggling and tapping on a Tihar drum, passing around a plate for coins. Is Hindu dharma, the tallest one said. Good luck give. Out the window, a translucent moon ducked behind a hidden peak. Shadows fell across the stubble field, studded with blue and orange tents. There was a peal of laughter, a muffled shout. Hebrew? Here? Susan squinted through the fogged-up glass. Yes, Hebrew, she was almost sure. A shadow passed, the low voice of a man.

Yo Susan, Ross said, waving a hand in front of her face. Gin.

Most Fridays, Dubi went home to Tel Aviv for Shabbat. He hitchhiked from the border or took the Egged bus. He carried a duffel bag stuffed with dirty laundry and his gun. When he could, he sat on the left side of the bus so he could watch the sun set into the sea. He'd count the seconds it took for it to slide behind the band of haze, flattening as if it were being squeezed beneath an enormous weight of sky. Faster than it seemed possible the earth could turn, the orange sphere would extrude itself into a liquid line, and then the sky and sea would turn dull and flat and it would be gone.

Dubi came home from his week in Gaza like a worker coming home from the factory or fields. He'd climb the steps of his apartment building, ring the doorbell as he fished in his pocket for his key. The bell chirped like a manic bird. Inside, he'd drop his bag, prop his M16 next to the door, call out that he was home. Usually his mother's boyfriend would be there, watching TV, drinking a Maccabi beer out of a can. He was a peacenik, a grizzled hippy type. Oh ho, here comes the big hero, he liked to say.

Dubi ached for home all week but once he got there everything felt wrong. He'd pull off his uniform, take a shower, but it made no difference at all. He couldn't bear his mother's anecdotes about her job at the insurance agency, couldn't care less about what was up with her boyfriend's snot-nosed kids. In the background, the baritone TV newscaster pronounced the word *Gaza* as if it were an outpost on the moon. But Gaza stuck to Dubi, got inside the creases of his skin like sand.

On summer Saturdays, Dubi went with his girlfriend, Maya, to the beach. They spread their towels on the sand. Maya was in the army, too. Her job was showing schoolchildren how to use gas masks. She was a skinny, large-boned girl with a halo of frizzy blondish hair, and she wore a too-short army skirt that gave Dubi a hard-on when he saw her in it, every time. But when she leaned her head against his shoulder, Dubi retracted like a snail. All along the beach, people laughed and played. They whacked racquet balls back and forth, dove into the waves, rubbed suntan lotion on their skin. Gaza was barely seventy kilometers away.

Susan spotted him again just past the crest of the steep hill along the trail to Namche, where the first glimpse of Everest hovered through the trees. He was sitting on a rock, playing a wooden flute. A small crowd of trekkers had gathered there to rest, snap photographs, buy cups of *kala chia* and bottles of Coke from the tea tent set up near the scenic overlook. He hopped down to the ground and picked up his pack as she drew near, fell into step alongside her on the trail. He had on the Bedouin pants again, a baseball cap, cheap Chinese sneakers on his feet. The muscle twitched beneath his eye as his jaw tensed. Not a wink.

Maybe I know you from someplace? he said.

Where are you from? she said, even though she knew.

He told her he was from Tel Aviv, that everybody called him Dubi although his real name was Dov, and that Dov meant "bear." He'd gotten out of the army just before coming to Nepal. He spoke in such a low tone that she had to strain to hear. She couldn't have said what it was, but there was something about him—that nervous energy, or that guttural accent, so like her cousin Gavi's, or the nakedness of the pale skin around his eyes that showed when he pushed his sunglasses up on his head—that kept her walking with him all that afternoon.

The sun was already fading when they rounded the bend to Namche Bazaar, with its terraced fields and red-roofed Sherpa houses built along the curved slope of the cirque. Dubi stopped to light a cigarette, cupping the flame between his hands. Strings of prayer flags fluttered along the houses' eaves, the words of the

Buddhist mantra shaking loose and flying out onto the wind. *Om Mani Padme Hum.* Up the hillside, in a stone-walled field next to a whitewashed house, Susan could see the Sherpas setting up their tents. She could hear the sound of singing, women's voices, high and clear. They were praying to Yama Raj, god of the underworld, for the long life of their brothers. It was the last night of Tihar.

Susan's parents' founding myth was this: that her father had caught one glimpse of her mother—then an NYU coed with long dark hair—and followed her around for the next year or two—back to Israel, around New York—until she finally gave in and agreed to go out with him. They were a sexy couple; there was no denying that. You could see it in the photographs—in the way her father folded his arm around her mother's waist, in the heavy-lidded, postcoital look in her mother's eyes. Within three months, they were married; seven months later, Susan was born. Not premature.

This myth—that Susan's mother was a flighty spirit whose feet needed to be held to the ground, that with a single glance, her father knew that they were meant to be—persisted, as such myths do, despite the transformations of the years, despite her father's infidelities, her mother's capacity to forgive, their tugs of war and fights. The myth provided roles for them to play: the skittish maiden, the dogged suitor; the one who pulled away, the one who reeled the other back again. It was possible that they stayed together because of the myth—so her mother could believe that she was free to leave, so her father could believe that he was, in fact, the constant one.

Susan sat in the Namche trekkers' lodge, trying to write a letter to her parents that she couldn't mail until she got back to Kathmandu, meaning she'd already be back in New York when it arrived. Their group leader was sitting across the table, flipping through a two-week-old copy of the *International Herald*

Tribune, the headphones of Joyce's Discman on his head. *Making love is a mental disease!* he exclaimed suddenly. For a moment, Susan thought he was talking to her, until she realized those were the lyrics to the song.

Clouds were rolling into the cirque and a fine snow had begun to fall. Susan touched the cornrows she'd let Ross braid in her hair since she wouldn't be able to wash it for the next two weeks. Her scalp felt strangely tight. Already it was hard to remember the smell of the subway, the feeling of high heels, the cursor blinking on her computer screen. She'd stopped feeling that she should check her voicemail or listen to the news. It was good to be away.

At first, Dubi and the others—the plodding Assaf, the kibbutznik Ofer, the Russian Sergei with the missing eyetooth—took the checkpoint seriously. They set their jaws beneath their sunglasses, squared their shoulders, shouted commands into their megaphones, fired warning shots into the air. But it wasn't long before the whole thing began to drive Dubi mad.

Little by little, it became a game, to see what he could make the Arabs do.

Hey, you.

Hand over those cigarettes.

Go on, sing us a song.

Get down on your hands and knees and bray like the ass you are.

No one stopped him. The commander of the unit leaned back in his chair and chewed on a matchstick and laughed, and everyone else laughed, too.

You're meshuga! they said, tapping a finger to their temples. Dubi took it as the compliment it was meant to be.

Gaza was a landscape made of borders: an IDF patrol line, rolls of electrified barbed wire, concrete blocks, a sandbag barricade, a bulldozed field, a concrete post, a road, a trench. Settlers here,

Arabs there, the army in between. There, in the borderland, he discovered you could cross the line.

Over the next six days, along the ascending trail to Khunde, Tengpoche, Pangboche, Dingboche, and into the moraine of Everest itself, Dubi kept showing up. He'd appear midmorning along the trail, or at night inside the trekkers' lodge in the hamlet where they'd camped. He slept in the lodge bunkrooms, ate the teahouse fare, drank the arrack *raksi* and the moonshine *chang*. He gave Susan a hard time about her cushy tent and catered meals. He said, How can you stand being waited on by the fucking Sherpas? They smile too much.

He made her laugh.

Each morning he said, So tell me something new, Suzy Q.

So she told him about the characters in her group: the truck driver's adventures trying to retrieve his glove that fell into a fetid charpi pit; the skull (human? monkey? yeti?) that the retired shrink bought from an old woman outside a village *gompa*; how one of the single girls developed acute mountain sickness at twelve thousand feet and had to be carried back to Lukla in a basket on their sardar's back. She told him about her family in Israel, about her cousin Gavi and how close they once had been. She answered his blunt questions (So why don't you come to live in Israel? Why aren't you married? Don't you want to have any kids?) and gave him daily plot updates from *Anna Karenina*, the one book she'd brought along on the trip. She never would have guessed that he'd take an interest in a literary Russian novel, but he was always eager to find out what had happened in the chapters she'd read the night before, as if they were episodes of a soap opera he'd missed. He couldn't get over that Karenin wouldn't give Anna a divorce, or that Vronsky would try to kill himself for love. Russians, he said dismissively. Such people he could not understand.

He told her about his girlfriend, about his mother and her latest man, about his dead father (the tank hero from the Sinai war). He told her he'd like to be a graphic designer, or a film director, or a high-tech entrepreneur. Sometimes he said he'd like to live in California for a while, learn to surf. Other times he said he'd never leave Israel, that all those Israelis living in the States, the *yoredim*, were copping out. She found his twitchy intensity compelling in a way she couldn't quite explain. Mostly, he struck her as being very young.

He's got a major crush on you, Joyce said.

They were arranging themselves for the night, tucking water bottles and contact lens cases deep into their sleeping bags so they wouldn't freeze, pulling on extra long underwear and their nighttime hats. It had been days since they'd taken off all their clothes.

Oh come on, Susan said. She checked the clasp on her watch, then snapped off her headlamp and pulled her mummy bag up around her face. She said, He's just a typical Israeli guy.

Well, Joyce said, he's cute.

Just that day, Susan and Dubi had been the first to arrive at a field where the Sherpas were setting out their lunch. They lay down on a tarp in the hot sun. A milk-green river flowed nearby, a string of spinning prayer wheels suspended in the stream. Out flowed the mantra, burbling on the rushing water: *Om Mani Padme Hum*. There were the sinuous muscles of his arms. There was the smooth skin along the side of his neck. The sun pulsed red behind her eyelids. The edges of their fingers touched. In the roiling green water, the prayer wheels whirled.

Souvenirs. That was the joke—they were collecting souvenirs. A watch. A pack of cigarettes. A photograph.

Ofer had the Polaroid. He took the picture of Dubi with the bloody Arab. The image was overexposed, so that even then, watching his own ghostly body emerge out of the Gaza haze, it already looked like a memory.

Right off, Dubi hadn't liked the look of him—those obsequious cow eyes, those cheeks all graying stubble topped with greasy hair. Put your arms up, Dubi said, and when the Arab did, Dubi hit him, hard. He felt his fist connect with bone, pain radiating through his knuckles, up his arm. The Arab stumbled backward and collapsed onto the road. Dubi cuffed his hands behind his back. Blood was running from the Arab's nose and he was making a low, whimpering sort of sound. When Dubi pulled the Arab up, the blue cloth of the man's jacket clenched in his throbbing hand, Ofer had the camera out and was pointing it at him.

Smile, he said.

When they got back to the post, everyone said what crazy fuckers they were. The truth was he felt happy then. He felt strong.

At Dingboche, 15,200 feet above sea level, Susan lay on her stomach inside her sleeping bag and tried to read. Anna had just told Vronsky that she was pregnant with his child. Levin was droning on about the beauties of a simple life on the land. Susan couldn't concentrate. She had a pounding altitude headache, the communal cough and runny nose. Even with her Russian soldier's fleece pants and the down jacket on over all her other clothes, she was cold. They were above tree level now, on a rubble-strewn plateau left by the glacier's retreating path. Ama Dablam was behind them and Everest dead ahead, a wisp of cloud snagged across its windy peak. Somewhere up there, people were inching their way across the ridge. Susan would never survive an expedition like that. She'd give anything for a shower, a real bed.

It was too dark to read. Susan crawled out of her sleeping bag and pushed back her tent flap to the cold. She could hear the others coughing, the barking of a dog. Suddenly, Lhotse appeared from behind a snake of cloud, its snowy flank gleaming golden-pink as if lit from within. Then in a swirl of wind, the vision disappeared. She could see why people invested mountains with mystical belief.

In the *thangka* paintings inside every village *gompa*, the Sakyamuni Buddha pointed to the ground, calling the earth to witness. The monks blew horns carved from human femurs. Here we are. See.

The light was almost gone. In front of the tents, Ross stood juggling limes borrowed from the cook. A group of dirty-faced children had gathered around to watch. In down overalls and a multipocket vest, his curly hair sticking out from under a knit cap pulled low over his brows, Ross looked like a ragged jester holding court. The limes flew up in a circle, over his head and around. The children laughed. *Ooooh, dai!* they cheered.

Inside the teahouse, a Sherpa girl was cooking rice and dal, while an old woman rocked an infant in a cradle on the floor. The yak-dung fire threw off a choking smoke into the chimneyless room, but at least it was fairly warm. The old woman rocked the cradle with her foot, rapidly back and forth, back and forth, in time to her muttered mantra. *Om Mani Padme Hum.* The grandmother looked ancient, hunched and lined, but the girl was surely no more than twenty and the baby just a few weeks old. How could anyone give birth in such a place, a six-day walk from anywhere? They were light-years from the sun, on a rocky, icebound moon.

He wasn't the only one.

When the Arab dropped his identity card, Sergei made him crawl after it in the dirt and then kicked him in the head.

Ofer posed two men naked in front of their wives and kids and took their photograph while the rest of the soldiers stood around and jeered.

Assaf let the one-armed merchant cross, but without his donkey cart. Today only one asshole gets through, he said.

They found ways to close the road and keep them waiting at the checkpoint for hours so they'd miss a day of work. They let through the old man who said he needed dialysis, but turned away the pregnant girl. They shot at the little boys who hurled stones at them from behind the concrete barricades. They said, That's the only way they'll learn.

They were average soldiers, average kids. They did the things they did because they could.

Now, here in Nepal, Dubi watched the trekkers—the young Americans and Australians and Japanese and Brits—partying in the teahouses late at night. On his way outside, he stepped over the Sherpa guides and porters who lay sleeping, curled up with the dogs, like dogs themselves, outside on the ground.

He watched them posing together along the trail, in front of tilted mani stones and snowy mountain backdrops, the trekkers and their Sherpa guides, arm in arm. He willed his body not to tense up as he watched them smile.

It came on in the middle of the night: stomach cramps, nausea, the runs. Susan stumbled to the latrine, clutching her jacket closed against the wind. Inside, her headlamp illuminated clumps of soiled toilet paper littered around the feces-smeared hole. She retched. Somewhere, not far away, a dogfight erupted into snarls. Back in the tent, Joyce slept, her breathing ragged in the oxygen-poor air, her mummy bag cinched around her face. Susan fought the urge to wake Joyce up. She lay feverish and shivering in the dark, listening to the rattle of the tent zippers in the wind.

At dawn, the group leader stuck his fur-covered head under the flap and touched her leg. Are you coming? he said. They were getting an alpine start on the climb to Kala Pattar, the black peak overlooking Everest, the Khumbu icefall and base camp. Today was the high point of the trip.

She could hear the others outside the tent, the sounds of Velcro and people spitting and stomping their feet on the frozen ground.

No, go on, she said, I'll just wait here for you all to get back.

She sipped some water from her Nalgene bottle, dizzy, and lay down again. The world had shrunk to the confines of this triangular burrow, this ripstop nylon sky.

Once, as a little girl, she'd gotten lost. They were in the transit lounge at Heathrow Airport, en route to Tel Aviv. Susan remembered waiting in a shop by a revolving rack of books. Her mother stood off to one side. She wore a light blue thigh-length coat. Susan followed the coat around the rack and across the lounge. She reached for the light blue hem—a pinwale corduroy—and held on. But when she looked up, there was a strange woman peering down at her, her eyes empty and surprised. Susan let go and the room tipped, the air squeezed from her lungs. There was an ocean of orange and blue carpet, a forest of bucket seats bolted to the floor. Outside the enormous plate glass windows, jets lifted off into the glare. Susan didn't remember the voice over the loudspeaker calling her name. There must have been shouting and tears, the smother of an embrace, but she didn't remember any of that. She didn't remember being found.

Here on the black shale crest of Kala Pattar, looking out onto the white sea of peaks that marked the border with Tibet, Dubi felt the energy rising like a snake. It rose through his chakras, from the root of his perineum to his head, with a burst of color and a receding rush of heat, like the Kabbalist Sefirot emanating from the void. Each chakra was a spinning lotus blossom wheel. The vibration quickened, his body aligning to true pitch. He was trembling, his tongue thick inside his mouth, a cracking sound inside his head. He was disintegrating into particles of light.

When he opened his eyes again, everything was clear.

When Dubi entered the Lobuche trekker's hut at midday, Susan's first thought was that he looked stoned—his pupils dilated, his eyes a little strange—but it could have just been the effect of coming indoors from the glare. She felt a rush at the sight of him. He was the first familiar face, other than their Sherpa cook, that she'd seen since dawn. When he sat down on the bench beside her, she held out her arms. He reached forward, pulling her against him so close that she could feel the thumping of his heart. He held her that way for so long that she had to disengage to breathe. She pushed back, but hung onto his arms. She felt that she would float away without him there to keep her on the ground. Despite her queasiness, despite the cold, she longed to feel his skin on hers. The weakness in her knees wasn't only from the stomach bug.

He was looking at her hard, the suntan lines around his eyes amplifying his stare. For a split second she had the strange impression that he was about to cry. But then his left eye twitched, his jaw contracted, and he looked away, patting down his pockets for his pack of cigarettes.

She knew then that Joyce was right. Here she was in three layers of unwashed clothes, a bandanna tied around her greasy cornrowed hair, her legs as hairy as a guy's, and he was looking at her that way. It wasn't a familiar sensation. Usually she was the one knocked off balance by romance.

It was only noon. Joyce and the others wouldn't be back for hours. Why shouldn't she do exactly what she wanted for once?

Hey, she said, reaching under the table for his hand. Come with me.

After Lobuche, everything changed.

The colors of the landscape grew more intense. Dubi could feel the music of his muscles and ligaments and joints, the swirling flows of blood and lymph and air. He could feel the harmony of the wind and stones and rustling trees, the vibration of the sunshine and the scudding clouds. He listened to the backbeat of his heart.

In Pangboche, he sat with the monks inside the *gompa* and watched them meditate. The Buddha smiled down at him in endless repetition from the walls, his thumb and middle finger pressed together, a swirl of blue and orange and green. Dubi took it as a sign. There was the drone of chanting, the chesty vibration of the gong, the clear tone of a silver bell. Afterward, outside the *gompa*, the letters carved into the mani stones floated loose and rearranged themselves before his eyes.

Dubi knew that what happened to him on Kala Pattar was real and not just another magic mushroom trip. Along the trail back down to Lukla, it came to him in little bursts, like flashes of white light.

After Lobuche, even though there was still a week left to the trek, every step was a return. They walked back the way they came, heading down through Pangboche, Tengboche, Namche, the names a musical refrain—*going home, going home*. The fact that the way was now imaginable changed everything. The intensity of the alpen-glow on a drifting peak, the mysticism of red-robed monks, the tableaux of Sherpa women digging roots out of the frozen fields had faded to the merely picturesque. They were sick of coughing and spitting, of dirty fingers and the runs, of the cold and dust and yak dung everywhere. They'd be home before Thanksgiving. They wanted hot showers, clean hair, a bed with sheets and a pillow, a newspaper, TV.

Namche Bazaar, with its whitewashed houses, electric light, trekkers' lodges, and street-side shops, felt like civilization now. They wandered through the crowds on market day, taking pictures of the Tibetans who'd come over the pass to trade meat and salt. The Tibetans wore rough sheepskin outfits and high felt boots, black braids wrapped around their heads and tied with bits of red cloth. They shopped for souvenirs: turquoise rings, woven carpets, *thangkas*, beaded bracelets, yak-wool sweaters, fur-trimmed embroidered hats. They waved to the smiling Sherpa girls, calling out *Namasté, didi!* the way the locals did. Susan took off her Russian soldier's pants and put on jeans. They were loose now at the waist, a good sign.

With Dubi, there was a studied effort on both their parts to behave as if everything was still the same—overly casual greetings and good-byes, a friction as their eyes met and shifted away. His feint of distance filled her with a delicate desire. At night, in the darkness of her tent, she replayed their afternoon together like a tape. The roughness of his tongue. The flex of muscles, the circle of his arms.

After Gaza, in those long weeks before he'd left for the Far East, all he'd done was sleep. He went to bed early and slept until noon. He slept with his pillow pressed over his head to block out sound. In the afternoons, he sat by the swimming pool at the Hilton, where Maya had a job, watched the tourists waddle past. His head felt dense as cotton wool. Even the air felt particulate, as if it had condensed to sand.

But now Dubi couldn't sleep. His eyes refused to close. His body cast a long shadow as he walked along the streets of Namche in the light of the full moon. He was gigantic, taller than the houses, taller than the trees.

He could see it clearly, the way things would be. He understood that everything up to now had been a trial, preparing him for this.

Back in Kathmandu at last, Susan shed the trek along with her smelly clothes. She stood under the shower for half an hour, letting the hot water flood her eyes and lips. Then Ross came to her hotel room with his scissors and trimmed six inches off her hair. Crescents of hair covered the bathroom floor.

Susan put on sandals and a sleeveless dress. Her hair swung against her neck. She sat down on the bed and turned the TV on to CNN. The stock market was still going up. Impeachment hearings for the president had begun. *Armageddon* was a huge box office hit. She hadn't thought about the news in days.

Dubi was standing in the lobby when she came downstairs. He

hadn't showered or changed, and she felt a small shiver of distaste. He was looking at her in that odd way again. The clenched-jaw grimace seemed more pronounced against the stubble of his suntanned face. In two days, she'd be back home. She wished she could have preserved her memory of him the way he was during the trek—a perfect souvenir. But here he was, looking at her like that.

Ooh-ah, he said. You are beautiful.

I was about to go out for a walk, she said. She knew he felt her distance. He was pulling her down, a heavy stone. She could see the pain fracture in his eyes.

He said, I'll come, too.

He reminded her of a boy in her fifth-grade class who used to follow her around, his tongue practically lolling out. He wrote her love notes and made his sister slip them into her desk. At recess, the other boys would beat him up and jeer and he would just lie there in the dirt, his arms and legs curled limply to his chest, until they were done. Come on, guys, don't, he'd whimper. Andrew. That was the boy's name.

Dubi pushed open the door and they stepped out of the air-conditioned lobby chill into the gritty heat. Sea level was a come-down. The smells of diesel exhaust and garbage settled like a weight.

Dubi said nothing as they walked but Susan could tell he was turning words around inside his head. He seemed to have lost his flirty humor, his aggressive Israeli style. In their place was that almost manic energy, those circles beneath his eyes. The image of her cousin Gavi rose in her mind before she could shut it out.

They were crossing a courtyard off Durbar Square when he pulled her to a stop, took her hands in his. She glanced up, over his shoulder, and recognized the balconies of the temple of the Kumari Devi, the same place she'd seen him, videotaping, back at the beginning of it all. The balconies were empty now, the windows reflecting the orange sun.

What he said was not what she expected. She wasn't sure she even understood it all. Something about a message he'd received, a sign. Something about the connection between them, how special she was—far more than she could know.

There is a reason we found each other, he said. It is not just a coincidence.

Coincidence. What was *coincidence*, really, but incidents randomly occupying the same place in space or time? Everything was a co-incidence, if you thought about it that way. The two of them were a case in point. Here they were, holding hands, but they'd never really touched at all.

Still, Susan felt herself softening a little bit. He was just a kid. He'd get over her soon enough. She reached up and kissed him on the cheek. She was feeling generous now.

Who knows, she said. Maybe some day we'll meet again.

B'seder, he said. Okay.

It was not so difficult. Her room was only on the second floor. He swung himself up to the balcony and crouched there in the darkness, listening. Below him, in the hotel garden, hibiscus flowers stretched their stamens up and spread their petals wide. The city's glow dimmed the stars. In the distance came the sound of a motorbike's high whine, the barking of a dog.

He pressed his forehead against the sliding door and let his eyes adjust. There was the dim outline of the bed. An uneven shape on top. He pushed gently against the glass. The door slid open, as he'd known it would.

He felt her before he could see her, the silent rise and fall of breath, the subtle movement of her shoulders, the faint flutter of her eyelids. He inhaled deep into his lungs, timing his own breath to hers. Blood pulsed through his limbs like light.

She turned, flinging an arm above her head, moaning softly in her sleep. The sheet pulled back across her chest; her skin glowed like the moon.

He crouched down, bracing himself against the wall as he slipped the lens cap off, lifted the video camera to his eye, pressed the button. Record.

He filmed until the tape ran out. He was so close that he could see the hairs along her bare arms, the soft down along her neck.

It was only then that he noticed the glint of light. It was a watch, round-faced, gold, lying on the night table next to the lamp. The hinged bracelet held in a circle by a chain. He put it to his ear, felt the beating of its tiny heart. Inside his shirt pocket, against his chest, it pulsed with his blood. Outside, a misshapen moon dangled in the sky. The air was warm as skin.

The hotel manager said he could not call the police since there was no sign that her room had been broken into or anything disturbed. Perhaps it has been misplaced, he said. He noted her address and phone number, tucked the paper into the pocket of his shirt. He said, Madam, we will certainly inform you if anything turns up, so Susan knew she'd never hear from him again.

It is not fucking misplaced, Susan told Joyce afterward as they waited for their midnight flight from Delhi to New York to board. My grandmother gave me that watch, Susan said, when I turned thirteen. I knew I should have left it at home.

She felt the thickness of the dark, the breathing of another body too close to hers, the violation of space. She pushed the thought from her mind.

In the windowless Delhi transit lounge, birds were twittering in the branches of an indoor ficus tree. Two lavatory attendants, squatting against the far wall by their buckets and brooms, took turns sipping from a thermos of tea. She rubbed her fingers over the tan line that marked where the watch should have been. Was it now on some Nepali chambermaid's wrist, or in a dusty pawnshop off Durbar Square? She missed its familiar face, its comforting soft tick. It seemed impossible that it was gone.

She closed her eyes and leaned back in the uncomfortable plastic chair. It was a sunny afternoon in a stubble field, prayer wheels spinning in a milky stream. Words were tumbling through the water, blowing through the air. The sun pulsed red against her eyelids. She felt the closeness of another hand beside her own.

Idyllic Little Bali

LORI OSTLUND

From *The Bigness of the World* (2009)

Calvin goes first, telling them about the time he was in Florida and decided to attend a Beach Boys concert, not really knowing anything about the Beach Boys except that they played music for basking in the sun to, which, Calvin being from Michigan, might explain why he knew so little about them. He hitched a ride up to Fort Lauderdale, which is where the concert was being held, with a guy in a convertible who dropped him off right at the stadium, and it wasn't until the band came on stage hours later that he realized the convertible guy, the guy with whom he'd scored the ride, was actually one of the Beach Boys, the drummer, whose name he couldn't recall.

This is exactly how Calvin tells the story, his clauses like tired acrobats, and though the others at the table have known Calvin only a day, they are disappointed. Joe goes next, then Martin, and after them, Noreen and Sylvie begin a long story about their first date, on which they went to a run-down bar on the west side of Albuquerque, the kind of place, Sylvie explains, where Hispanic butch-femme couples show up in wedding gear on Saturday nights to hold their receptions, the butches playing pool in their tuxedos, the femmes taking over the bathrooms, where, in a never-ending cycle, they fix their makeup and cry with happiness.

"So," Sylvie says in a voice thick with drama. "There we are on our first date, and Noreen invites this woman Deb to play pool with us."

Noreen cuts in, explaining that this Deb woman had actually struck up a conversation with *her* while Sylvie was off in the bathroom. She describes Deb as a massive-thighed Amazon who raised horses and engaged in competitive weight lifting, details that, in her mind, make clear that Deb had posed no threat to their date. She even tells them how Deb, who was wearing shorts, had said, "Go ahead. Feel it," flexing her very large thigh for Noreen, and how she, Noreen, had of course refused.

"I didn't even know her," she reports earnestly. "So why would I feel her thigh?" She actually seems to be soliciting their input, though it is not clear whether she is seeking plausible reasons that she (or anyone in that position) might have opted to feel the thigh or their approval for not having done so.

"It's irrelevant anyway," announces Sylvie, but Noreen doesn't reply because she is thinking about Deb's thigh, about the way that Deb had first extended her foot delicately, like someone testing the water in a pool, but then had ground her toes hard into the floor, making the leg muscles leap to the surface. There is absolutely nothing sexual about the memory. On the contrary, the thigh had been far too large, too freakish, to find appealing. Noreen had felt the way she did the first time that she saw the penis of an aroused farm animal, fascinated and repulsed, actually unable to look away, but with no sense that what she was seeing had anything to do with her.

"She gave me the creeps. Immediately," continues Sylvie, by way of letting these relative strangers know that her instincts are keener than Noreen's. "But Noreen invited her to play pool with us, so what could I say? Then, halfway through the game, this really blond, granola-y type walks in and sits down at the bar. She's watching us play, so finally I go over and invite her to join the next game, and it turns out that she's Australian." She pauses as though she has revealed something significant.

"Olivia Newton-John?" suggests Calvin dryly, and the others laugh because, boring Beach Boys story aside, Calvin is funny.

"What?" says Sylvie nervously, bewildered by the laughter but still joining in, assuming that if others are laughing, then something must be funny. Perhaps because they have spent so much time around strangers on this trip, Noreen has begun to notice just how often Sylvie does this—laughs when she has no idea what is funny, her hand flying up to her mouth to hide the way that confusion tugs it downward.

Noreen suddenly feels tired, tired of the story itself as well as of the way that Sylvie keeps talking over her, keeps saying, "That's not what happened" when it is, in fact, what happened. Then, there's the way that Sylvie steered the story right past the particulars of Noreen's meeting with Deb, had somehow gotten her talking about Deb's thighs when the meeting was really the important part.

What had happened was that Noreen was sitting at the bar, Sylvie's stool empty beside her, when Deb sat down on it, leaned toward her, and said, "You know why the Jews didn't leave Germany?" Noreen had been put off at first, thinking that Deb was telling a joke, some one-liner about the Holocaust. After all, it was at this very bar that the DJ had, between songs, once asked, "How many Polacks does it take to rape a lesbian?" and when Noreen complained to the owner, a pudgy man in running shorts, he had said, "What? Are there Polacks here?"

But Deb was not telling a joke. She was relating an anecdote that she had read somewhere, a reply that a Jewish man had given after the war, after he had survived and been asked to explain, in retrospect, why it was that the Jews had not left when they had the chance. "Because we had pianos," the man had said, at least according to Deb. Deb was slightly tipsy but not at all drunk, and so she did not go on and on about this in an overly sentimental way, which Noreen appreciated, yet it was obvious that the man's response had meant something to her. Later, Noreen told Sylvie about the exchange and Sylvie had seemed impressed, so how, Noreen wonders, could Sylvie tell the story without beginning there, with the Jews and their pianos?

The others are still laughing at Calvin's Olivia Newton-John crack, everyone except for Noreen and Martin. They have just added Martin, so there are six of them now, sitting at a table beside a pool in a tiny hotel in Yogyakarta, drinking beer and taking turns describing their oddest brush with fame. When it was his turn, Martin, who grew up in Washington, had shrugged and said, "I don't know," and then, as though it were a question: "Ted Bundy used to be my parents' paperboy?" Martin is forty-five, the oldest of the group, and the others sense that he would not have joined them back home, that he has joined them now precisely because they are not in the United States.

The truth of it is, they are all tired of dealing with non-Americans, tired of having to explain themselves and of having to work so hard to understand what others are explaining to them. They are tired and what they want, crave actually, is just to sit around with a bunch of other Americans playing silly games like this, games that do not require them to stop constantly and explain, to say things like "Ted Bundy? Are you kidding? He's famous." Because, of course, the explanations never stop there. If they were talking to an Asian, they'd have to explain the whole concept of serial killers (unless the person were from Japan, of course) and if the other person were European, forget it—they'd spend the next half hour discussing why Americans were all so damn violent.

This tiredness is what attuned them to accent as they overheard one another soliciting directions from the hotel employees and ordering eggs sunny-side up, though it was Calvin who finally brought them together, yesterday afternoon as they lounged around the pool with the other hotel guests, eyeing one another. He had thrown out some ridiculous sports question, something about American football, and they had all clamored to respond—even those who had no interest in sports—because they understood that sports was not the point. They stayed up until midnight drinking and discussing where they were from, without having to stop to explain that Minnesota was cold, or worse, having to fumble around trying to figure out what thirty-below Fahrenheit translated into for the rest of the world. And they would have kept going had the front desk guy not warned them that other guests were starting to complain.

"The loud Americans," they called out in stage whispers as they disbanded, laughing and giddy after a night of drinking, happy to have found each other, a feeling that they all share, though one that they haven't verbalized for various reasons—Noreen because she feels that it would make them seem provincial to acknowledge such a thing and Joe, on the other hand, simply because he sees it as a given, and Joe's belief is that people who state givens are either insecure or stupid.

That was last night, and now they have reconvened, adding Martin, whom Joe overhead discussing flight reservations with the front desk man when he got up to use the restroom. "That's the guy," Joe said, indicating Martin with a nod as Martin passed their table, and Sylvie called out to him, politely but with the slightly patronizing tone that people in groups sometimes adopt when addressing someone alone. "Hey! Excuse me. May I ask where you're from?" she asked, even though they already knew where he was from, knew, that is, that he was American.

Martin turned and looked at them; *sizing them up* was how Joe saw it, which is how Joe generally sees such things, just to be clear about Joe. Joe is, as his name suggests, an average guy—

moderate in habit and opinion with uninspired taste. He grew up in a rural, slightly-depressed-though-no-more-so-than-the-towns-around-it town in Minnesota, where he was a mediocre student, of average intelligence and in possession of no real talents that set him above others, that marked him, that is, as someone destined to rise above his humble beginnings (as such beginnings are always described after a person has done a little rising). But what Joe did possess was a desire to do just that, to leave that town behind entirely, a desire, moreover, that wedded itself to no one plan for doing so, which actually made the whole thing far more accomplishable than had he hoped to achieve it, say, by becoming a doctor or wowing everyone with his athletic prowess.

Instead, Joe accomplished it by lying, by packing his bags and moving to California, where he knew nobody, which meant that there was nobody to point out that he was lying. Once there, he lied his way into a progression of increasingly better-paying jobs, his favorite for the chamber of commerce, where he was the guy that got sent out with giant scissors to cut the ribbon when new businesses opened, from which he learned that women really gravitate toward a man with big scissors. When it was Joe's turn to discuss his brush with fame, he described meeting Dorothy Hamill, a lie, of course, and an easy one at that, for Joe knows the trick to lying well, which is either to go really big or, as is the case here, really small—to talk about sharing a ski lift with a figure skater who was last known for her haircut.

Besides lying, or perhaps hand in hand with it, what Joe does have a talent for is sizing people up. Thus, as he sat watching Martin size them up and sizing him up back, he sensed immediately that Martin was disdainful of them, of their need to be together. Disdain is one of those things that hits too close to home with Joe (perhaps because of the humble beginnings) and is, therefore, one of the few things that diminishes his objectivity, which is why he failed to consider that Martin might simply be distracted, might be focusing on his own problems to the exclusion of what is going on around him, a state of mind that can easily be mistaken for disdain.

This is precisely the case with Martin, who has come to Indonesia with his wife of thirteen years, a trip that the two of them began planning even before they were married and which it has taken them all this time to bring to fruition. Martin has always been vaguely distrustful of success, a disposition that allows him to now feel vindicated because here in Indonesia, things have fallen quickly apart for Martin, starting in Bali of all places, where he and his wife began their vacation because everyone back home told them that Bali was *the* place to start: Bali was paradise, these people said, an Eden of smiling, happy people, and the dances, especially the *barong* dance, were simply the most beautiful things they would ever see.

During the long flight to Bali, his wife had started out in a state of wine-drinking jubilation, but as the hours went by, she developed a terrible headache, the result of caffeine withdrawal, which neither aspirin nor a belated cup of weak airline coffee could assuage. Then, as they flew over the turbulent Strait of Malacca, she became nauseated as well. Martin was sure that she would feel better once they landed, but as they entered the airport, they were met with the sweet, cloying smell of jasmine and the overwhelming humidity of the tropics, and she rushed to the nearest garbage can and exploded into it, the entire history of the flight recorded in her vomit as she held weakly to the can with one hand and pushed back her stringy brown hair with the other. And through it all, Martin stayed frozen where he was, perhaps fifty feet away, watching as several young soldiers looked on impassively from the exits and the other members of their flight, strangers with whom they had spent the last thirty hours, passed by and stared at his wife, bearing witness to the contents of her stomach and seeing her hunched over, her mouth smeared with something pink, the wine that she had consumed thousands of miles ago when she was still feeling festive.

Finally, a saronged woman about his wife's age approached her and, in what sounded like an Irish accent, said, "Get it all out, luv. It's the only way." She handed his wife several tissues, looking discreetly away as his wife cleaned her face. "All better, isn't it then?" the woman said encouragingly, his wife thanking her weakly as she went on her way. Only then had Martin spun into action, coming up behind his wife as though he had been there all along, whispering, "Do you need the bathroom" and "No? Are you sure? Because there's one right here." Later, as they rode in a taxi through the streets of Denpasar, he had wanted to acknowledge his failure, or, even better, he had wanted her to acknowledge it, to scold him in the loud voice that he hated, but she had said nothing, her head thrown back, eyes closed, as the taxi sped along.

Three days later, they checked into a hotel in Singaraja along the northern coast of Bali, a hotel that catered to Indonesian businessmen and where they were the only tourists and, as such, were accorded the dubious honor of being placed in a room directly across from the hotel desk. There, with the night receptionist just outside their door and Indonesian businessmen snoring away behind the paper-thin walls on either side of them, his wife had wakened him in the middle of the night to tell him that she was thoroughly and profoundly miserable, that she had been for years and had been concealing it from him, and that she now understood that he was to blame for all of it, even the fact that she had been concealing it. He switched on the lamp next to the bed because it felt wrong to be discussing such things in the dark, and when he did, she began sobbing, but all Martin could think about was the night receptionist outside his door, listening to his wife cry.

Hoping to discuss the situation more rationally, Martin got

out of the narrow bed and sat in a chair beside the armoire, leaning back with his arms crossed in front of him. He knew, of course, what crossed arms conveyed—inapproachability, an unwillingness to listen, outright hostility—for he had the sort of job, a middle-management position with a company that produced copiers, where people were always going on about things like teamwork and communication and body language, but he also knew that his arms were incapable of doing anything else at that moment but reaching toward each other and holding on.

After listening to his wife sob and curse him for nearly an hour, he asked in a low voice that he hoped she might imitate, "What can I do?"

He had meant what could he do at that moment to make her stop crying, but she had looked up at him incredulously and said, "Can you learn to cry when you hear sad songs? Can you learn to articulate why you prefer radishes to cucumbers? Can you learn to appreciate irony? Wait. Can you learn to even *understand* irony? No? Well, then there is absolutely nothing you can do, Martin."

He slept sitting upright in the chair, and the next morning, with no mention of what had happened during the night, they packed and moved on to Ubud. During the day, they walked around the town, visiting the monkeys and stopping, it seemed to him, at every shop they passed. At one of them, his wife bought a carving that was heavy and round like a softball, the wood cut into the shape of a man with his legs pulled up to his chest, his head and shoulders curled over his knees.

"Is weeping Buddha," the shopkeeper told Martin's wife. She sighed and gave the man the exact amount of money that he asked for, and Martin kept his mouth shut.

That night, they ate dinner at an outdoor restaurant called Kodok, which, according to a poorly written explanation on the front of the menu, was the Indonesian word for *frog*. Martin supposed that the word was an onomatopoeia, and he marveled at the fact that *kodok* was nothing like the English word for the sound that frogs made, *ribit*, yet both words seemed exactly right to him somehow. Normally, he would have shared this observation with his wife, but he didn't, just as normally she would have commented on how beautiful the garden was, with candles nestled in beds of woven banana leaves and flowers everywhere and a pond near their table, but she didn't.

In keeping with the restaurant's theme, Martin ordered frog legs, which he had never had before. Several minutes after placing his order, as the two of them sat rolling their bamboo placemats up like tiny carpets and letting them unfurl, he watched as a boy bent over the little pool and, hands flashing, grabbed two plump, kicking frogs and rushed back to the kitchen with them. Martin was horrified. He thought that if he hurried, he could change his order before the damage was done, but when he looked up, his wife was staring at him with such naked revulsion that he did nothing, nothing, that is, except suck the frog legs clear down to the bone when they arrived.

The trip had gone on like this, the two of them speaking only about small matters such as who would request more toilet paper and what bus seats they had been assigned. They continued to sleep in the same bed, not talking, not touching, not even accidentally, and finally, after a week of this, Martin gathered his courage one morning at breakfast and asked, "Is it because of what happened in the airport?" For even though it was impossible to change things, he felt that he had to know.

His wife had stared at him blankly for a moment. She was eating papaya, which she loved but which they rarely had back home in Ohio.

"Perhaps we should go our separate ways?" he said then because as he watched her eat the papaya and smack her lips, he understood that she was content, perhaps even happy.

"Think about the money," she scolded. "How can we afford another two weeks if we don't share expenses?" Then, after a moment, she added, "Besides, what's so different, Martin, really?" She asked this almost gently, which made it worse, for it meant that she felt secure enough to consider his feelings.

At least here in Yogyakarta they have begun spending their days apart. She has hooked up with four grown siblings, three sisters and a brother, who are staying at their hotel, and though Martin feels that she is intruding upon the siblings' family reunion, he does not say this to her, knowing that she would scoff at him, would say something like, "Poor Martin. How does it feel to always think you're in the way?"

In a few days, they are supposed to leave for Jakarta, and from there, they are to fly to Sumatra, and it is not until two weeks from now, an interminable amount of time, that they are scheduled to return to Jakarta and begin their trip back home, but Martin has realized that he can't continue on like this. He simply cannot. That is what he had been speaking to the front desk man about when Joe wandered by. The front desk man, it turned out, was actually the manager, a helpful fellow with the unfortunate facial features of a toad: darting tongue, lidless eyes, and thin lips that cut far back into his cheeks. Martin felt immediately apologetic when he faced him, which he later understood to be residual guilt over the frog legs.

"I must change my flight," he told him, forming the story as he went along. He laid out his ticket, Garuda Airlines, Jakarta to Singapore, for the man to see. "I read about the Garuda crash in September, and quite frankly, I've become nervous." He began his request in this way to conceal his real motive, which was to change the flight date from two weeks hence to tomorrow, though why he felt he needed this bit of subterfuge, he could not say. However, as he spoke, he realized that there was truth to what he was saying. He had never been the sort that gave flying any thought, that questioned the ability of planes to stay aloft, but he saw then that things were not as he had always thought them to be.

"Sir, there is nothing to worry about. Garuda is our national airline. It is very safe. That accident, it was caused by the forest fires—the smoke—but that was months ago. I think there is no need to worry." The man studied the ticket. "Also, sir, your flight is not for two weeks." He added this quietly.

"I see," said Martin, quietly also. "Well, I was thinking that as long as I'm making such a big change anyway, perhaps I might change the dates as well. In fact, I would like to take a flight tomorrow afternoon, from Jakarta. Can this be arranged?"

"I am not sure, sir," the man said, flustered for some reason by the request. "You see, it is rather short notice. And your wife? Mrs. Stein?" he said, pronouncing Martin's surname so that it sounded like the mark that dropped food leaves on one's clothing, but Martin did not bother to correct him because he couldn't image that it made any difference to either of them.

"My wife will be staying. Only I must return early. You understand." And to be sure that the man did understand, he placed a twenty-dollar bill on the counter, which, he had read in his guidebook, was the way that things got done in Indonesia. The man seemed embarrassed by the bill's appearance and in no way acknowledged it, but neither did he return it. Instead, it sat on the counter between them as he made his calls, first to Singapore Air, arranging a shuttle flight from Yogyakarta to Jakarta for the next morning, followed by an afternoon flight to Singapore, and then to Garuda Airlines, canceling the original flight. Only after hanging up the telephone for the final time did he place his hand on the counter between them, over the twenty-dollar bill, and, still mispronouncing Martin's name, he declared, "Everything is arranged, Mr. Stein."

"Thank you," Martin replied, but looking at the kindly, toadlike features, he felt suddenly ill. He walked quickly away from the desk, and as he passed the nearby pool area, which doubled as a bar, a woman called out to him from one of the tables, asking where he was from.

He turned and stared at the woman and her companions for a long moment, thinking to himself, "Where *am* I from?" and finally, he took a deep breath and said, "Cleveland," and then, as though these people might not know where that was, he added, "Cleveland, Ohio," and they all nodded and smiled.

"Of course we know Cleveland. We're Americans," they said, and they invited him to sit down.

They are playing a game, the fame game. Martin hates games, and when it is his turn, he tells them about his parents' paperboy, Ted Bundy, though hesitantly, for he is still not sure that he understands the point of the game. The two lesbians go next, relating a very long and increasingly convoluted story about a woman with big thighs and an Australian who might or might not have been Olivia Newton-John. The thigh woman was raised by Satan worshippers in Minot, North Dakota, but had escaped when she was seventeen. Now, she raises horses and lifts weights and is a lesbian also.

Suddenly, or so it seems to him, Sylvie, the lesbian who is doing most of the talking, pushes her hands against her own throat as she explains that the thigh woman had threatened to kill the Australian woman with a pool cue, claiming that the Australian had been sent by the Satan worshippers to retrieve her. Martin is sure that he has missed something, some crucial detail, and he studies the others, hoping for a clue, but the waiter approaches their table with another round of drinks, and Sylvie pauses while everyone pays, a chaotic undertaking because they are all distracted by trying to convert rupiahs into dollars in their heads.

Joe, seeing an opportunity to get the conversation away from this god-awful story that, as far as he can tell, has nothing remotely to do with a brush with fame, turns to Martin and asks, "Did I hear you discussing flights with the desk guy?"

Martin considers explaining that the "desk guy" is actually the manager, but he is tired, so he simply says yes, he is leaving the next day. He does not mention that he moved his flight up two weeks, only that he has made the change to Singapore Air. "I'm feeling a little nervous about this Garuda Air," he says. "They had a crash in September. Now, Singapore Airlines—you *know* how things are in that country. They cane pilots for crashing." They all laugh because it is the only thing they do know about Singapore—that it's that little country that's always caning people.

Amanda, the sixth and youngest member of the group, says softly,
"I think you're very wise, Martin." She is the sort of woman that men describe as *sweet*, which simply means that she listens far more than she talks and that she is prone to comments like this, comments that reinforce their opinions of themselves in very uncomplicated ways. She is the only one who has not yet described a brush with fame and who is actually interested in Sylvie's story, partly because she has a cousin in Minot, North Dakota.

There is another thing to know about Amanda, a secret that she has maintained successfully over the last two days, largely by keeping track of her vowels. Amanda is not American. She is Canadian, though her mother is American, a Minnesotan who fell in love with Amanda's father years ago over the course of a weekend getaway to Winnipeg with a group of friends. "With my girlfriends," her mother says when she tells the story, though Amanda has told her mother repeatedly, and at times petulantly, to stop using *girlfriends* like that—to talk about the women with whom she bowls and shops.

"Only lesbians call other women *girlfriends* these days," she explains, "and they *don't* mean friends." But her mother disregards everything she says, every attempt she makes to offer advice that might save her mother from future embarrassment.

Once, for example, during their annual visit to Minnesota, she overheard her mother telling a group of relatives that Warren—Warren was Amanda's father—had to "really Jew down" the used car salesman from whom they had just purchased a car. Amanda was sitting on the sofa nearby reading a book about lighthouses. She always read books about strange topics when she visited her relatives because she secretly liked promoting the notion that they already had of her—as *different*. *Different* was not meant as a compliment, but because she considered her relatives backward, she clamored after the label as though it were. She lowered the lighthouse book and said, "Mother, I cannot believe you said that."

"What?" said her mother.

"'Jew him down.' I cannot believe you would use an expression like that."

The conversation had stopped as they all turned to look at her, seventeen-year-old Amanda, their flesh and blood, who was being raised in Canada. No wonder she had such odd ideas. No wonder she read books about lighthouses. But her mother just laughed. "Honestly, Amanda," she said. "Sometimes you have the most peculiar ideas. Next you're going to tell me that the Dutch are up in arms about 'going Dutch.'" The relatives laughed then also, laughed because even though Amanda's mother had moved to Canada, she still had her sense of humor.

Amanda hopes to sleep with Calvin, though Calvin is not yet aware of her interest, a state of affairs that would normally suggest that nothing is going to happen between them. Calvin, however, does not work that way, does not allow himself the luxury of choosing friends or sexual partners. Calvin waits to be chosen. Today is Calvin's birthday, but he has not yet decided whether he will tell the others, afraid that they might find him weird, even pathetic, if they learn that he is here celebrating alone. Back home in Michigan, the story of his trip to Indonesia will play differently. His friends and coworkers will say, "That's Calvin for you, trotting off just like that to celebrate his birthday in Java—wherever the hell that is." Back home, he is funny, risk-taking Calvin, spontaneous Calvin who runs off to places like Java and

Florida and Belize, warm places, at the drop of a hat. Calvin has worked hard to create his own myth.

By the time the group begins to break up for the night, Calvin has finally noticed the way that Amanda's hand creeps across the table when she addresses him, the way it sits demurely in her lap when she speaks to everyone else. Then, too, there is the way that she laughs at his jokes, heartily, with a whispered, breathy "Oh, Calvin" at the end. He thinks that all they need is one more good session of drinking and chatting as a group, one more chance for him to showcase his humor for her, and so, as they stand to go off to bed, he says, "Tomorrow, folks? Same table? Four-ish?"

Everyone nods except Martin, of course, who will be in Singapore by then. Even Noreen nods, though she is tired of everyone, but she is most tired of Sylvie—Sylvie, who never knows when to stop talking. Even when they are finally in bed, lying side by side with books in their hands, Sylvie cannot stop talking. "Do you see these books in our hands? That means we're reading," she said to Sylvie a few nights earlier, her voice straining to make it sound lighthearted, like a joke. And tonight will surely be worse because tonight, frustrated by having her story cut short, Sylvie will feel compelled to finish it again and again as they lie in bed.

Sylvie, she suspects, did not notice that the others were alternately puzzled and amused by the story, not to mention annoyed by the pace at which it was told. Noreen tries to imagine the story from their point of view, a story heard over drinks around a pool in a hot, bright country, and though she had sympathized with their impatience, she still cannot make sense of their reactions, for she cannot find amusement in anything about that night, certainly not in the fear she felt as Deb pressed the Australian woman against the bar, pool cue twitching in her red, meaty hands, and announced, "In two minutes, if you are still here, I am going to kill you," not screaming the words as an exaggerated expression of anger but stating them clearly and matter-of-factly, attaching a time frame, making them a promise.

Is it possible, Noreen wonders, to locate the exact moment that fear (or hate or love) takes shape? And is there ever a way to convey that feeling to another person, to describe the memory of it so perfectly that it is like performing a transplant, your heart beating frantically in the body of that other person? That night, after the Australian fled, Deb turned to Noreen and Sylvie and remarked nonchalantly, "She knew," and Noreen, looking fully into Deb's eyes for the first time, saw in them something distant and unmoored, like a small boat far out at sea.

When it was Noreen's turn at the pool table, her hands shook as they held the cue, which felt different to her now—like something capable of smashing open a head or boring through a heart. As Deb racked the balls for the next game, her back turned to them, Noreen grabbed Sylvie's hand, and they fled the bar also, sprinting across the vast, dark parking lot, glancing around nervously as they fumbled to open the doors of Noreen's car. Once inside, they locked the doors and flung themselves on each other for just a moment, their hearts thudding crazily against the other's groping hands, before Noreen started the car and sped out of the parking lot, not turning on the headlights until they reached the street. Halfway home, they pulled over on a dark street and finished each other off quickly right there in the car, not even bothering to silence the engine.

On the third afternoon, shortly after the five of them convene and order their first round of drinks, a sweaty woman approaches their table and asks whether they have seen Martin. "Martin?" they repeat in a sort of lackadaisical chorus.

"Yes," she says impatiently. "Martin. I saw him having drinks with you yesterday. I'm his wife."

They look at one another nervously. Martin had not mentioned a wife. "We haven't seen Martin today," Joe says at last.

Martin's wife picks up a napkin from their table and wipes her face with it. "I've been out all day with friends," she explains.

"Man, is this place muggy." She studies the napkin for a moment, then says, "Well, I better run up to the room and get myself into a shower." But she does not commit herself to action; instead, she continues to hover over them, and so they feel obligated to ask her to sit down.

"I must look a fright," she says, falling quickly into a chair. She eyes them suspiciously, as though she suspects them of harboring a loyalty to Martin, and then launches immediately into the story of how Martin ordered frog legs in Ubud. Amanda, with a drawn-out Canadian "oh" that almost gives her secret away, shrieks, "Oh no, the poor frogs." The others say nothing, especially Calvin, who does not think that Amanda would be impressed by a joke about the dead, legless frogs.

In the midst of this, the front desk man appears beside their table. "Mrs. Stein," he says quietly, addressing Martin's wife and mispronouncing her name.

"Stein," she corrects him curtly.

"Stein," he repeats dully. "I am very sorry, Mrs. Stein. I do not know how to say this, but the plane has crashed." He does not know when he decided to begin in this way, by referring to *the* plane, a pretense suggesting that they share between them the knowledge of her husband's departure.

"I'm afraid that you must have me confused with another guest. I don't know anything about a plane," says Martin's wife, speaking stiffly, almost angrily.

He puts his hand nervously into his pocket, seeking out Martin's twenty-dollar bill, which feels different from Indonesian money, sturdier. Yes, it's there. It exists, which means that everything else exists—Martin, the flight change, the plane—but, he realizes as he gets to the end of this chain of associations, what this means is that none of them exists.

"The plane that your husband was on," he croaks. "I switched him yesterday because he was nervous about flying our local airline. I called the Singapore office myself. He flew to Jakarta this morning, and from there he was going to Singapore." His seemingly lidless eyes blink once, slowly, and then focus on the table.

"It's true," says Noreen. "Martin told us yesterday that he was leaving this morning, that he had just changed his flight because Garuda made him nervous."

"Why didn't you mention this a minute ago when I asked?" Martin's wife asks, widening the scope of her anger to include all of them.

"I guess we thought that maybe he'd changed his mind," explains Calvin.

"He did not," says the manager sadly. "I took him in the hotel van myself."

"It really was none of our business," adds Joe.

Martin's wife stands then, stands and takes another napkin from the table and passes it across her face, and when she is done, it is as though she has wiped away the angry expression, and in its place a new expression struggles to take shape, her face like a television screen as one fiddles with the antennae, all blurs and fuzziness and glimpses.

The manager has begun to cry, quietly and without embarrassment. "Come," he says to Martin's wife gently, reaching for her arm. "The families are gathering at the airport to grieve. I will take you."

The five Americans watch them walk away from the table together, too shocked to speak. They order one round of drinks and then another, and finally Calvin says, "That front desk guy's a heck of a nice guy," and because they are a little tipsy by now, they drink a toast to the front desk guy.

"His English is really good also," says Sylvie. "I mean, he knows a word like *grieve*?" She holds up her glass, and they drink a second toast—this time, to the front desk man's English.

Only then do they discuss Martin, shaking their heads finally at the irony of the situation: how Martin died as a result of his desire to live. "Yep, old Martin would have liked that," Calvin says, and they nod together, agreeing that their friend would have appreciated the irony, for that is how they have come to think of Martin—as a friend—because he is dead and they were the last to know him.

"Well," says Noreen after a moment, stretching to signal that she is done for the night. She stands, and Sylvie rises as well. "It was nice meeting you all. We're leaving for Bali tomorrow." She does not look at Sylvie as she says this.

"Idyllic little Bali," Joe replies.

"What?" says Noreen.

"Idyllic little Bali," repeats Joe. "Don't you remember yesterday, when Martin first sat down and I asked him where he was coming from? He said: 'I've just spent eight days in idyllic little Bali.'" From very far away, which is how yesterday seems now that it has become a time when Martin was still alive, Noreen can hear him intoning the words, like a man in a trance, like a man exhausted by the task of putting paradise into words.

Montauk

SANDRA THOMPSON

From *Close-Ups* (1984)

It's a long drive back to the city from Montauk. I'm sitting shotgun next to Norton, who is driving his mother's Cadillac. My husband and my two-year-old daughter, OD'ed on sun, are asleep in the backseat. The Doo Wop Shop is on the radio. *Those oldies but goodies remind me of you. The songs of the past bring back memories of you.* Norton and I are singing along with the oldies but goodies. We know the words of almost every song. I grew up in the Midwest, so I don't know some of the regional hits. I try to pick up the words from Norton, coming in a little behind him but trying to keep up.

Norton has one arm draped over the steering wheel, half-driving. I'm sitting with my bare feet on the dash. The traffic is bumper-to-bumper on the westbound L.I.E., the way it always is on a late Sunday afternoon in July. If my husband were driving, he would be weaving in and out of lanes or driving on the shoulder past the line of traffic, then nosing his way back in when the shoulder ran out. I would be in a hurry to get home.

But I'm not now. I like singing along with Norton. I never listen to rock anymore. It annoys me to hear the same songs I listened to in high school, hanging over the radio in my mother's kitchen, mooning over some guy or another. Now I only listen to WRVR All Jazz Radio. Jazz doesn't have words, and I like that. But because I'm not musically inclined, I can't remember the tunes without the words. I have an ex-husband who can scat, but I can't.

Oh, I wonder, wonder who ba doo oh who! Who wrote the book of love? I slap my knees on the offbeat. Norton taps on the steering wheel with his palm. Our voices are similar: weak, off-key, but determined, reaching for but never making high notes, straining but sounding like we're clearing our throats at low notes. Norton doesn't look at me. I can look at him because I know he won't look back at me. He looks handsome in his Hawaiian shirt. His knees are pink and tender with sunburn.

My husband, the one who's sleeping in the backseat, is ten years older than I am. He doesn't know the words to any rock and roll. When I used to sing along with the radio, he'd say, "How can you remember the words? I can't even hear the words." I wonder if I left something behind with Buddy Holly and the Platters and Fats Domino and Norton. It probably wasn't anything good, but I miss it just the same.

Problems, problems, problems all day long. Will my problems work out right or wrong? Norton and I sing the words in a sustained whine. I'm smiling because the song is perfect for Norton and perfect for me.

Friday night I am supposed to be driving out to Montauk for the weekend with my husband, my daughter, and some friends, but when their car pulls up and I see myself packed into the backseat of the Peugeot between my husband and my daughter in her car seat, I can't let myself be so crowded for so long. I watch my daughter's sweet, oval face framed by the back window, the triangular pane of glass between us. I wave goodbye until my arm hurts and the car rounds the corner.

In the apartment I sit on the couch and listen to nothing, and I like it.

But at 7:20 the next morning the telephone rings.

"Did I wake you?" Norton says. Four hours ago he has broken up with the woman he left his wife for, and he has been waiting since then to call me. So I ask him if he wants to drive me out to Montauk.

Norton pulls up in front of my apartment in his mother's Cadillac. He waits, slumped over, with his forehead on the steering wheel, his fingers spreading his blonde, frizzy hair out from his head. The back of his neck is pale. I want to touch it. Norton looks up, and his eyes below his wild, light hair are somber; his dark beard, tragic. He looks like a cross between an Hasidic rabbi and Harpo Marx. I want to stroke his uncombed beard, kiss his swollen eyelids. I am upset by wanting to do these things.

"Well, here we are again," Norton says in a high sing-song as he pulls away from the curb. "Do you remember when you and I went to Montauk together?"

I show him where to turn off Atlantic Avenue to get onto the B.Q.E. He makes a sharp left, cutting off a Brunckhorst's delivery truck, its red lacquered side with the boar's hairy snout flashing past the window as he slams the brakes. His right arm extends stiff in front of my chest to keep me from flying into the windshield. But I'm wearing a seatbelt. He isn't.

"Whew," I say, and sink down into the seat. I'm angry that Norton almost killed me, but I'm grateful that he tried to save me.

"That wasn't even close," he says.

"How many years ago?" I ask Norton. "You still can't drive a car. It was the same Cadillac, right?"

"Uh huh." Norton is driving in the right-hand lane of the B.Q.E. with the pickup trucks and the senior citizens.

"We took your mother's dog with us. What was its name?"

"Froufrou."

"Froufrou. Does she still have it?"

"It died. It had a heart attack at the Puppy Palace. I told you that."

"I forgot. It was a nice dog. It was trained to use the toilet in your mother's apartment, wasn't it?"

Norton nods.

"I was pissed off at you that weekend."

Norton raises his hands. His shoulders take on his long-suffering slump. "So what's new?" he says.

"We had to leave the beach at two in the afternoon. You wanted to beat the traffic. I wanted to stay. We ate lobster at Gosman's, and you said to me, 'You have the most beautiful eyes I have ever seen.' The Pepperidge Farm rolls were cold. They must have been refrigerated."

"You still do," Norton says.

"What?"

"Have the most beautiful eyes. *You* know."

"Your ex-wife had beautiful eyes."

"It was makeup."

It's so early there's no traffic on the L.I.E., but I hate the L.I.E. It slices right through the front yards of split-levels and two-family houses that all have the same facade. The L.I.E. is divided by a low metal bar bent out of shape by cars crashing into it. I prefer the Southern State Parkway. It cuts through what looks like forests with the backs of suburban houses only barely visible through the trees. If you squint your eyes you can't see the houses at all. The highway dividers are of rough-hewn wood. They are intact.

We are approaching Lefrak City where you can turn off the L.I.E. and get on the Grand Central Parkway that takes you to the Southern State. If my husband were driving, he would edge the car to the right-hand side of the right lane of the L.I.E., and he would say, "Should I stay on the L.I.E.?" I would say what I always say: "No." And he would straddle the V in the highway that separates the L.I.E. from the Grand Central Parkway, turning his head to the left to see if there's traffic on the L.I.E., driving up the narrowing horizontal lines until he either had to turn to the right or to the left or drive into a strip of dried-up grass, and then he would jerk the wheel to the left and continue on the L.I.E.

I ask Norton, "Would you take the Grand Central to the Southern State? I don't know if it will get us where we're going, but it goes in the general direction."

Norton says, "Sure."

I look for a road map in the glove compartment so I can figure out where we're going from here. But there's no road map. There's a pair of sunglasses with one lens missing and a half-eaten roll of Certs.

"I never heard of a glove compartment without a map," I say.

"No one in New York uses road maps."

"How do they get any place?"

Norton shrugs. "You've got me."

"Norton, the day you and your ex-wife signed your separation agreement, she came over to my apartment. She told me you used to say to her, 'Why don't you go to the movies or something with Molly?'"

"Well, *I* didn't want to go to the movies with her."

"And she said she used to tell you, 'But I hardly know Molly, and she lives in Brooklyn, and she has a baby. She can't just drop everything and go to the movies with me.' She was wringing her hands."

Norton says, "You know when I first started going with you, it was like I had just discovered sex. It was so terrific. I mean, it was really extraordinary."

I try to remember. Images of Norton and me shuttle across my mind: Norton pressing me into the white wall of my bedroom; Norton and me sitting on the Morton Street pier in the afternoon, my sweater on Norton's lap and my hand under my sweater; Norton lying on top of me on the cool parquet floor in his apartment during our lunch hour; Norton and me wrapped around each other in some uptown movie theater while *Closely Watched Trains* plays on the screen. I never think about these things. I tend to think Norton and I have always been the way we are now.

"What happened?" I ask him.

"About two blocks before we'd get to your apartment you would start getting a headache or a stomachache or you would start to sneeze. When we got in bed, you were only interested in cuddling."

"And you started getting up in the middle of the night and bringing Sara Lee banana cake into bed with us."

"I don't remember that," Norton says.

"It's true. Your hips started to spread." I think about it for a minute. "But I mean before all that. What happened?"

We reach the end of the Southern State and stop at a gas station to pick up a road map. I like reading road maps. I am amazed that by looking at colored lines on a piece of paper you can get anywhere you want to go. If it had been left to me, there would be no road maps. I would get on one road and go into someone's house and stay there, trying to figure out what's going on. My father once said to me, "If everyone in this country were like you, there would be no roads or bridges built." He was right. On the other hand, so what?

I want to take the road that has the thinnest line on the map. When I was a girl on the way from Illinois to Florida, my mother took over the driving from my father and got on a dirt road in Georgia that led us into a cemetery. A little circle of black people stood around a grave as we passed by in our Oldsmobile.

I tell Norton, "We can get on 27 and pick up 27A near Sayville. 27A runs into 27 anyway, but if we take 27A it might be a more picturesque ride."

"I'm in no hurry," Norton says.

On 27A we are caught in a steady stream of Saturday shoppers. Traffic is bumper-to-bumper with cars turning in where it says Enter and coming out where it says Exit. In the parking lots, people are wheeling giant metal carts right up to their cars and unloading into the trunks. Whole families stand around watching.

"Maybe this wasn't such a good idea," I say.

"It's all right," Norton says.

The air-conditioned air in the Cadillac is singeing my nostrils. I push the button and the window on my side of the car goes down with a whine. I let my bare arm hang out the window in the hot, thick air. Norton doesn't put his window down, and he doesn't turn off the air conditioning.

"You know the first time you introduced me to your friends, you said, 'This is Molly. She's from Illinois. She used to be a twirler.'"

Norton laughs a high he he he he.

"It made me feel like I had six fingers or was a pinhead."

Norton doubles over. He has always found the word "pinhead" funny.

"You didn't take me seriously," I say.

"Neither did you." He's not laughing anymore, but his cheeks are still wet.

"Take you seriously? Or take myself seriously?"

"I bought you acrylic paints and canvasses. I took you more seriously than you took you seriously."

"I didn't want to paint. I wanted to get married."

Norton lets out some air between his teeth. "I was twenty-two years old. You wanted to get married and move to Westchester. You had never even been to Westchester. Anyway, I said I'd do it."

"But you were lying. You wouldn't have, would you?"

"Maybe."

We stop at the McDonald's on the outskirts of Southampton. In high school, my girlfriends and I used to drive through the Mc-

Donald's parking lot all night looking for the guys who were driving through looking for us. We always missed each other. They didn't have Big Macs then, just small hamburgers. I feel silly standing in line with Norton.

We take our Big Macs and sit at a stone table at the edge of the parking lot surrounded by trash cans that say THANK YOU.

Norton takes large, ragged bites out of his Big Mac. I can see he is really very hungry. His hands are shaking, and that scares me. Maybe there's more to all of this than we're making out.

"Are you okay?" I ask him.

He nods, but I can see that he's not and that he's grateful I asked.

"I'll drive the rest of the way," I say.

"You don't have to."

The first thing I do when I get in the car is turn off the air conditioning and press down all the window buttons. The window on the driver's side and the two back windows sink simultaneously. I press the gas pedal just to test it, and the Cadillac lurches onto the highway. I look over at Norton to see if he's going to say anything, but his eyes are half closed.

Norton sleeps all the way through Amagansett. We are on the flat open road that follows the ocean along Napeaque Beach to Montauk. The clear, cool, salty air blows through the car into my face. I sit up a little straighter and shake my hair down my back. I look over at Norton. He's awake now. I ask him if he had a nice nap.

"I wasn't asleep," he says. "I was just resting."

We pass the motel where Norton and I stayed for the weekend with his mother's dog. "How many years ago was it?" I ask him.

"Seven."

"Seven?"

"You're my oldest friend."

Norton's head is erect, but his shoulders are drooping. The left side of his cheek is red and wrinkled from pressing against the leather seat back while he was asleep. We're almost to Montauk. All of a sudden I feel generous towards Norton. I want to give him something.

"I ate my first mango with you," I tell him. "We were stoned. You had this fruit that looked like a football with the air let out, and you cut me a slice. It was a carnival in my mouth. The oily taste and the sweet taste fighting each other and merging. I'll never forget it. Of course I was stoned."

Norton clears his throat. He has a look of passionate annoyance. He's staring straight ahead, not looking at me. "We're almost there," he says. "No one knows we're coming. We could turn around right now. You could just pull off the road and turn around. We could stay at one of the motels we passed, or we could drive back to the city. Anything you want."

But I'm concentrating on my driving. We're on the Old Montauk Highway now, a two-lane road that rises and falls through winding hills. The Cadillac climbs the road, its hood far in front of me, and I can't see anything ahead but the top of the hill and beyond that, sky. When I was a girl and my father was driving, I was afraid he would drive right over the edge, and I held my breath. I hold my breath now as the front of the Cadillac rises up on air where there is no more road. Then the road levels off and I can see ahead. There's no drop-off, not even a sharp curve, just more of the same road.

Chiclets

ANNE PANNING

From *Super America* (2007)

The Whites' room was in a hotel in Taxco, Mexico, which, until 1620, had been a monastery. Toby, Alice's husband, had mentioned this several times. Once inside their room, Alice collapsed on the bed. Above her, large black beams supported a red clay ceiling.

"Do you think those tiles could fall on us?" she asked. "Do you think they've been up there since 1620?"

Toby emptied his pockets of loose change, keys, receipts, pesos. "Do you want some water?" he asked.

Alice sat up and marveled at the medieval cast-iron door latches. She imagined small Spanish monks pulling them open, their dark robes brushing the cool floor. "Is it purified?" she asked. "Because I can't get sick right now. I can't. Not now, not when we're so close to—"

Alice had brought along not only a basal body thermometer but a five-day ovulation test kit. She'd urinated onto a small white stick in the Mexico City bus station. At first she'd been confused, not realizing she was supposed to pay two pesos just to use the *sanitarios*. Then, when she realized there was no toilet paper, she'd had to step out of the stall and pay a small girl two more pesos for a small wad of tissue. She'd crouched over the seatless toilet, her sandals wet, the hem of her dress grazing the wet, dirty floor. The felt strip had shown two dark purple lines. She had felt her cheeks flush with nervousness and excitement.

On the bus to Taxco, she'd tried deciding on the best position in which to become impregnated. Not with her on top, which was their customary position and pleasurable for both of them. Perhaps with Toby coming from behind would be the best. But the bus ride had been long and curvy, and she'd grown exhausted. She'd tried to ignore the booming movie on the tiny television screen above her, while the sharp scent of the toilet mint in back made her head ache. Toby had insisted on buying Primero Plus bus tickets, complete with air-conditioning, plush reclining seats, movies, and a bag of snacks, which included chili-dusted peanuts and a can of Squirt. He'd said he didn't want *bandidos* to stop them, rob them, or harass them, as he'd read could happen. Alice did not fear such things, but she'd agreed simply because sometimes it was just easier to let Toby win.

Alice got up to investigate the bathroom and ran her hands over the blue and yellow painted tiles. "Oh," she said, "I love these! I'd like some in our bathroom at home. Aren't they gorgeous?"

"In our Queen Anne Victorian?" Toby said, and stepped out of his khakis. He was nothing if not a culturally sensitive and appropriately dressed traveler. He folded them and hung them carefully over the chair.

"Well, I know," Alice said. "I just meant . . ." Toby took everything literally. Of course she wouldn't *really* want Mexican tiles in their high-ceilinged, period-wallpapered bathroom back in Rochester, New York. The 1880 house now felt too large and ornate, too complicated in comparison to the simple white walls of Hotel Los Arcos. Who needed so much space? she thought. Five bedrooms, two living rooms, and two baths for just the two of them. When college was in session and they were both teaching, often Alice would find herself grading quietly in her study—

the moss green north bedroom—and realize she could not hear a sound from Toby in the entire house.

Alice had been the only one in her family to break away from her hometown of River Falls, Wisconsin, and go to college, much less graduate school. Being a psychology professor who researched attachment relationships between parents and children, she knew there was some guilt associated with her transcendence, which she sometimes confused with abandonment. Her parents had still not visited in the five years she'd been married to Toby, and the most they could say about her job as associate professor of psychology was what an awful lot of days off she seemed to have. Alice felt it was better for her to disassociate, though she often dreamed at night of her parents' small pink house as a symbol, she suspected, of her desire to return to the safety of the womb.

In actuality, a simple three-bedroom house would have sufficed for her and Toby—always working, reading, writing, preparing for classes. But Toby, who taught architectural history, had bought the house the year before they'd married, and Alice had simply moved in with him after vacating her small but cozy two-bedroom apartment on East Avenue. There was definitely something of herself she'd left behind as she'd rolled up her tatami mats and taken down her vintage movie posters. Her life, which had previously been a collage and collision of influences, had changed into something serious and dignified, as represented by their beautiful, well-appointed Victorian home.

"So, *vamos mirar el zócalo*," Toby said. He'd changed into khaki shorts of modest length and had already brushed his teeth and splashed cool water on his face. His shirt still looked crisp.

Alice's Spanish was terrible; she admitted it but wasn't proud of it. She spoke some Italian from a year's study abroad back in college, which sometimes helped her Spanish, but most often confused her.

"*Inglés, por favor*," she said. On the airplane down to Mexico, she had joked with Toby that her ugly American gambit was going to be "*Inglés, por favor!*" Toby had laughed, too, and so she'd said it over and over, loving it when he found her funny. "They'll ask me, '*Cómo está usted?*' and I'll say, '*Inglés, por favor!*' They'll say, '*Buenos días*,' and I'll say, '*Inglés, por favor!*'"

"Let's go check out the town square," Toby said, and looked at his watch. Why would he look at his watch? Alice wondered. And why must they immediately storm out into the town and investigate when they had all day, and the next day, and the next day, which would be their five-year wedding anniversary? "Or do you want to wait here? Rest?" Toby smiled at her, but Alice sensed he was forcing himself to be patient and pleasant.

Alice sighed. She walked to the window that boasted a view of twisting cobblestone streets, a hodgepodge of chalky white buildings with clay roofs seemingly built on top of one another. Streams of white VW Bugs, the ubiquitous Taxco taxis, groaned and sped up the tiny winding streets.

Toby came up behind her and held her. She leaned back against his solid chest and enjoyed the sense of being enveloped by something larger than herself. He smelled brightly of the hotel soap and of slightly worn deodorant. She rubbed his arms, dry and hairy and familiar. "Did you know," he said, and she could feel his warm breath on her hair, "that Taxco is a historic district? The entire city. There are actually rules that state residents can't paint their homes—or rather, the exterior of their homes—anything other than white. It's a Spanish colonial city, and you can see how the roof lines reflect . . ."

Alice let him go on, amazed by his inability to turn off his professor-lecturer role, even with her. She could hear his voice change into a smoother pitch; he paused more emphatically and drew out the ends of his sentences.

"Toby, please," she said, and he stopped. Although she was also a professor, she welcomed the opportunity to abandon her role of Dr. White whenever possible. Whenever a student called her

Dr. White, she felt as if a surgeon should come rushing around the corner, ready to perform emergency surgery. "Call me Alice," she'd tell them at the beginning of each semester, but they would never dare. A couple kind-hearted but dim students, always female, would routinely call her Mrs. White, which she didn't like either, but she never had the energy to correct them.

"Don't you care about the history of the place?" Toby asked, suddenly sounding angry. "There's a quote by someone about travel—I can't remember now who said it, but it goes something like: 'He that would bring home the wealth of the Indies must carry the wealth of the Indies with him. A man must carry knowledge with him if he would bring home knowledge.' I believe it goes something like that." Toby pulled open the curtains of the other window, which overlooked garbage cans and dust mops.

"What if you're a woman?" Alice asked. She fished out her Ziploc of Tylenol and shook two into her palm.

"What?"

"If you're a woman?" she said, and swallowed the pills dry. "It says a man must carry knowledge, but what if you're a woman?"

Toby sat on the edge of the bed beside her, and the rocklike mattress barely budged. For a moment, he hung his head. "Come on," he said. "Let's not do this. We're tired. Let's go get something to eat."

He reached for her hand and she took it.

The only place they could find to eat with a balcony was called Vicky Cafeteria. To reach the restaurant, Alice followed Toby up a tiny spiral staircase inside a silver shop. Toby hit his head at the landing, and Alice cooed with him to be careful. Their small table overlooked the busy town square, and Alice was so distracted she couldn't focus on the menu. She looked out over the *zócalo*, which was full of people listening to an odd vocal medley from *Cats*, in Spanish. Three people dressed like cats sang into a fuzzy microphone, spun in circles, and clapped their hands.

On the corner, a man with upwards of thirty straw hats atop his head yawned and stretched. Another man sold bright pink cotton candy, and Alice could see, even from this distance, how it melted in the humidity.

The waitress came by, and after Toby handled the formalities in Spanish, Alice was pressured to order. "Burritos with *queso*," she said. She always ordered the easy items she could pronounce: tacos, burritos, enchiladas.

The waitress, a plump young woman with large curled bangs, looked at her eagerly. "*Con jamón?*" she asked.

Alice looked at Toby for translation. He asked her did she want ham. Did she want ham in her cheese burrito?

"Well, I suppose," she said. "Okay."

When Toby said *sí*, the girl walked away quickly.

"Sounds kind of breakfasty, though," Alice said. "A little like McDonald's."

"Maybe," Toby said.

The burrito that came for Alice was nothing like the fold-and-wrap variety to which Alice was accustomed. These tortillas were smashed flat and flipped in half like a taco. The cheese was a bright yellow spread; the ham was a single smooth sheet. Toby's meal looked luscious. Two large fried tortillas smothered in a rich brown sauce called *mole*. It came with a dollop of bright green guacamole, a circle of dark refried beans with a single tortilla chip sailing in its center, and a gravy boat full of green salsa. The waitress uncapped two bottles of Corona for them and was about to pour them into glasses with ice.

"Please, no thank you," Toby said. He looked at Alice to instruct her also to refuse the ice, for health reasons, but her hand already covered the glass.

At last, they ate.

"So, I'm about to ovulate," Alice said. "If ever there was a more perfect time." She squeezed lime and sprinkled salt in her Corona. She figured this would be the last of her drinking.

Toby raised his eyebrows, and Alice thought she saw him wink. "So tonight's the night," he said.

"Or this afternoon," Alice said. "The sooner the better, really."

This endeavor was not new; still, Alice felt a manic glee, a certain boisterous anticipation at the sheer *maybe* of it all. So far, nothing was "wrong" with either of them. Their doctor had told them to just keep trying, even though Alice feared it was almost too late for her, at age thirty-six, with so many good, unused eggs gone to waste ever since she was fourteen. The doctor told her that 80 percent of healthy couples took up to a full year to conceive a child. The important thing, she'd said, was to relax and just keep trying. They'd agreed a trip to Mexico might be just what they needed.

A small girl in a yellow dress wandered up to their table, selling tiny packets of Chiclets: purple, pink, red, white, and green squares the size of postage stamps.

"*Señora*," she said, and looked up at Alice with big, pleading eyes. "*Chiclet. Barato. Por favor. Barato.*" She rubbed Alice's arm softly with her hand.

"Toby," Alice said, "ask how much. How much for one pack."

He did, and told Alice in English.

"Ten," Alice said. "I'll take ten little packs." The girl didn't respond to her English but looked as if she knew she was in for a good sale. She leaned her elbows on the table and waited patiently. Alice could see her flip-flops had been many times repaired with tape.

"It would be three pesos," Toby said. "For ten."

"That's thirty cents, right?" Alice said.

"More or less," Toby said.

"Let's give her twenty pesos," Alice said. "That's only two dollars." She fished through her trim black travel pouch, which she kept inconspicuously inside her dress, strung around her neck. "Here," she said.

"Don't flash all your money around," Toby said, and physically shielded her from the street, even though they were up two stories.

"I'm not," she said. She paid the girl, scooped up her ten packs of Chiclets, mostly pink and maroon, and set them by her plate. She didn't even like gum, but the girl was so charming and such a convincing little salesperson. What was two dollars to Alice?

She gave Toby a look that said *what?* but soon a group of children flooded around Alice, hawking their wares: beaded necklaces, silver chains, brightly painted ashtrays shaped like sombreros, Aztec paintings on sheets of bark paper, clay vases banded in cobalt blue, bags of fried pork rind drenched in hot sauce like splattered blood.

"No thanks," Alice said. But the children wouldn't go away. One of them pointed to Alice's plate, where the ham and cheese burrito sat cooling, hardening, and Alice could feel a pained expression cross her own face.

"I'd give it to her," she told Toby, and crossed her legs uncomfortably. "But then the others—"

"It's okay for you to eat your meal, Alice," Toby said. "I'm sure they scam all the tourists. They don't look emaciated or anything."

Eventually, much to Alice's relief, the waitress sent the children back down the curving black staircase, and Alice watched them spill into the street below and zero in on other easy targets.

How she hated to say no to children, to anyone for that matter.

On the way back to their hotel, Alice feared they'd be run down by the white taxis constantly speeding through the narrow streets. She pulled herself up against buildings whenever one passed. She never turned her back on the traffic. She leapt into open doorways when a taxi got too close. As it turned out, it was Toby who got hurt. He did not get run down but lost his footing on the steeply pitched, wet brick street and twisted his ankle. Luckily there'd been a break in the taxi traffic. Alice had never seen him in such a state before. He lay on the ground, grimacing, gripping his leg at midshin, his face a dark shade of red. Fortunately they were just two doors down from Hotel Los Arcos, and the proprietor came rushing out and helped Toby hop down the street and into the hotel courtyard.

"I think it's sprained," Toby said, back in their room. Alice pulled the drapes closed and sat on the opposite bed, unsure what to do.

"Should we try to find a doctor?" she asked.

Toby tried moving his ankle around but winced. "No," he said. "Maybe just an Ace bandage. I think there's a little pharmacy around the corner. Do you think you could do that? It's really swelling. Maybe some ice, too."

Alice panicked at the idea of venturing out on a shopping trip, alone, with her poor Spanish skills. "Sure," she said, then fished the dictionary out of her bag. "I just need to look a few things up. Give me a sec."

Toby lay on the bed with his eyes closed as Alice frantically flipped through pages. Even the simplest request, the simplest sentence, caused her stress. She wanted to be good at it, to blend in, even though it was impossible with her rich, red, bobbed hair, her green eyes, and her milky white, obviously North American skin.

Finally, when she felt ready, Alice grabbed her money pouch and slid into her sandals. It was almost dark outside, and loud salsa music drifted in through the windows. Maybe she would buy an ice-cream treat, or a couple bottles of beer, or some garlic fried peanuts. She felt the Chiclets in her pocket as she reached for the door.

"Babe?" Toby said, startling her. He opened his eyes, sat up, and looked at her with an odd combination of apology and love. His beard, she noticed, had gone more gray than black, and she wondered, if she ran into him on the street, a total stranger, if she'd be attracted to him. It was his eyes, those piercing dark brown eyes, that got to people. He was dashing, you could say. He looked smart. He looked like someone who took good care of his belongings and drove a sensible but not unattractive car.

"Yes?" she said.

"It's probably not going to happen," he said. "I mean, with this ankle and everything. I'm good for nothing at this point."

"Right," she said, and although she tried to sound upbeat, she couldn't help the disappointed flatness that lingered in her voice. "It's just—I mean, of all possible times. You know? This is it," she said. "I mean, the doctor said as soon as the ovulation test is positive . . . I was just so hoping this time."

"I know," Toby said. He held up his hands in surrender. "I'm really sorry."

"Don't be silly," she said. "There's nothing to be sorry about. It was an accident! At least you didn't get run over by those crazy taxis." She strode over and planted a quick kiss on his cheek, which landed more on his ear. "We'll try again next time."

"I love you, you know," Toby said, and blew her a kiss with two fingers.

"You, too," Alice said, but her heart fell.

Out in the street, Alice imagined herself a single, reclusive expatriate. She exchanged knowing glances with a couple of young backpackers who had to be in their twenties. At home, they could be her students. They would hate her for giving them poor grades. They would call her Dr. White and complain about her difficult Introduction to Psychology exams. Here, they nodded at her in solidarity as if to say: This travel thing's a trip, isn't it? Around the corner, dogs barked and growled at her. Men glanced at her in her linen sundress as if she were merchandise for sale. Her new sandals creaked and groaned at the straps.

At the pharmacy's glass counter, a woman dressed in nurse's whites looked at her expectantly and asked what Alice assumed to be "May I help you?"

Alice's carefully practiced Spanish melted away. She was without words, utterly incapable of asking for anything, much less an Ace bandage or ice. She couldn't remember the verbs or the nouns. Nothing. Without Toby as her guide, she was rendered mute and ridiculous. Here, all her education couldn't get her a single bag of ice. The woman spoke again, in Spanish, this time more rapidly.

"*Inglés, por favor*," Alice said, her own worst joke, but the woman wrinkled up her nose and shook her head.

"Okay," Alice said, in English, and slowly. "I need some ice and an Ace bandage. For a foot?" She lifted up her own ankle and pointed to it.

The woman looked at her blankly, then produced a small package of Band-Aids from underneath the counter.

Alice shook her head but felt they were finally getting somewhere. She acted out walking and then twisting her ankle. She made a painful face, then pointed to her wedding ring. "*Mi amor*," she said. She didn't know if that was the right word, but the woman's eyes lit up.

"*Sí, sí*," the woman said, and walked purposefully back among shelves of supplies. She returned quickly, placing a bright red condom packet in front of Alice. *Profiláctico*, it read, the absolute last thing Alice needed. Clearly, they'd reached an impasse.

Alice was about to give up but couldn't stand the thought of Toby's disappointment at her returning empty handed. Hands in her pockets, Alice came upon the Chiclets and fished them out, as if they could explain something. She set them on the counter, pink and maroon, like little valentines, sweet nothings. "You can have these," Alice said. "Give them to your kids. You have kids, right? Everyone in this country seems to have plenty." The woman looked at her suspiciously, then said something else that Alice didn't understand.

Alice shrugged her shoulders apologetically. The woman finally produced a small notepad from under the counter; she pushed a pen towards Alice and stood back. Alice took the pen, thought for a second, then wrote, in English, "I'm out of luck. It's not your fault." She lay the pen down and left.

On the short walk back to the hotel, she gave money to every beggar who asked for it. She gave until her pockets were empty, then went back to Toby, who lay waiting in the dark.

Jimi Hendrix, Bluegrass Star

GEOFFREY BECKER

From *Black Elvis* (2009)

In front of the Pompidou Center, a pretty redheaded girl with a violin case took a position about fifteen yards to my left. She wore tight jeans and a black cowboy shirt with pearly buttons, and I kept one eye on her as she took out her instrument and applied rosin to the bow in brisk, short strokes. I finished up "All Along the Watchtower," nodded to the family from Peoria who had stopped to stare at me as if I were a roadside accident, laid down my Strat, and went over.

She launched into something lively and Irish sounding, her eyes closed, her head tilted thoughtfully to one side. I maintained my position as her entire audience until I was joined by a few skinny Parisian teenagers in black clothes, generating their own weather system of Gauloises smoke and attending to the music as if it were a philosophy lecture. When she finished, I tossed a few of my coins into her case to set an example, but it didn't make much of an impression on my associates, who moved quickly on down the line toward the guy who was walking on broken glass and eating fire. That bastard always had the crowd, and it had crossed my mind more than once to think up something a little more dangerous for myself, too. I didn't know how he did it. The glass was real, jagged and sharp—I'd checked it out.

"I know some bluegrass," I said to her, when it was just the two of us. "You want to play together? We'll double our income."

"You do? What do you know?"

I knew exactly four tunes, all of them learned to help out my college roommate with his senior thesis, "The Dave Katz Project." Katz had completed a music major without developing facility with any instrument, bravely working his way through the trumpet, the piano, and the upright bass, before finally settling on the banjo.

"'Sally Goodin'?" I said. "'Rocky Top?'" I didn't want to give her all four at once.

"'Sally Goodin.'"

She came over to my spot and stood beside me as I slid my guitar back on. It was a midseventies model in a particularly ugly color called "Antigua," a kind of puke-and-cigarette-ash sunburst. I'd picked it up cheap from a guy I met in a record store who claimed he wanted to get rid of all his worldly possessions. It had a sawn-in-half baseball bat neck, and gouged into the back of the body was the legend "Satin Lives"—the work of some former owner with either poor spelling or a shiny wardrobe. I turned off my distortion and tried to get the cleanest, most mountain-pure sound I could. A few minutes earlier, I'd been blasting nuclear holocaust through that runt speaker. Now I wanted pine trees, moonshine whiskey, cold running streams. "There," I said, strumming a bright, open G.

"Wendy," she said, meeting my eyes briefly, without much interest. "I like to go fast." She stomped her foot three times.

Playing with The Dave Katz Project had always left me slightly depressed, since we never went fast—it was like sitting for the SATs. But Wendy took off like a bottle rocket. I thumped along, careful not to be too loud, trying to emphasize the bass notes and not let the pace drag. The Parisian teenagers came back. A small crowd began to gather.

The money rained in, copper, silver, even some notes. I asked her where she'd learned to play like that.

"Suzuki method. How about 'Cotton-eyed Joe'? It's just A-E-A."

When we'd done all we could to that one, a man with a bad hairpiece asked us if we wanted a job. He wore a suit and seemed reasonably believable when he said he could offer us 750 francs to play for the night, plus room and board. Wendy's French was slightly better than mine, and between the three of us we managed to clarify that the place we were going to was a sort of retreat for *les travailleurs* of the Renault automobile company. "They like very much the American music," he assured us. "John Denver."

In the van, I let my hand rest against Wendy's leg, which she didn't seem to notice. "I'm Phil," I said. She was staring out the window, so I did, too. The day had started out sunny and warm, but had been disintegrating since noon, and now it looked like rain. Jean, our host, drove us first to my hotel, where I grabbed my pack from the front desk—I'd checked out after breakfast and hadn't made any plan yet for tonight—then on to the youth hostel, where Wendy had her things. I'd learned she was from Baltimore, but that was about it. She seemed intent on not sharing much. I thought about what I might say to make myself seem interesting.

"How do you like France?"

"It's OK," she said. "I'm running out of money."

"We could make a killing together. We're eclectic."

"That's what that thing is? An eclectic guitar?" Her eyes were light green, almost feline. "I'm getting married in December."

"Good for you. Where is he, now?"

"Back home. Mad at me for being here."

"He should have come along. Does he play anything?"

"No. He doesn't really like music."

"And you want to marry him? Have you thought this thing through?"

She smiled, one side of her mouth going up higher than the other. "He voted for Reagan, too," she said. "It's sort of a problem."

It took about an hour to get where we were going, which was out in the country, and to the south. What we passed through to get there confirmed my suspicions that much of Europe was just an extension of the New Jersey Turnpike. Train tracks, concrete-bunker-style warehouses, power lines, freight yards, and ratty fields where they appeared to be raising weeds. Eventually we slid off into prettier territory, with farmhouses and trees. Then we were getting out in front of a big white house. Jean took us upstairs and showed us to our room.

We explored our quarters—twin beds with orange spreads on them, a sink in the room, a small bathroom off it with a toilet, tub (no bidet). I had found out a few things: she was twenty-four. She smoked Marlboros, lighting them with a World War II–vintage stainless steel Zippo. She had been traveling three weeks on an Inter-Rail Pass in France and Italy, busking infrequently, and with mixed success.

"They think we're together," she said, sitting on the edge of one bed.

I sat down beside her, but she got right up, went into the bathroom and brushed her teeth.

In the time we had before dinner, she showed me three more songs. I kept trying to rock-and-roll around underneath her traditional melodies, but she was having none of it. "Straight," she warned me. "Please, just keep the beat and hit the right chords."

Dinner was five courses of cafeteria-quality food, served to us at a table downstairs by a tiny blonde girl in a white jacket. I took it that this, the main house, was where Jean himself lived. Perhaps the girl was his daughter. It was meat, potatoes, green beans the color of army fatigues, cheese, fruit, and wine that tasted the way our family basement smelled, back before we'd had it fixed up and the carpeting installed. But it also wasn't pâté out of a can, and I paid attention, thinking I might live to tell someone about it sometime. *A five-course French meal!*

A path ran alongside the house and back to three one-story, concrete dormitories, as well as a central recreation building. They had a stage for us, with lights, even a small sound system. I gathered from a poster on the wall that we were the last-minute replacement for a ventriloquist who had canceled. Maybe Jean figured the broken-glass guy was too much of a fire hazard.

Our crowd was so drunk we could have been playing in different keys and they wouldn't have minded. There were about fifty of them, men and women, on foldout metal seats. Dress was casual. We played close to an hour.

Jean paid us in cash and told us when he'd take us back to the city in the morning. "I return you to the Beaubourg, yes?" he asked.

After he left us, Wendy grabbed my arm. "Come on," she said. "Let me show you something."

There was a phone booth in the courtyard. She took the receiver off and held her thumb over the button that turned the phone on and off. "You have to get it just right," she said. "OK. Who do you want to talk to?"

"No one."

"Don't you have a girlfriend or something?"

"No, not just now."

"Well, there must be someone you want to call. Give me a number." I told her my mother's. Keeping her thumb over the button, she used the forefinger of her other hand to tap sharply on it. "It's all in the rhythm," she said. She must have tapped fifty times. "Yes! Take it—it's ringing."

I huddled up next to her. The answering machine came on, and I left a cheery message—I was OK, I was making money, I'd write soon. Then I nodded and Wendy let up her thumb. "How does that work?"

"You can only do it with this kind of phone, but they have them all over. You keep the button out just far enough to get a dial tone, then tap the numbers. It takes some practice, but if you get the rhythm right, you can call anyplace for free."

She showed me, and for the next few minutes, I tried unsuccessfully to call my own number in Brooklyn. She told me to think in triplets—a nine was just a series of three threes—and that helped, but I eventually gave up. The whole business just reminded me that I had no one to talk to anyway. I'd illegally sublet my place to a guy named Clem who was a video technician down at CBS TV, in charge of making sure the right tapes ran between 2:00 a.m. and 6:00 a.m., when it was all just prerecorded programming. His bald head reminded me of a mushroom, and his dilated pupils and oddly timed way of speaking made me suspect he did a lot of hallucinogens, but he was the only person who had responded to my ad, and he'd paid cash in advance.

Back in the room, we smoked cigarettes by the window, the cool air bathing our hot faces, our bodies inches from each other. I told her about trying to be a musician in New York. I told her about how the house I'd grown up in, in New Jersey, was now for sale. My mom was moving in with Re-Pete, a bearded guy she'd met on the tennis courts, and my dad—Original Pete—had a new apartment.

"This friend of mine I knew from high school, Adam Gordon, comes in to this place where I'm waiting tables," I said. "He'd just spent a year playing his way around Europe. Paid for his whole trip. He gave me his map." I dug it out to show her. It was a Michelin one, with the good money towns circled in red, and it had been folded and refolded so often that it had the integrity of a laundered Kleenex.

"Been there," she said, studying it. "There, too. Want to go there, there, and there."

I thought about what else to tell her. My life seemed deeply uninteresting. This, right now, was probably the high point. My best friend might as well have been married—I never saw him anymore. I had one guy I hung out with back home, a Vietnam vet named Doggie John who washed dishes at the cafe. He and I would get stoned, go to Prospect Park, and throw the Frisbee to his Doberman pinscher, Ralph. Ralph had an inoperable brain tumor that made him blind in one eye, and as often as not, the Frisbee smacked him right in the side of the head.

"*Original Pete*," she said. "That's pretty funny."

"Not to him it isn't."

"No, I guess not."

"I'm glad we met," I said.

"I might go to law school. That's the other thing I'm thinking over. This is my thinking summer. Do you like martinis?"

"Not so much. I'm more of a shot-and-a-beer guy." I thought this might be the kind of thing a girl from Baltimore would like to hear.

"I love how they look. I love how the word sounds. And I've never had one. I'm not sure I want to. Then I'd have nothing to look forward to."

"There might be other things," I said.

"You understand that I couldn't possibly have sex with you?"

The moon was descending from a cloud, a big silver coin. I could feel the weather clearing. "What's he do? Your fiancé."

"Artist."

"Like a painter? A sculptor?"

"Yeah, like that."

"Does he at least have a name?"

"Tomislav."

"That sounds made up. Did he make it up?

"No, it's real. He's Serbian. From Yugoslavia."

"Ah," I said. "And votes Republican and hates music."

"He doesn't hate it. It's just not something he notices. It's funny when you think about it, because he's a gifted artist."

I stared at my boot, the toe of which had begun to come apart from the sole, and thought about how much I hated the word *gifted*.

"What?"

"Nothing."

"You can tell me." She reached out and touched my knee. "We ought to get to know each other."

"I'm not looking for sympathy."

"No one said you were."

"So, forget it."

"Forget what?"

"I'm not going to say."

"Sure you are." She exhaled through the screen. "Otherwise, I'm going to tickle you."

There was a bulge in the plaster where it had been resealed and painted over. The scar ran diagonally from the ceiling to the bottom of the window. "I have a tumor on the brain," I said, and then added, "inoperable."

"Are you serious? You're joking, aren't you?"

An uptown bus of a moment passed by, but I didn't get on. "You're right," I said. "I'm joking."

"Oh, my God." She took my hand. "You *aren't* joking. I knew a girl that happened to, back home, but they were able to operate. She was okay after the surgery. No hair, though." She touched mine, which hadn't been cut in a while, and was looking fairly wild. I hadn't shaved in a week. In general, I was pleased with how disreputable I looked. "Does it hurt?"

"Not usually. I feel like it's focused me, though."

"I'll bet."

"Sometimes I have visions. Brief ones."

"I get migraines, and right before, everything takes on an aura. Is it like that, or do you actually see things?"

"More like that."

"Brains are weird."

"Yes," I agreed. "They are."

"I'm really sorry about your head." She stood up, pushed her hair back behind her ears. "I'm going to take a bath."

"Knock yourself out." This was something Katz and I used to say.

She proceeded to take off all her clothes, right in front of me, then went into the bathroom and closed the door. I listened to the water as it fell into the tub, watched the light on my little amp in the corner where I'd plugged it in to recharge.

I'm ashamed to say that what followed was not a period of regret, or self-loathing, or anything like that—I found the role of dying musician fit me well. I almost began to believe it myself. Life took on a heightened quality—individual moments seemed artificially lit and oversaturated with color, like in a fifties musical. Occasionally I caught my own reflection in something—a bus window, the side-view mirror of a parked car—and noticed with satisfaction how nobly I seemed to be bearing up.

After Jean dropped us back in Paris, we went straight to the train station and headed to Switzerland, where the really good money towns were. Since what you earn as a street musician is the change in folks' pockets, you want to situate yourself in a country where the pocket change means something. Also, the Swiss are so orderly, so painfully aware of anything remotely out of place in their little windup towns, that they tend to throw money at you out of a kind of civic duty; they think if they pay enough, you'll go away. On a busy street in Bern, our first stop, we made nearly two hundred francs, and no one watched us for more than thirty seconds at a time.

We camped. Most towns had campgrounds on their outskirts, with reasonable facilities, a laundry room, perhaps even a Ping-Pong table or a bar. Wendy had a small tent, and every night, after a few hours of partying and maybe practicing a new song, we'd lay out our sleeping bags. I'd watch her kick out of her jeans, roll them up into a ball, then slide in. I grew to know her smell, which reminded me of sourdough bread. I learned the rhythm of her breathing when she slept, deep and even and a bit like surf. Occasionally, I'd make some kind of gesture—rub her shoulders, maybe, or try to nibble her ear—but although she'd let it go on for a minute or two, eventually she'd always push me away. When a campground had the right kind of phone, I'd practice my technique, calling the number of this nurse I'd gone out with one time, Rita, but with no luck. Foreign voices spoke to me, and I'd quickly hang up. I had no plan for what to do if I ever did get through, if Rita ever did answer. I knew she'd remember me. She was nice enough, older, maybe thirty, and had a kid. We'd eaten Chinese food at a place in the neighborhood. We'd just had nothing to say. Our waitress had taken our order, then disappeared for a long time. We'd heard shouting from the kitchen. We were the only people in the place. Finally, after another twenty minutes, during which she told me all about that evening's episode of *Wheel of Fortune*, the cook had come out to retake our order, very apologetically. He had almost no English at all, and we'd pointed to the items of the menu. For some reason, I still had Rita's number in my pocket.

A week passed, then another. We went up to Amsterdam, where I'd started my trip. The tall ships were coming, which meant crowds, which meant money. Money was the thing that kept us together, the subject of most of our conversations, the closest thing we had to a direction or goal. We stayed with Wild Bill, who ran a flophouse-style hostel, with strictly enforced house rules about being out of the house between 9:00 a.m. and 4:30 p.m., and required attendance at an afternoon tea at 5:00

p.m. He was Dutch, but long ago he had lived for a while in New York. Underneath his bossiness and generally irritable veneer, I suspected he was actually a nice guy. "Hey, look who it is," he said, when we showed up on his doorstep. "The Voodoo Child."

He gave us a room all to ourselves. It was tiny—there was barely space to stand up, but it had an actual bed in it, and even a tiny dresser. "Weren't you embarrassed?" she asked. "Going around pretending to be Hendrix?"

"It was like being in a tribute band," I said. "Just without the band. One of the few things I do well is imitating Jimi. I've been working on it since I was twelve. In high school, I was a god."

"You are *so* much better off with me." She broke off a piece of a Toblerone and popped it in her mouth, offered me the rest. "Listen, the Gnats are planning a big jam tomorrow night. They asked us to play." The Cashville Gnats were a bluegrass quartet made up of two Americans, upright bass and guitar, and a star banjo player named Jens, who was German and all of about sixteen. They had a mandolinist, too; I didn't know where he was from. We'd seen them in Bern and also Zurich—they always seemed to be leaving a town when we got there, or vice versa. It figured they'd come for the tall ships.

"How do you know?"

"I ran into Matt, the bass player, at the train station."

"You did?"

"When I went to get French fries. He was getting some, too."

"How come I didn't see him?"

"I don't know. Because you're oblivious? Anyway, I told him we'd come play."

"I don't want to play with them. We won't make any money."

"Maybe not, but it will be fun. Don't be a baby. Now, let's go see if we can find something to eat."

"Matt? How do you even know his name?"

"He told me. What's your problem?"

We played all the next morning down by the harbor. Two teenage girls had a stand selling soft ice cream cones, and around noon they brought us over a couple. The tall ships were due in the following morning, and the city was filling up with tourists. According to a headline I'd seen outside a newsstand, Iraq had just attacked Iran, but both these places seemed so remote to me as to almost be fictional. My jeans pockets were stuffed to bursting with guilders, so heavy I'd had to crank my belt another notch to keep my pants up.

A young couple was making out on a bench, really going at it. Wendy took an extra-long lick at her ice cream, then cleared chocolate from the corner of her mouth with the end of her finger. "I should call Tomislav," she said.

"Why haven't you?" I'd been wondering this for a while. I'd even begun hopefully to entertain the idea that there might not *be* a Tomislav.

"That wasn't our deal. Our deal was time apart. You aren't apart if you keep checking in."

I crunched the rest of my cone, swallowed. "I'm going to have to leave," I said. "We're going to have to split up."

She licked again and thought some more. A group of big, black birds pecked at the cobblestones a few yards away. "You mean it?"

"I have to live life to its fullest. Carpe diem."

"Don't T-shirt philosophy me. Speaking of time, yours is improving."

"I didn't know anything was wrong with it."

"You drag a little. More than a little, actually. But you are getting better."

"Well, that's nice." I checked my watch. "We don't want to be late for tea. Bill will toss us out on our asses."

"What?" she said.

"Nothing."

"I told Matt we'd be there."

"I might hit Greece," I said. "Go lie on a beach someplace and eat grape leaves."

She was studying me. "All right."

"All right, what?"

"You know. Maybe the normal rules don't apply to us."

One of the crows took a vicious swipe at another. Then the lot of them took off over a warehouse like a gust of sooty wind.

In theory the things you want most, the things you've waited longest for, ought to be the sweetest, but everyone knows this isn't always true. The apples reddening so attractively on the tree turn out to be mushy or tasteless; the fantasized-about, dreamed-of career turns out to be just another desk in a cubicle in an office with bad air. The dope so delicately traced with red fibers turns out to give you a massive headache, the big game is a blowout, the expensive shoes just make your feet hurt.

I thought about getting a hotel or something, but we didn't have so much saved that we could afford to blow a lot of guilders. Plus, that would have made it a big deal, and the idea was that it was not. People assumed we were a couple anyway—certainly Bill did. To go check into some fancy place would have upped the stakes too much. This was casual. We just needed each other, and the bottle of Côtes du Rhône we picked up on the way back.

We'd had tea; we'd had dinner. There was still some pastel light coming through the tiny window by the bed. It all went reasonably well. She told me she'd remember me. "How?" I said. I was happy the way I was happy once on Halloween, when I'd gone out twice, in different costumes, spread out double the candy I deserved on the floor of my room and started to divide it taxonomically: Snickers and Baby Ruths, 3 Musketeers, Hershey's, right on down to the lowly boxed raisins and worthless candy corn. But she never answered. After a while, I realized she'd fallen asleep.

The next day we went out and made some money in the late morning, but then she wanted to rest, and I went for a long walk around the city. I was furious with myself, because I was pretty sure I was in love. I wanted more nights like last night. I thought about ways of fixing things. Did tumors ever just go away by themselves? I tried to imagine how that might happen. It wasn't something you just coughed up like a hairball. Perhaps I could be the recipient of miraculous news from the States. *It was a mistake. We mixed your X-rays up with someone else's! All is forgiven!*

I didn't want to play with the Gnats, and I was reasonably sure they didn't want me to play with them, either. One guitar is plenty for bluegrass. Plus, Wendy was right about my time—I couldn't even get the phone trick right. What they needed was a fiddle. I'd seen them watching us back in Zurich, enemy faces among the tourists, appraising, scouting our little Division III team for its pro-quality running back.

At 7:30 p.m., we all met down by the docks. Wendy had put on a sleeveless black top that showed off her figure, and she had a purple scarf that fluttered in the evening breeze. The ships had arrived, a leafless forest of masts and rigging. I remembered a book my father had bought for me when I was twelve, called simply *Pirates*. I searched the decks of these enormous vessels for men in breeches and blousy shirts. "They were ruthless," he'd told me. "They took what they wanted. They made up their own rules."

The air held the mingled harbor scents of fish and diesel exhaust and open ocean. I looked at her, I looked at the gathering Gnats, and then it hit me—the fix was already in. She hadn't just run in to the bass player—she'd made a deal with him. It was why she'd finally agreed to sleep with me—out of guilt. When we started up, I stood on the far side of the action, watching and listening as the five of them burned their way through some very professional-sounding stuff. I'd learned a lot from Wendy over the past weeks. We did "Uncle Pen," and "Salt Creek," and "Way Downtown." They had other, more complicated material up their sleeves, too, including "Take Five," and a banjo version of "Flight of the Bumblebee." I sat those out, resentment growing in me. When it came my turn to solo on "Foggy Mountain Breakdown," I stomped on the fuzz pedal, and started playing Jimi's solo from the Woodstock version of "Fire." A couple of people cheered.

In a jam, it's customary to take two choruses, then shut up and let the next guy go. Maybe if you're all having a good time, you go around again. But I wouldn't stop. I did all my tricks: between the legs, behind the back, playing with my teeth (you don't actually get your teeth on the strings, but it looks that way). From "Fire," I segued into "The Star-Spangled Banner." Mostly, I was just making noise. There were maybe a hundred people watching, hundreds more moving past along the waterfront behind them, enjoying the cool evening, happy to be out and about where people were alive and mingling, and where there were tall ships.

By the time I was done the Strat was out of tune and I was sweating profusely. I stepped back and avoided Dennis's icy stare. Wendy was clearly mortified, but I didn't care. I unstomped my pedal and tried to strum along, but it sounded so bad that I just turned down the volume and stood there, watching as Jens took center stage again, sending busy, silvery ladders of notes up into the night sky.

"You are a jerk," she told me, when we took a break.

"I knew what was going on as soon as I saw that scarf."

"You're crazy."

"It's like a signal or something."

"Was that one of your visions? It's a *scarf*. I thought it would look nice."

Jens was signing autographs. The other Gnats were popping open bottles of Grolsch, with those cute little porcelain stoppers.

"I'm not dying," I said. She just stared at me. "The cancer thing is a dog I know, Ralph. I just borrowed it." The perspiration at my collar was getting chilly with the breeze coming in off the water. "So, I'm a jerk. Proven. It was a stupid lie, but I didn't think it mattered because we'd never see each other again anyway, and now I see that it does matter and I can't do anything about it." I hoisted my gig bag over my shoulder and picked up the amp. "I'm going back to Bill's," I said. "Have fun with your new friends." After a few steps, I stopped and turned. "Aren't you going to say anything?"

"Like what? That I'm disappointed?"

"You didn't say I was wrong."

"Maybe I knew all along," she said. "Did you ever think of that?"

She came in very late that night, smelling of beer, climbed into bed, and turned her back to me. I listened to her sleep and thought this must be what a marriage feels like after it's gone past the point of repair.

In the morning, Bill's houseboy brought us coffee and a cinnamon muffin as he always did. "They're invited to three festivals in the States next summer," said Wendy, brushing crumbs off her napkin and writing her address and phone number down for me. "I'm playing with them tomorrow at the Leidseplein. Then, in a week, I'm going home."

I did the same for her with mine. It seemed we were done talking about it, which was probably best anyway. "Just remember," I pointed out, "now you're looking at a five-way split."

I went to Germany. For eight humid days, I traveled and busked with a harp player I met in Heidelberg, a short Austrian named Ernst, but he smelled bad and sang even worse, and one night I woke up in the park where we were sleeping to find him attempting to make off with Satin Lives. I tackled him, but he surprised me with a head-butt, grabbed the guitar and ran off into the night. I figured it was a sign.

The number Wendy had given me turned out to be for a bar at a driving range outside of Bel Air, Maryland. "Nineteenth Hole," the guy said, when I called from the Brussels airport. Our connection had a bad echo. Three days since my fight with Ernst and my head still hurt. I couldn't believe I'd finally gotten the phone trick to work.

I asked anyway.

"Windy?" he shouted. "I don't know—I'm inside. They were talking rain for later on. You sound long distance. Are you long distance?"

I let my thumb up and broke the connection. I was across from the duty-free shop, the window of which displayed a new brand of vodka, cobalt-blue bottles lined up at attention and shimmering in the terminal light. About thirty yards further along toward the gates, in a waiting area, a skinny guy with dreadlocks and a bad complexion was juggling beanbags. I went over and watched him for a while. He was good with three and with four, but with five he kept dropping bags. Before I left, I unloaded the rest of my change into his hat.

Lost in Rancho Mirage

DENNIS HATHAWAY

From *The Consequences of Desire* (1992)

Nobody approved of Jill. Not Denton's mother and father, not his sister Claire, not even his best friend Mark, who said that even if times had changed in most respects a man without an appropriate wife was still a stray dog, something that would only get scraps and leftovers, a creature that you would feel leery about getting close to. "What about David Felter?" Denton wanted to know, thinking the dog metaphor not only inappropriate but lacking imagination. "It's okay to be gay," Mark asserted. "It can even be an advantage, as long as there aren't too many of you. But a bachelor . . ." He shook his head remorsefully at the utter unfortunate sadness of the idea.

Denton's father said that marrying a previously married woman was like buying a used car, you could never be sure how well it had been taken care of. "It's almost the twenty-first century, Dad," said Denton, suspecting that his father knew nothing beyond what he read in certain sections of the *Wall Street Journal* and the quarterly reports of companies whose stock he was thinking of buying or selling. "Nobody stays married to the same person all their life anymore. Besides, you can't compare a woman to a car."

"Why not?" Denton's father lit his pipe in defiance of any new conventions that might presume to displace the old, the perfectly serviceable, the tried and true. "Some are fast and some are slow." He smirked through eddies of smoke. "Some don't cost you a penny, while others bleed you dry, like your mother . . ."

"What in the world are you talking about?" Denton's mother's tone lifted to a high enough register that Denton could imagine a scene he didn't want to be anywhere near the middle of. She didn't approve of Jill either, not because of the previous husband and child, but because of the fact that the child lived with the father, not with Jill. "I don't care what you say," she said, in response to Denton's explication of this arrangement. "A normal, balanced woman is not going to give up her child under any circumstance. You would have to be a mother to understand."

Denton decided to call Claire. He said, "They assume that anyone who isn't rich is after money," and Claire said, "Yeah, well . . . ," as if she agreed. Claire had met Jill when Denton and Jill stopped at Monterey on a trip to San Francisco, and Jill had irritated Claire by complaining at length about the weather that had turned gloomy during their drive up the coast and rendered what she had expected to be the stunning vistas of Big Sur into gray, sodden disappointments. Jill, who had grown up in the Midwest, loved the perpetual sunlight of L.A., while Claire, who spent her first twenty-one years there, professed to hate the city and all of its inhabitants.

"Why is it that you have to have their approval, Denton?" she said. "They're dinosaurs. They're not on the verge of changing."

"What do you think?" Denton imagined a familiar scowl of impatience on his sister's face.

"It doesn't matter what I think, Denton. Do what you want to do. You're an adult."

"I guess I'm not 100 percent certain," Denton said.

"What do *her* parents think?" Claire's tone flipped up a little red flag in Denton's head. "Do they approve of you?"

"We haven't met," said Denton. "She hardly ever mentions them. I don't think they know about me."

"I'd say she's conflicted," Claire said.

"What's that supposed to mean?"

"She wants to be independent, but she's carrying around all this baggage—her background, her kid, the fact that her husband was abusive, verbally and physically . . ."

"What?" Denton felt that he had just walked into the middle of a movie. "Do you know something?"

"Yeah," said Claire. "We talked."

"She didn't tell me," Denton said, uncertain of what to blame for his feeling appalled, the fact that Jill had kept things from him or that she had been a victim of something tawdry.

"I'm a woman," said Claire, with a declarative assuredness that further sank Denton's self-regard and confidence. "We understand one another."

The sun predictably appeared each day until the week after New Year's, when, without sound or fury, the sky turned a rubbery gray and blessed the earth with cold, mechanical rain. Jill told Denton in a rueful tone that wind and lightning and thunder were the only midwestern phenomena for which she felt nostalgia. She acknowledged an ongoing state of irritability brought on by the weather, and he began to think about the condominium that his parents owned in the desert. An image of its red tile roof and sandstone stucco walls transformed into a picture of himself and Jill stretched out on the patio lounges beneath a curative sun. By habit, his mind turned to logistics: a real estate deal had bogged down at the bank and he could safely leave town; Jill did clerical work out of an agency and could get off when she wanted, so that if they left on a Friday afternoon and returned at the end of the following week they would have time, between eating and making love and lying in the sun, for a trip to the mountains to ski. He might give her lessons in golf, or tennis, neither of which she had ever attempted. They could hike in the desert, ride the tramway, sneak out late at night to swim naked in the pool, watch movies on TV. The prospect glowed like sunlight through the wet, dispirited sky.

Jill had more or less moved into Denton's place, although she kept things in the apartment that she shared with another woman, an apartment in a building that allowed children and was perpetually defaced with graffiti. She had gone to the apartment to get a certain sweater and Denton waited with growing impatience for her to return. Without reflection upon possible consequence, he dialed her number. She sounded sleepy, and in a mumbling, childish fashion told him that she had lain down to rest and the very next moment discovered herself the victim of a nightmare in which a telephone rang and rang and rang, an instrument of torture. "Now I can hear somebody's stereo," she complained. "Like it's in the next room." Not wanting to dwell upon Jill's annoyance with cosmic circumstance, Denton described the imagined trip to the desert.

"I'll think about it," she said, indifferently.

"Wow," said Denton. "I really sold you on this one."

"I'm tired," she said, her tone defensive. "And Jenny called."

"Yeah?" The flat, resigned invocation of this name implied that something unpleasant was involved.

"She said her father won't let her eat pizza because the cheese is crammed with cholesterol and will clog up her veins."

"Jeez," said Denton. "She's seven years old." Jill's ex-husband was a chiropractor, unreasonably obsessed, it seemed to Denton, with matters of health. He lived with Jenny in Indiana, a state that Denton had never set foot in but that he guessed to be like the agricultural parts of California, entirely flat and green. The denial of pizza struck him as a form of abuse. He said this to Jill, with the possibly defective expectation that she would laugh, or at least giggle.

"Denton," she said, in a tone that warned him to be careful. "It isn't funny. The poor baby. I feel like such a heel." The thickening quality of her voice meant that she had either begun or was about to cry, and Denton suddenly felt self-conscious, as if the telephone in his hand had turned into an embarrassing revelation. He heard her sniffle.

"I'm glad that he cares about her." There was shuffling, rustling, then a blowing of the nose. Denton rummaged his mind for an appropriate remark.

"Maybe I should go back," she said. "Maybe I could work at the turkey plant. They're always hiring. I could take her horseback riding on weekends. My best friend in high school married this guy and they live out on the edge of town where you're allowed to keep horses."

"Jill," said Denton, not because he had a response to this but because he felt themselves, the two ends of this electronic connection, fading in opposite directions. She had arrived in L.A. with a commonplace desire—to become an actress, to get into movies, TV. He had met her when she was working for Mark selling real estate, a job that couldn't have lasted, Mark explained to Denton later, because of her unfortunate propensity to offer clients her honest opinion of the houses she showed them. When Denton first met her he told her that she looked like Meryl Streep, although he didn't know then about her aspirations. As it turned out, she didn't consider Meryl Streep the least bit attractive, so it hadn't been the perfect thing to say.

"There's a jacuzzi," he said. "There's a thirty-six-inch TV. We can rent all the Bette Davis movies."

"Oh Denton." He heard in her voice a softening, a yielding. He felt suddenly giddy.

"We can go dancing." Jill had a thing about ballroom dancing, and although Denton found everything but the Samba boring, he was fairly light on his feet. "It's still the fifties there, Jill. Everyone drives around in Cadillacs."

"Denton," she said, "my big goal in life at this point is to play Mother Courage. Do you think that's unrealistic? Silly?"

"I don't know." Questions like this, impossible to answer, tended to irritate him. Jill was undeniably attractive, and possessed an unselfconscious ability to draw attention to herself, but thinking of the variety of circumstances, accidents, coincidences necessary for her to actually become a successful actress made him almost dizzy. With dogged persistence she went to auditions, called up agents, concocted schemes for getting into invitation-only events, but Denton regarded as midwestern naivete the belief that she would succeed if only she worked hard enough. Telephone one more agent, run out to one more casting call. Denton's father once said, "If hard work was all anyone needed to get rich, then the guys who pick up the garbage would be millionaires." Denton might, himself, have been picking up garbage or digging ditches if his grandfather hadn't left his father a piece of real estate that turned out to be directly in the path of a freeway. "You got to have luck," Denton's father said. "Your mother and I were going to live in that dump, but instead I had this dough in my hand and I thought, I ought to do something with it. Invest it. Buy another piece of property. That's how it all got started."

"The condo," Denton said, trying to divest his voice of a tone he knew to be impatient and unappealing. "It's in this place called Rancho Mirage. Right on a golf course. You can sit on the patio and watch the golfers go by in their carts."

"Mother Courage," Jill sighed. "And Cordelia. 'If for I want that glib and oily art . . .'"

"Jill." Denton squeezed the phone, frowning, trying to summon her attention. "The sun shines every day. It never rains. There's a sauna. There's an exercise room with a rowing machine. What more could you possibly want, Jill?"

"Money," she said, her voice now floating on a cloud above the tawdry details of the present and real. "Fame. Love."

"I love you," Denton said.

"Yes," she said, in dreamy affirmation. "I know you do."

She adored the TV and pool, hated the exercise room because the carpeting gave off an odor, and found the plush green of the golf course to be, in some inexplicable way, annoying. "I could never spend my time like that," she said, staring from the living room window at a pair of middle-aged women in visors gliding down the fairway in a cart. Denton wanted to sleep in the guest room but she refused, on the obvious grounds that the master suite was larger and more luxurious. The idea of making love in his parents' bed made Denton a little queasy, although he didn't say so. They sat in the jacuzzi at night, under a cloud of stars such as she hadn't seen since she left Indiana. She slept until ten or eleven and then spent the afternoon on the bed, flipping channels between three or four soap operas with a P. D. James as thick as a dictionary in her lap. "If that woman's an actress, I'm the Duchess of Kent," she would comment, or things to that effect.

Even though he had bought her a racket, she decided that tennis would be impossibly difficult and therefore boring. She was irritated by the golfers, who could sometimes be seen or heard stirring around in the rough outside the windows, and a populist inclination seemed to be awakened by the sight of Cadillacs and Mercedes-Benzes and women wearing what she described as tons of jewelry in the middle of the day. "If I were you," said Denton, feeling helpless, "I wouldn't be so quick to judge things just by appearance," but of course she said that wasn't what she was doing at all; she didn't even expect him to understand, having had a Mummy and Dad with oodles of money, and never anything serious to worry about.

On the morning of the third day he left her asleep in the fading darkness of dawn, drove his car beyond the golf courses and condos, and found a spot where he could pull off the road and hike a short way into the desert. He climbed to the top of a flat rock and sat staring at the glow of the impending sunrise, wishing that Jill were with him, snuggled against him in the air so chilled that when he opened his mouth a cloud of vapor blurred his view. He waited, shivering and impatient, and finally an arc of liquid orange appeared above the ragged line of distant mountains. He had almost begged her to come but she had emphatically declined, saying that getting up at such an hour was entirely inimical to her idea of vacation. The arc grew into a half-circle and then a complete disk of radiant heat and light that dissolved the darkness of the sky, making Denton feel like a witness to a miraculous event that would never be repeated, at least not in his lifetime. He watched a lizard dart between two twisted pieces of vegetation that may or may not have been alive. His eyes followed the rim of the mountains and descended to a sea of roofs all white and glittering in the shower of oblique light.

"Just think," he had said to Jill when they first descended into the valley, into a long irregular shadow the mountains cast over the habitation. "A hundred years ago there was nobody here but Indians." The change inspired him to think of his business as invested with the power and significance of history. He was involved in nothing less, he thought, than transformation. He wanted to say as much to Jill but feared that she would find him pompous. She seemed to find people who spoke too freely of their own accomplishments pompous—a peculiarly midwestern trait, Denton suspected. And perhaps she was right. After all, he thought, as the perceptible ascent of the sun began to drive the chill from the air, I have been involved only in the transfer of some pieces of property, the construction of some buildings devoted to purposes of minor importance. Of the millions in the city, Denton reflected, only a few hundred enter these buildings, and perhaps a handful know my name, or care who I am. As the shadow of the mountains retreated, exposing more of the sparkling gravel of identical roofs, his exultation expired and he felt depressed and hungry.

With the sun like a nosy eye in the rearview mirror he drove back to the condo where he made coffee, ate cereal from a box, and got out his tennis racket and took some practice swings in front of the sliding glass door that opened onto the patio and the verdant, deserted fairway. The chance of meeting someone looking for a partner on a weekday morning was highly unlikely, and he practiced spinning the racket on his finger for a few minutes before letting it drop to the floor. He opened a closet and stared at his golf bag. He took out a putter and ball and stood in the middle of the living room, trying to smooth out his jerky, unconfident stroke. He returned the putter to the bag, the mute heads of the clubs speaking the truth that golf attracted him only as a social event—some badinage with friends, some harmless gambling, now and then the conduct of some piece of business. He was typically inept and unlucky, and the idea of scouring the rough for his ball or endlessly putting while others waited impatiently behind was distinctly unappealing. He gazed with a sentimental longing at his skis, which leaned above the golf bag. Jill had not expressed the slightest interest in waking up early enough to get to the lifts at a reasonable hour, and while Denton was not opposed to going by himself, and in fact found the imagined solitude of cold and height and descent acceptable, some elemental fear or need to encircle and protect made him loathe to abandon her.

He lay on the sofa, thinking of a golf ball nestled like an egg in grass, and he fell asleep, to be awakened from a vaguely sensual dream by the cascade of water in the toilet and then the steamy hiss of the shower. He got up and went into the bedroom and lay on his back on the mussed-up bed, staring at the vaulted ceiling upon which unfolded a hazy vision of a future—Jill, older and plumper; children of indeterminate sex and number; a house with trees and grass. The bathroom door clicked and from a mist emerged a miracle—Jill, wearing only a towel wrapped into a turban about her head and flowing like a cape to the small of her back. She saw him and smiled a prim, girlish smile that made her look innocent and somehow inviolable.

"Denton," she said, her voice perking up as she spoke, "do you think I should cut my hair?"

He thought a moment, but the lingering confusion of sleep rendered him incapable of visualizing what was beneath the towel. It was almost eleven o'clock. She waited for him to answer and an idea blew like a gust of desert wind into his head.

"I made coffee, Jill. Want some?"

"Thanks" she said, "I'm tired of my hair."

"I don't want to talk about your hair," said Denton.

"Oh. Okay." Silence was threaded with a faint, electronic hum, and far away, the resonant whack of a golf club. "You'd look good with a beard, Denton. Cover your chin."

"What's wrong with my chin?" He had begun to feel a swarmy, feverish desire.

"Nothing's wrong with it. It just recedes a little. With a beard it would look stronger."

"Jill." With a shock of adolescent fervor he almost said, "I want us to get married, Jill," but he stopped himself, because he had already decided upon the accoutrements to a proposal—the particular restaurant, the kind of wine, the shirt and jacket he would wear, the moment within the afterglow of the meal when he would lift her hand and gaze into her eyes. It's true, he thought, about my chin. Juvenile longings to the contrary, he knew that he would always resemble most closely his father, not Richard Gere. He had once grown a beard but it had looked unclean, a smear of charcoal on his cheeks, and after enduring a few weeks of comment he had shaved it off.

"I watched the sunrise," he said, delving for suitable adjectives to bring alive this phenomenon. But she did not find his description remarkable enough to comment upon. His passion began to leak like air from a punctured tire. He left the bedroom to get her a cup of coffee and when he returned she had put on a robe and was sanding her nails with the P. D. James open once more in her lap, and when he bent to kiss her she offered her cheek and not her lips, which were pursed in thoughtful, enigmatic speculation.

"I want to go out," he said. She turned her head as if on cue and produced a smile that Denton felt was meant not only for him but for some larger audience. "This babe is in a different world," Mark had said, shortly after Denton and Jill had been introduced. Denton suspected that an actor or actress might sometimes have trouble distinguishing between the artifice of the stage or set and the reality of the everyday, but when he tried to say as much to Mark he got a condescending look in return, along with the suggestion that Denton give a certain female architect that they both knew a whirl. The architect's face passed like a shadow through Denton's mind. His desire to play tennis or ski had been displaced by an urgent need to drink a martini in a bar with low smoky light and the tinkle of a loungey piano, but he knew without asking that Jill would decline—she had resolved to lose five pounds and therefore alcohol, along with butter, potato chips, even pizza, was forbidden.

He left the bedroom and walked down the hall and through the door into the garage, where he started his car and backed into the street without a clear idea of destination. The sky was a faded blue, completely free of clouds, and he drove for a few miles, listening to country and western music on the radio. *My man's gone off somewhere to play, and left me with the bills to pay*, a woman sang in a voice that reminded Denton of Jill's imitation of Patsy Cline. He began to think that perhaps he should have turned left instead of right, or vice versa. The street became a highway that seemed to lead toward the open end of the valley, but he felt loathe to stop and turn around and gradually the houses and condos receded in his rearview mirror like a fading dream. "She's got a nice pair of bazookas," Mark had said of Jill, as if little else about her merited observation. The highway of diminishing width bored onward through a landscape absolutely flat and empty save for groves of palm trees and an occasional roadside stand that advertised dates for sale. "She's beautiful," Claire had said, in a tone not of admiration but rebuke, as if the unremarkable features she possessed in common with Denton had been held up to ridicule by the presence of Jill. Denton pulled the visor down against the inquisitive glare of the sun. He felt a need to articulate to himself all the reasons that he loved Jill, but before he could begin a sign appeared, implying the existence of civilization, and then the road abruptly curved and he was on the main street of a town, a town of an entirely different nature, a place where a scattering of dusty vehicles sat at various angles against a curb that wasn't a real curb at all but a strip of gravel interrupted here and there with tufts of yellow vegetation.

Denton drove slowly, staring at buildings that all seemed to be in a mild state of dilapidation. He saw the word BEER in blocky, unlit neon in front of a window framing a murky scene of backs at a counter, a tableau that promoted a sense of having arrived in a new and possibly dangerous country. He parked beside a truck that appeared to have just brought someone from the deepest recesses of the desert, a Power Wagon the color of the dirty gravel without any top, with a single seat nearly bereft of upholstery, a dirty windshield with a spider's web of cracks that led in diminishing concentric circles, he observed with a little bump of fear, to a hole the size of his finger.

He stood inside the door, trying to size up the unfamiliar situation. He was glad that he hadn't changed clothes after his hike to view the sunrise—his Levi's, his boots, the jacket that he had bought at a place that sold backpacks and sleeping bags, made him feel that he belonged. He looked around at men who all seemed to be wearing cowboy hats or caps with bills. He smelled cigarette smoke and the fermented odor of beer. No one appeared to stare, or even to notice him, as he walked to the far end of the bar that formed a narrow horseshoe in a long room lined on opposing walls with wooden booths. The booths appeared to be empty, but nearly all the stools at the bar were occupied. Denton wondered where these people lived—the town had seemed no more than a handful of buildings and houses scattered without any sense of order, as if blown there by the desert wind, by accident.

He felt both wary and excited by the strange surroundings. He sat on a worn and polished stool between a heavy young man and a much older man with jowls and forehead so ruggedly crevassed that his face didn't look entirely human. Neither man turned his head to look at Denton. The younger man was systematically going at something on a plate in front of him, while the older man held a glass in both hands and stared intently into it as if the liquid contained a vision of compelling grandeur or complexity. Denton looked at the double row of bottles reflected in the mirror, the cash register of an obsolete style, the faded signs dispensing aphorisms and a sort of humor that he considered rustic and unfunny. A woman in jeans and T-shirt knotted above her waist appeared and waited indifferently for him to speak, and unable to make up his mind conclusively he asked for a common brand of beer, thinking that in this place, perhaps, he might be able to discover something authentic. She didn't pour the beer, but merely pushed a glass and bottle toward him. It was lukewarm. In the city, he thought, in another sort of place, he would refuse it, but then he confirmed for himself that he wasn't in the city, he was somewhere in the desert, possibly lost, possibly in some sort of trouble that he had yet to perceive. In the mirror he saw himself, and the barmaid, who looked bored, and the magnitude of the distance between this place and the bars that he found himself in from time to time caused him to feel, in successive little jolts, exhilaration and fear. He heard a voice. For a second he thought it was Jill, doing another of the imitations she was fond of; for a moment he did not know where the voice came from, or that its lascivious message was intended for him.

The voice droned loudly on and then abruptly stopped, as if controlled by a switch. Denton felt that everyone's eyes had lifted from the ardent attraction of the liquid in their glasses or bottles to fix upon him. He tried to maintain an aloof and consciously bemused expression. The voice belonged to a woman seated at the opposite end of the bar, a woman with brassy hair and a face puffed up as if by gas, with bloody eyes that gazed at him with infantile directness. Denton guessed that she was drunk, and that no one would expect him to take her seriously. He briefly imagined in general detail the melodramatic elements of a life that would permit her to get drunk in the middle of the day, to humiliate herself in front of what he guessed were acquaintances, to offer herself to a total stranger. The beer, the stale odor of the place, the smoke, made him feel slightly ill. The barmaid, he observed, was the only other female in the place, and as he stared at the slightly flaccid girdle of flesh between her jeans and T-shirt he wondered why she hadn't said anything, hadn't attempted to divert the other woman's attention, tell her that she already had enough, that she ought to go home, lie down, sleep. Denton observed the wale of a scar just to the left of the barmaid's deeply hollow navel, and with a mildly nauseous unease he imagined blood and tissue and a circle of hot white lights above an operating table. He wondered why no one else had spoken. The silence seemed dangerous, evil. He decided to leave, immediately, even though he hadn't finished the beer. An impulse he didn't reflect upon led him to put on the bar an overly generous tip, and he sensed with a little tug of trepidation that the men between whom he sat had watched him delve into his wallet, had guessed at the amount of money in it, had suspected this amount to be considerable, and had arrived at some conclusion and possibly even an idea.

The slatternly woman's voice switched on again as the heat and light of the outdoors embraced him, and he desperately hoped that she would not get up and follow, create a situation from which he would have to extricate himself. He walked back past the Power Wagon, hurrying, and with a snap of elemental fear he saw that his car was gone. He was suddenly transported back to the condo, back to bed, where he had tossed the previous night in the turgid, sweaty grip of a nightmare. "Jill," he had moaned, unable to reach the solace of her heat and form. He blinked. The windshield of the Power Wagon was intact, there was no provocative series of cracks, no portentous hole. The color of the vehicle, in fact, wasn't exactly right, and instead of the springs and tufts of gray sticking out of the seat there was a worn green blanket. He heard a crack of indeterminate cause and location and spun in a panic to see, in gradually reassuring detail, an identical vehicle, the one with the hole in the windshield, and beyond it, a section of the bumper and grille of his car, a sight so reassuring that he smiled, then chuckled, then laughed aloud. In a rush to escape a complication so minor that he could already laugh about it he had turned the wrong way, been momentarily disoriented. No one had followed. He heard a murmur of voices and the click of a glass. Jill appeared in his mind, as she was when she emerged from the shower, a conglomeration of genetic accidents so sublime as to inspire awe and worship, and Denton felt happy, even as he knew that it was her languor that had brought him to this alien place. He peeled off his jacket and threw it into the backseat of the car as the sun poured its blessing freely down upon his head.

Bored with soap operas, Jill had put a movie in the VCR. In three nights they had worked their way from *All About Eve* to *Deception*, with Jill murmuring certain lines and pointing out how a sudden drop in register could convey an infinite volume of meaning. "Did you see the way she lifts one shoulder?" she would say, excited by discovery. They would then have to rewind, play the scene two or three times. "God," Jill said softly. "Was she a brilliant actress or what?"

Denton didn't know. He didn't know what constituted a brilliant performance, only what he liked and didn't like, and he knew that despite occasional tugs of interest he found what he saw to be dated, a vestige of a distant, irrelevant past. He stared with indifference at what seemed unhappy goings on. He looked at Jill's knee, a promise exposed by a parting of her robe. He saw Bette Davis nearly swoon into the arms of an actor he did not recognize, and the sight of their heads together awakened a thought that glided to his tongue.

"Did you ever do a scene like that?"

"Of course." Jill pulled both her knees up to her chin, causing a flutter in Denton's chest.

"Did you feel anything?"

"Huh?"

"I mean, kissing a stranger. Does it make you feel anything in particular?"

"Well, he wouldn't be a stranger, exactly." Jill stared straight ahead, studying the scene as if she expected to be quizzed upon it later. "It would be somebody you had rehearsed with. It might be somebody you knew real well."

"I was just wondering," Denton felt compelled to explain, although he was in fact uncertain of what he was actually digging for. "I was wondering if you get turned on doing scenes like that."

"Sometimes," said Jill, in a disinterested voice. On the screen a door shut, locations changed, Claude Rains appeared. Jill stretched out her legs and leaned back against the headboard. "Sometimes not. I don't know. It depends."

"On what?"

"Huh?"

"What does it depend on?"

"I don't know. The guy." She leaned forward and the front of her robe sagged open, freezing Denton's mind with a vision of smoothness and curvature and a deep, mysterious divide. "There was this guy one time who was really great-looking. I mean, totally gorgeous, but kissing him was like kissing a rock." The memory caused her to frown, then giggle. Denton laughed, too, and Jill suddenly clutched the robe, as if aware of her exposure and Denton's leer, a liberty improperly taken despite the fact of their intimacy. Denton thought of the savagely handsome actor and despite her description of his stonelike lips he felt a small tongue of jealousy lick at the edge of his ardor.

"Jill?" he said.

Her throat made a slight humming sound.

"You don't really look like Meryl Streep. More like Faye Dunaway." With a shudder of fear and expectation he slid a hand between the halves of her robe, a hand which encountered an efficient, virginal reflex. She wasn't flattered, amused, anything—she had reentered the gray screen and stood next to Bette Davis, so overwhelmed with awe that she couldn't speak. Denton rolled away, in a paroxysm of need and despair.

"Faye Dunaway is old," said Jill, without turning her head from the apparently climactic moment. The acuteness of his desire caused Denton to groan at the same time she said, softly but distinctly, "I'm trying to figure out exactly what it is she's doing."

Denton swung his feet over the side of the bed and tested the carpet. He saw himself tiptoe away, then run, flee through the sliding glass door and down the center of the golf course, startling a cartload of women identically dressed in pleated skirts and visors and tasseled shoes. He stared at Jill's hair, revealed now, a woodsy damp confusion of brown that he thought, yes, should be cut very short, so that her oversized ears, one of her most unattractive features, would be revealed and mitigate the oppressive perfection of her eyes and nose and mouth. He had commented once on these ears—a serious mistake. He thought of her body, rendered shapeless by the robe, and then of her mind, a discrete and separate entity like something electronic on a shelf, with gauges and dials, something that could be tuned and adjusted.

"I want to go back," he said, reaching for the boots that he had kicked off. The simple verities of passion burning like gasoline in the engine of their togetherness, Denton thought, had transformed into ashlike elements tiny and lost in a vast and unknowable universe. His love, despite his belief in his own maturity, was puppy love, an adolescent crush, nothing more. He felt distraught, embarrassed, angry.

He put on his jacket, giving her time to respond, but she just lay on the bed, clutching her robe beneath her chin as if on guard against any more improper advances. He stood unhappily between the bed and door, the beer slightly gaseous and sour, rising to his throat. She turned to look at him, her eyes shaded as if from sunlight by a long, slender hand that terminated in vermilion nails. The opal ring he had bought for her on the trip to San Francisco, he noticed with an irrational little shock, was still on her finger.

"Why? I thought we were having a good time. I mean, I'm having a good time. Is it still raining in L.A.?"

"I don't know," Denton said, even though he had heard on the radio that the sun, indeed, was not yet expected to appear. His lie was a means to avoid the complication of discussion, of deviation into subjects mundane and therefore suggestive of normality, a world immutable and unchanged. The imaginary sunlight bathing Jill, he realized, was a microcosm of a world in which she would always be the center; he would always be standing a little off, in a shadow, where he belonged. He did not want to be in this shadow, and yet the sun was far too hot and bright. "I want to leave, Jill," he said.

A glimmer of possibility stirred in him, an image of some past moment sublime in his bedroom, in a sailboat, in his car, at a party, on the street. Perhaps they were lost, he thought, and once they found their way back everything would return to the way it was before. Indeed, there was something artificial and disheartening in this place with its relentless heat and sun and people diligently engaged in such pursuits as golf and tennis rather than going to work, pumping gas, reading meters, delivering mail, selling, buying, arranging, detailing. It was a place for his parents, who in spite of their incessant quarrels seemed more firmly bound together than Denton could imagine being with Jill, or any other woman that he had met, or known. A place where nothing extreme would ever happen, where if you got lost it didn't matter, you wouldn't even know it. Like the incident in the little town and bar, any dislocation would flatten out and quickly fade from the mind.

"I'm afraid," she said softly, shutting the P. D. James in her lap.

"Of what?" Denton attempted with partial success to feign disinterest.

"Jenny's father." With her perfectly white, perfectly even teeth she bit her little finger. "He wanted to buy this house, out in this subdivision, but I said I wouldn't move. I mean, Jenny liked her school, and where this house was there weren't any trees or anything, just these cornfields."

The transparency of a tear beside her nose caused Denton to feel a loss of freedom, a sense of being caught in the net of her emotion. Small, ungallant remarks came to his mind.

"We were arguing about whether or not I would move to this house and he told me to shut up or something and when I didn't he hit me." She sobbed suddenly, turning her head away from Denton, seeking some solace or comfort that he was obviously incapable of giving. Then she sat up straight, stiffened herself into an attitude of exaggerated dignity, and rubbed a fist in her eyes. "What if he hits Jenny?" she said in a plaintive tone.

"Did he ever?" Denton managed to say.

"No. I mean, she would have told me." She sighed deeply, looking up at him as if she had just then noticed him, contemplating him with an expression he felt to be evaluative. "I guess he gave her a swat on her bottom once in a while. I mean, *my* father did that." She puckered her lips and planted an exaggerated kiss on the air.

What did that mean? Denton thought.

"If you ever hit me, Denton, I'm not kidding, I'll call the police." She glared at him with huge wet eyes, as if he had already committed this crime. Then her voice dropped to an introspective murmur. "I should have called the police." The tips of her long fingers brushed her cheek. "There's still something wrong with my jaw." Her mouth opened wide and slowly closed, a gesture that beckoned him against his will. "Sometimes there's this catch. And a pain . . ." Distracted, her mouth opened again to hint at the soft mysteries within, she seemed even more desirable than ever. But Denton, who could not remember the last time he had lost his temper, who believed that violence directed toward women or anyone else was an evil deserving of harshly punitive measures, managed to resist the charm that wafted like the odor of perfume from Jill's agitation. He sat down on a corner of the bed, an undeliberated action that did not immediately suggest another. He felt confused by the mixture of grief and ardor that hung in the air, and after a moment in which the silence threatened to expand and engulf them he reached out and touched her arm. "I want us to get married," he said. The words poured out of his mouth so suddenly that he was stunned, and if she hadn't turned her head and raised her damp, inquisitive eyes he might have been able to convince himself that the idea had simply been whispered in the dark captivity of his mind.

Her lips parted slightly and her tongue glimmered, causing a nerve in the back of his neck to tingle. He decided that if she responded at all she would say, "I'll think about it," in the same indifferent tone with which she had reacted to his idea of this vacation, but just as he was about to surrender to humiliation and despair her body suddenly melted, one arm flopped over his leg, and her long hair brushed his face and hand as her head descended to his lap. A murmur arose from his thigh, a neural dance made the skin jump on the back of his head. A river of details flowed through his mind. Details concerning change—alterations of furniture, decoration, perhaps of the very place where they would live. He imagined once more the house, Jenny coming to stay, some legal action concerning custody, a newer car for Jill, a honeymoon in Hawaii, Europe, Japan. A squirmy, childish excitement made it almost impossible for Denton to sit still. He took a deep breath and inserted his fingers into the unbrushed wilderness of Jill's hair. He stroked this miraculous hair, wondering how it would look if cut, if styled differently. He wondered if he would be able to approve.

Rosie

PHILIP F. DEAVER

From *Silent Retreats* (1988)

Here I was, or part of me, trying to explain to someone, Rosie T., why there's no God, and I was drinking. Almost always on the road I'm drinking—usually Johnny Walker black from a silver hip-flask McClure gave me before he died of the good life—all of this on top of black beans and beer.

"I think about the blood," I was saying. Over the years, I'd become accustomed to the mean anger I could now feel getting loose from me. "Here's God's son, sent to the world to save us. He's going to do this by, what they say, 'dying for our sins'—but first he says 'Do this in remembrance of me' and he starts eating his own body and drinking his own blood. This I'm supposed to explain to my children. Rosie—are you with me? I swear, what in hell was that guy doing? We're talking about the New Testament here."

There sat Rosie, drinking imported beer, gold earrings glinting in the partial light when a breeze lifted her hair. Her eyes were focused down, and her feet were bare.

"I don't know," I said. "When I was in college, I'd get in these arguments with the priests. They drove me whacko with their opposition to abortion, a belief they held up right next to their patriotic tolerance for napalming the citizenry of small . . . never mind, you remember all that. Abortion was bad, but arming ourselves so that we were second to none in our ability to fry the whole planet—*that* was okay. I said, 'Guys, try to look at it like this: maybe you don't care so much for the already born but instead are genuinely concerned about the unborn. But look here,' I said, 'if we fry the whole planet, think how many unborn babies we might kill.' Of course, this was a wise-ass oversimplification if there ever was one."

Rosie was peeling the label off her bottle. Sometimes her expression would change. I'd see an edge of a smile, an edge of a nod. Faint as these responses were, I chose to accept them as rapt appreciation for the wit of my argument. We were out by the tennis courts, under stars visible through the city haze. Off some distance behind her, the vaguely lit and looming old style hotel waited like a mother ship anchored offshore.

"I'm telling you," I told her, "there's nothing more unsatisfying than trying to nail a bunch of priests for inconsistency."

It's lucky I was drinking, because God is a big topic—bigger than sex, bigger than fossil fuels, I tried to tell myself, bigger than ennui, consternation, thwartment, and other characteristics of my professional life. To address the nonexistence of God, or to presume to address it, required drinking, which in turn provided me with a good excuse for the quality of my argument.

"Now, the idea was that he was going to save us by letting us hang him on the cross and bleed to death, or, I guess, God was going to save us by letting us do that to his son. We hang him up there between a couple of thugs and the whole business comes to pass just like the prophets had predicted. Naturally, since they had predicted it, we had to go ahead and do it."

Rosie's crisp gray skirt and white blouse glowed, her gold necklace, long and graceful, glittered in the light and shadow.

"Then—let me know when I'm being offensive—he rises again on the third day, opening the question of 'Is it really such a sacrifice to send your only begotten son to die on the cross if you have the power to bring him back in glory three days later at the drop of a hat?' You with me?"

Rosie was in the company, out of Boston. I was from Dallas. She took a sip from her green bottle and smiled. On other trips, before this evening, I'd seen her at meetings. She had one of those faces I'd keep seeing, and sometimes we'd even exchange glances. I'd been surprised this evening when, after the last afternoon panel discussion had ended, suddenly it was just the two of us drifting down Connecticut toward a Mexican restaurant she knew about, beyond the embassies, the arches, the long bridge.

"Don't misunderstand me," I said. "I oppose abortion too."

I watched her peel the label, and took another hit from the flask.

"God," I said. "Is that me? Is that my breath I smell?"

Rosie laughed abruptly, her eyes flashing up to mine, bright, clear, very pretty. "You could have said you don't like Mexican food," she muttered, razzing me. Finally, a verbal response.

"I love Mexican food. I was just checking to see if you're listening. I love Mexican food." I relaxed a moment. I could smell her perfume when the cool breeze came around just right. "Jesus," I said, "I'm starting to depress myself."

Rosie brushed at her dark hair. She was a beautiful girl. When in the past I had seen her, she would be sitting in corners of hotel bars, in intense conversations with someone, or striding down hallways among her friends, laughing and gesturing big. There was something captivating about her movement—bold, confident, but still very soft.

"I don't drink like this at home," I told her. Her eyes were down again now. "The blitherings of a drunk. By the way, I don't mean to run roughshod over whatever it is you believe—I'm not doing that, am I? You have to look at these as the blitherings of a corporate drunk or whatever—quick, change the subject. Extricate me."

She was looking down, no signals. Her hands folded now, motionless in her lap. Her beer on the table almost gone.

"I told those priests, I said, 'Look guys, if there's a God, why isn't war a sin? What do you want?' I said. 'War contains rape and lying, insanity—sometimes people even get killed. There's inebriation and profanity, stealing, promiscuity—what do you want?'"

I heard myself resort to old letters-to-the-editor, old complaining missives to the draft board, old 1960's runnings-off-of-the-mouth.

"'So where's the mainstream American church which follows the footsteps of the Prince of Peace and says absolutely no to war?' I said to them, 'Some churches say no to dancing. A lot of them take very brave stands on gambling and birth control. On the topic of frying the planet, however, there's some question. Right? You get high-level debate on that one. You get damned near to the Amish before you find religions extreme enough to oppose war.'" Rosie just sat there. I was wearing out.

Now she looked up and muttered, "So you say there's no God because of what churches do?"

"Hell," I said, "I don't know. There probably *is* a God. He probably planned all this as a test."

I was now beginning to feel like I'd been drinking the scotch through my eyes. Rosie remained at rest, her legs up on the wrought-iron table (skirt perfectly tucked and folded for modesty), her face rosy-cheeked from imported beer and the night air.

"Oh well." I was trying to back myself down. "Talk, talk—how did I get on this godforsaken subject?" I put the bottom of the flask against the sky. Out came the last of the Johnny Walker, down my throat sore from raving.

"My goodness, but you sure told those priests, didn't you, at your college, back in the good old sixties." Rosie was looking down, as always, at the bottle, at her hands.

"Okay, sorry—I'm wound up." I smiled, trying to slide off the hook with a flanking maneuver. "If I offended you, I'm sorry."

"Not at all," she said. "Actually, I don't know what in hell you've been talking about."

My face froze in a waxy half-grin. I tried to push a chuckle out through the wax, but it wouldn't go. I was leaning forward, a posture left over from my last glorious moments as a religion bullshitter. I had the need to swallow, but I was afraid I would gulp audibly so I resisted, but this made me almost choke. She was right, of course. When I'd started the conversation, it had been ordinary and banal subliminal seduction fare, getting to know one another and so on. But I'd caught an old ideological thermal, and the thermal and the scotch conspired to ruin me. Now Rosie's face wore a polite, perhaps even a shy, smile. She knew she got me.

What a strange test. Two people otherwise married, out by the courts in the middle of the night. Was it my imagination, or had the growth in the number of business meetings held in hotels exactly paralleled the growth in the number of professional women in business?

What a life. Waiting or hurrying in the airports, waving big at the taxi stands, hopping in and out of friends' cars at the various bars after meetings, that's the way things were, and in the hotels thousands of faces passed by me, thousands, motivated at cross-purposes, full of plans and secrets and wondering. Their briefcases and careful choice of clothes, the unspoken whole life behind their eyes—home, where the reality was, where the real, not plastic, loves were—home, behind them somewhere, or half thought of in the half-finished letter in the breast pocket or worthless little toy picked up in the airport gift shop.

I leaned back in my chair and sweated out my penance. The air was getting damp, and there was a chill. The morning fog, it appeared, would not be confined inside my head but would spread to the streets, bridges, alleys between tall buildings, would hover on the Potomac.

After a while she said, "You seem so angry at something." She looked at me. "Are you like that? Seriously. Your whole face changes."

"Doesn't sound like me to me," I said, trying to laugh it off.

"I don't know," she said.

It seemed like that was about it. Time to pack it in. Count it as a miss—attribute it to anger in the eye of the beholder.

After a while Rosie took a long sigh, and her chin came up, her eyes, and she was saying something, almost too quietly. "My mother died three months ago."

She quickly waved off a gesture of mine that I was so sorry, and she was going on.

"She was fifty-five and no great friend of my father. I have memories of loud fights. But, anyway, she had cancer, which had been in whatever they call it—remission—for a couple of years, then came back.

"She knew she was dying, but the doctors tell you not to think that way, so every time she did she had to do it with guilt, as if the *fact* wasn't bad enough. We sort of thought she'd come to terms with dying—I guess people can. But right at the end she was real disturbed, wild in her eyes—she was grabbing out at things next to her bed, shouting, crying. God, that's with me forever.

"The doctor said she was really unconscious, couldn't feel a thing, bullshit, bullshit—she was supremely lucid.

"My father was in and out—he couldn't stay still. He had this kind of automatic chant, 'Everything's going to be okay, okay, okay. Everything's going to be all right.' He'd say it not to tell her the truth—I had the feeling it was to keep her quiet. I'll never forget when the priest was giving her extreme unction—now they call it 'anointing of the sick.' The whole room got cool and smelled like candles and feminine hygiene deodorant.

"'Am I going to die, Al?' she'd ask him, and he'd say, 'Why no, honey. Of course not. C'mon.'

"The priest who gave her the last rites, he came and talked to her—many times. They talked alone. He held her hand. Sometimes they prayed, and from the hall you could hear this low monotone duet. His visits would always give her some peace, they really would. If you could have seen that, you'd have thought, 'I don't *care* whether or not there's a God, get that guy back in there!'

"But my father—I could tell he wanted to be warm toward her, but something stopped him, the same thing that had stopped him since day one. She'd look right at him sometimes, all eyes, you know the way they get? She weighed about seventy-five pounds.

"Dad was the detail man, finding out what nurse was on duty, what doctor, holding the priest's oils, always away from her, back behind the candles, keeping busy. He was down the hall when she died.

"At the last, she was horror-struck—and what kills me is, I could tell she wasn't afraid out of pain or delirium or any of that but because she was seeing things *clearly*. She'd never be loved. She'd never have a love story. She was one little woman with this whole life behind her, nothing panning out, dying in a hospital where pulling the sheet over somebody was nothing—they did that *a few times* every day.

"Anyway, he was down the hall. I'd never seen anyone die. Have you? I guess I always thought that in hospitals they went in one of these slow, drugged-out swoons."

Rosie sighed, and I thought she might stop. But she went on.

"She kept saying in this loud, desperate whisper, 'If only he cared. If only he cared.'"

Rosie drank her beer down and clanked the bottle on the wrought-iron table. Then she folded her hands in her lap, staring down.

"I think about that. When Dad comes up on the train to visit so he can what he calls 'relate to' the kids."

When she looked down, her hair would fall forward. I had an impulse to put my arm around her, stayed where I was.

"We're probably the only ones not in bed," she said, wiping her nose, looking at her watch.

Her blouse fit loosely and casually around her. Her hands were large and expressive, not dainty. Her eyes could be hard just before these tears, and there was a scar intruding itself in the arrangement of her hair and the available light. Even in this discussion, I could pick out the aspects of Rosie that made it possible for her to deal in a business world, tough corners of herself she'd developed into tools of her trade.

"Well," I said after a while, "at least your mom had you. *You* were with her."

Rosie passed this off. In fact, her gesture seemed to deny it. "It wasn't even that simple," she said, dabbing at her eyes with this pink hanky she found in her handbag. "Sorry;" she said as an aside. "I don't cry like this when I'm at home.

"Mom and I hadn't been friends for a long time. When I was sixteen, she caught me in bed with a boy. Walked in on me. My dad was out in New Mexico buying a ranch or something, and Mom and I had this great admiration-and-trust thing going. She thought it was admiration and trust. I thought it was admiration and tacit permission—well, anyway, an opportunity—to be free. One afternoon she came home from shopping and caught me. I was in *her* bed with Michael Hannah. Truly, I don't think there's anything, at that angle, that she did not see in that short moment. She slammed the bedroom door and stomped down the hall. *Her* bed, isn't that a beaut?"

"Yikes," I said. It was the best I could do.

Rosie chuckled. "Michael Hannah's a lawyer in Florida now. I'll bet that scene replays with him from time to time." She brought her legs down and sat forward, pulling on a sandal. It was close to two-thirty. "I just want to say I didn't mean to be impolite when I said I wasn't listening."

"Not at all. I really got going. Sorry. I understand."

"And," she said. "I really enjoyed supper."

She was standing up. When she picked up her purse, I heard the clink of at least two more green bottles. "I'm certain you enjoyed hearing about my dead mother and the great primal saga of Michael Hannah, right?"

She was taking my arm, whether out of affection or weariness I couldn't tell, and as we walked the sides of our legs would brush and bump and I could actually feel the curve of her thigh. She was talking in a low voice, but I wasn't listening. I was wondering about the next five minutes.

We had to walk across a dark patio that led through double doors into the bar, which was closed. In the dim of high-ceiling light, workers bent over the tables and stacked chairs, ran large barrel vacuums over the thick, royal-blue carpet. They were dressed in brown clothes, and the men wore hats stained through at the sweatband. They seemed to stoop so naturally, from the waist, like picking cotton; and their voices were low and sleepy. The room was still rank with the smell of stale barroom smoke. The door from the lounge led into the hotel lobby, where the lights were bright. Standing next to the column in the center of the room were two of my people, out of Dallas, and my first impulse was to duck. But they were just separating from a conversation, no doubt concerning prices at the pump, what's stored, and what we've still got in the ground.

"Here we go," I groaned to Rosie as Crazy Bob Price noticed us. He was coming.

"Oh no, this I don't believe!" Price shouted. "Harold!" he yelled back at his friend and mine, Harold Atwood. "Harold! Do you see this? Check this out, this company's only liberal meets Rose Targus, the Boston flash!" Harold disappeared on the elevator before Price finished getting this out. Bob and I worked closely and had

had many talks. For him it was axiomatic that anyone who opposes human slaughter is liberal.

"I'm serious," Bob said, grinning, joining us for the short stroll down the corridor to the elevator for the west wing. "There should be media coverage of this. Movietone highlights, something. This is either a match made in heaven or the most unlikely combination I could summon myself to imagine in the whole company, coast to coast! I'm not kidding." Bob was one of those people who has known for twenty years that he can get by with this kind of talk because of the grin he has.

"Why aren't you in bed?" I asked him. I could see that he and Rosie knew each other, but, actually, everyone knew Bob Price. He seemed to have done all the groundwork for getting himself well promoted several years before, and even though the promotion never came, the groundwork remained. The promotion never came because of Bob's love of the night. The question was rhetorical.

He grinned. "I made a cardinal error, is why I'm not in bed. I called someone I knew from the old days, who lives out in Arlington. I received an invitation for supper—what could I say? How was tonight's session?"

We paused one count too long. "Never mind, never mind, wrong question, forget I asked." He was winking at us, loosening his tie.

"Hey," he said, a different tone now. "Was I as loud as I think down there when I shouted to you just now?"

"We understood," Rosie said, scoring back, and the elevator was opening for Bob's floor. I was relieved that he would be gone and I could say good night to her in private, even though I had no idea how.

Bob was getting out. "Listen, Flash," he said, "good to see you, no kidding. You too, big guy," he said to me, "but I see you all the time anyway. Sorry if I was loud down there. I'm working on that stuff. Even I get tired of being a buffoon."

"No problem," I was saying, reassuring him, but then I noticed something strange happening in the corner of my eye. Rosie was getting off the elevator on the same floor.

"This is my floor, too." She grinned at Bob. Then she half turned to me, about to speak. Bob was holding the elevator doors, just letting them go.

"Amazing," he was saying. He was a little drunk, but there was something warm and engaging about him, a kind of unabashedness-about-everything. It made him seem innocent of business, even though he'd once done six months at Danforth for a specialized piece of market research—he'd been caught in the middle of the night microfilming abstracts of Sun's aerial propane surveys.

"Martin, is this amazing? Flash's room is on the same floor as mine." The doors were almost closed.

"For a hung-up old Catholic like myself, and a Texan, you make good company," Rosie said to me through the narrowing gap, and she was gone.

"I'm not a Texan," I said.

"He's not a Texan," I heard Bob tell her as their voices dropped away below me. The elevator was taking me up to seventeen.

"I don't even sound like a Texan," I said, staring at the menu for the restaurant on the roof, posted on the wall of the elevator behind plexiglass. The bell dinged and I stepped off into a long hallway whose length and repetition of carpet pattern combined to upset my stomach.

"I don't like Texas very much, in fact," I said, trying to find my room key. "There's too much stress in Dallas. Too much rain in Houston."

The world is full of people, many of them at cross-purposes. When you encounter someone like Rosie and talk half the night, and you're on the open road, so to speak, and so is she, this business of saying good night is such a problem, the whole business so futile, that veterans of the road hesitate to go through it at all.

I know many guys who have been on the road for years, and most of them eventually learn it's best to have one glass of wine, go to your room, turn on the Carson show, and lapse into sleep. For others, the puzzling game of instant intimacy goes on, futile and sad. Everybody's married and everybody knows the problem, and yet the game occurs just enough beneath the surface of the things that are happening so that it keeps happening.

So I was thinking about the game and hating myself in my room, washing my face and brushing my teeth and avoiding the dresser mirror, trying to hang up my pants without dumping the change from the pockets. I confess that I felt some relief. In a way, I was glad she was gone. The good-bye in the elevator had been all wrong, yes, but I was going to make it to morning without the waftings of guilt. Lights out, I stretched out on the high double bed closest to the window and looked at the city. The amber lights on the expressways and bathing Capitol Hill gave an eerie cast to the night, with the low, thin haze seeming to dampen everything. I could see National Airport in the distance. I thought of my kids, how they reacted the first time we took a trip on a plane, something routine for me but seen through new eyes when I went with them. Thinking of them, as always, relaxed me. I closed my eyes and began my usual custom of stopping the room from its drunken spin by muttering the Lord's Prayer over and over unto sleep.

But the phone rang.

"Hello."

"Martin?"

"Hi."

"I wanted to tell you, it wasn't really my floor. It's just that goddamned Bob Price. Such a loudmouth. I know him from way back. I decided not to take any chances."

"Protecting your good name, as we say in Texas."

"Seems odd to you maybe."

"I'm not from Texas."

"That's what I hear. No, really, I never thought you were. I was just keeping the conversation rolling. You know?"

I didn't say anything.

"I acted like I was walking to my room, past his room, then doubled back. I'm too tired for intrigue, but I had to do it."

"Quick thinking," I said. You've come a long way since Michael Hannah, I was thinking, but luckily didn't say it.

"I guess, too, I wanted to thank you properly for the evening," she said. "Tolerating Mexican food and my crying." There was a long pause. "I just wanted to tell you that."

"That's real nice of you, Rosie. I enjoyed it, too. I am sorry about your mother. I got rolling with my old religion thing, and there you were, still in mourning for your mom."

"You didn't do anything wrong."

She was quiet then. I was elated she called, and could smell her perfume over the phone, but I couldn't get myself to start the whole process again. I flattened out on the bed and enjoyed simply listening to her breath over the phone line.

"Martin?" she said after a while. I was staring at the ceiling. It was stucco-looking, or was that stuff asbestos?

"Martin? Are you there?"

"Yes."

"You going to sleep?"

"Nope. Just resting."

"How's your view?"

"Well, I've got the Potomac. I've your Jefferson Monument, your Capitol dome. The two eerie red lights in windows on top of the Washington monument. How about you?"

"Foliage mostly. Treetops. Your deciduous and your native conifers. And there's a *very* tall tulip . . ." I could hear her moving, maybe stretching the phone cord. She was laughing. "Hold it, it's a flower box outside my window."

I laughed too.

"Martin?" she said to me then.

"Hmm?"

"Do you have pure blue ice in your veins, or what?"

She came to the door dressed in cut-off jeans, the same blouse, only not tucked in, and she carried a large plastic department store shopping bag which contained a robe and a few other things. We held each other by the window, her face against my chest.

I showed her all the sights through my window. I felt chatty. There was that feeling again that I always forget. The feeling that you've been out there alone all your life until now, and you want to explain to this woman how you've been feeling, go over all the stuff, the torment of work, the stress and the isolation. You want to thank her for being with you.

"Rosie . . ." I began.

"Don't start trying to talk about this," she said. "I'm only here to be held. And to hold you. I'm sleeping in the other bed—say so if you can't handle it."

I could feel the warm breath on my arm when she spoke. There was a desperate kind of trust she had, very sad. Under ordinary circumstances I'd have contrived to get past this little last-minute hesitation. I could handle the terms because of the vulnerable expressions of trust, but it wasn't easy. I didn't sleep much, but stared across the gap between the beds.

And then here I was, the sun on me and my headache—I was wide awake; and there was Rosie T., deep in blankets and still asleep, across the great divide. I couldn't see her face at all for her brown hair. I reached way over and spread it away so I could see the pretty brows and dark, shy lashes, the long straight nose. Recalling that encounter now, I find that I remember vividly the heat in the room that morning. I was fascinated by the little-girl wisps of hair at the scalp line, near her face, which I lightly touched with my fingers as she slept. I could hear her breathing, wonderful girl. In that skin and how those lips were, in the distinctive character of her hands, somewhere in there invisible to me was Rosie's mom, gone to her maker.

I looked at my watch on the table next to the bed. Outside the window and far away, a 727 rocked off the airport runway, plowed up into the capital sky and disappeared beyond the Capitol dome, conveying people like me, and wonderful people like Rosie T., home.

From Bremerton

TOM KEALEY

From *Thieves I've Known* (2013)

Shelby woke before sunrise, dressed in her warmest clothes in the dark. In the kitchen, she packed her book bag with apples and bread, some peanut butter. She added a map of Seattle, a carton of cigarettes she'd hidden at the top of a cabinet, and then brewed some coffee on the stove. She walked barefoot in the trailer so as not to wake her sister and the boyfriend. It was still dark outside by the time she poured the coffee into her thermos, and out through the window she could see the dull yellow glow of a streetlamp at the edge of the trailer park. Rain fell in the lamp glow, and she could hear the drops clicking against the top of the trailer. She wished she were back in bed, but she'd made a promise the week before, to a boy that she was in love with, although she was not now sure if she was still in love. Lots of things—her love for the boy, her grades in school, her future, or what she hoped to be her future—were in doubt. Wisps of fog disappeared in the rain. Before leaving, and because it was her nature, she put away the beer cans and the pizza boxes from the night before, emptied the ashtrays, wiped down the counters. She slipped into her boots, pulled her woolen cap over her ears, and closed the door, quietly, on her way out.

In the puddles of mud and slush outside she caught a blurred, distant reflection of her own gaze, a reflection that she liked: dark and small, without many features, a work in progress it seemed. She stepped around the puddles when she could, leaning over them, kicking a soda bottle across the park, listening to the rattle across rocks and broken glass. Outside Phillip's trailer, she could see a light on in the kitchen. A cat, wet and muddy, eyed her from under a small porch as she made her way toward the light.

She knocked, listened to a series of loud thumps from inside the trailer, entered when no one came to the door. Inside, Phillip knelt in a corner holding a shoe above his head. A dozen or so brown splotches—roaches—were scattered on the floor around him. The kitchen smelled of mold and baked chicken.

Phillip turned as she slid a chair out from the table and sat down. His eyes were large, a little irregular, and his bony elbows and wrists seemed like knots on a straight line. He was not a good-looking boy, but Shelby—who was similarly thin, and who'd had painful acne since she was twelve—could find the beautiful parts of him when she put her mind to it. His hair, which was long and smelled of smoke and lemon soap, his lips, his neck and fingers. She liked all of these things, and liked him. Believed him to be good, if not good-looking. She felt a turn in her breathing as she sat watching his large eyes. The boy reached into his pocket, took out a roll of dollar bills, tossed them to her.

"How much?" she said.

"Enough to get us there."

Under the streetlamp, they sat on an overturned apple crate, watched the first blue-pink rays of the sun appear from across the water. The Olympic Mountains were snow-capped and gray. A half-dozen men and one woman sat on similar crates, on seats torn from old cars. One old man drank from a coffee mug, the steam fogging the man's glasses each time he sipped. Nothing was said. They all watched the road that led from the trailer park, and those that had them shielded themselves from the rain with umbrellas. Others wore ponchos. Phillip and Shelby sat under a plastic trash bag cut lengthwise down the sides. Phillip slipped a square sheet of white paper from his pocket, unfolded it on his knee. He creased new lines as he refolded it in triangles from each corner, bent those folds inside out and down until he'd made what looked like a fisherman's rain cap. The man with the coffee mug watched him. Phillip folded two opposite corners together, and then the remaining corners up, folded what was left in half, pressed his finger against the angles to keep the creases. He set the paper right side up and placed it on Shelby's knee.

"What's that?" said the old man.

"It's a sailboat," said Shelby.

The man squinted and looked doubtful. The woman next to him stamped her boots in the mud, for warmth it seemed, still looking down the road. Behind her, in the distance, the pine trees swayed with the wind.

Shelby placed the sailboat at the edge of one of the puddles, flicked it lightly with her finger. The paper turned back at the motion, the bow pointing up at the sky, but the vessel floated in the red water.

"Nice trick," said the man. He pulled his poncho closer around his shoulders. "Maybe you can make a roof next."

Shelby picked up the sailboat, shook out the water as best she could. She unfolded the sail first, watched Phillip out of the corner of her eye as he shook his head. He'd taught her the next folds the week before. She liked that about him: he knew things, even if it was only paper folding and the like. He'd made a compass from a needle and magnet, Halloween masks from feathers, glue, and cardboard. He knew how to draw well and seemed content to teach her what she could learn. She doubled the paper back, refolded the sail, and turned the bow of the boat inside itself. She took out a pen. In the center of the fold she drew a dot within a circle, added some waved lines and shading at the bird's neck.

She looked over at the man.

"A dinosaur?" he said.

"A rooster."

"Hmm."

In the distance, the headlights of a pickup truck appeared through the fog. The woman stood up from the crate and shook out her umbrella, but the men stayed seated, looked out through the rain. Phillip unfolded the rooster, set the paper flat on his knee again, tore slits along some of the folds. They listened to a dog bark in the distance.

When the truck entered the park, they could see three men already in the back huddled against the wooden slats and a driver, sitting alone, in the cab. Rainwater kicked from the tires. Phillip folded and refolded as the truck approached the collection of crates and the window rolled down. A bearded man peered out into the rain.

"I got work for four. Bring you back around eight."

"How much?" said the woman.

"Fifty."

"What're we to do?" she said.

He pointed his thumb at her. "Not you then. I'll take three of you men and the boy. Decide and get in."

The woman sat back down on the crate, gave the man a look, although there'd likely be other trucks to come along. The old man and two others shook out their ponchos and umbrellas and climbed into the back of the truck. One of the men remaining lit a cigarette.

"You give my friend a lift?" said Phillip. "Wherever we're going?"

"Going where I always take you," the man said. "I said I'd pay for four, now get in or get out."

"No pay," said Phillip. "Just a lift."

The man shifted the truck into gear. "If there's room," he said. The window rolled up.

In the back of the truck, Shelby and Phillip stood against the cab, tried to hold the plastic bag against the wind as the truck made its way up the road. The backs of their shirts were wet through their jackets, and they shivered with the cold. In the gray wood, previous workers had carved their initials or nicknames. A few hearts were scattered here and there between the cracks, an etching of an airplane. Next to Shelby's head, an inscription read *Tony hates Eloise.*

"Hey," Phillip said to the man with the coffee mug. "You got any kids?"

The man looked up out of his poncho. "What's that to you?"

Phillip took out the piece of folded paper, handed it down. The man took it with the tips of his fingers, turned it over in his hands, examined it.

"Brontosaurus," he said.

"Sure."

"They're likely to swallow it," the man said, but he slipped the paper into his shirt pocket.

During the ride, Shelby imagined a truck much like this, one in her future perhaps, a warmer ride even in Alaska. It would be summertime, and she'd be headed west from the train station in Anchorage, to work the fish lines in a small harbor town. She'd picked some of these towns out on a map, names that she liked: Kasilof, Ninilchik, Port Graham; and she'd read a slim book by a woman who'd done what Shelby hoped to do: worked the lines in the summers, saved her money in the winters, invested in a boat after that—the woman, like Shelby, was no fisher-woman, she'd had others work for her—made her fortune and was making more. The woman, like Shelby, liked the water. Phillip thought it a strange, unlikely wish.

"This woman made it," Shelby'd said.

"Make sure you read about the ones that didn't," he'd said.

They rode the seven miles toward Bremerton, caught a

glimpse of the bay during one stretch, the vessels making their way down Saratoga Pass. The rain fell harder the closer they came. Eventually the men made some room and the two teenagers knelt against the cab, covered their heads with the plastic, watched the raindrops through the thin black covering. The light of the sky was becoming a brighter gray.

In Bremerton, they jumped out at a traffic stop, waved back at the men in the truck, who stared dully after them. They cut down an alleyway, past a diner window fogged up from the rain, past the lines of ships moored at the docks, their white masts bobbing in the air like a row of birthday candles, past the stacks of netting. In the ferry terminal they opened a pack from the cigarette carton, lit up, counted out their money. Phillip paid at the counter for his ticket, boarded alone. Shelby waited on the dock, out of sight, she hoped, behind a wall of crab traps and crates. On the ferry, Phillip rolled his ticket stub into a ball, leaned over the railing, looked behind him. He'd hoped to be sly, but he looked guilty as the damned. He threw the stub out over the water, just a few yards, wondered if he'd been spotted. Shelby found the balled stub in a crack between the crates, slipped her hand inside, nabbed it between the tips of her two longest fingers. She held her breath at the gate, held up the ticket, folded flat but looking worn and wet. The teenager, about Shelby's age, looked to get out of the rain, waved her on, tore the next ticket.

They sat in the cabin, sharing coffee from the thermos, set their socks and sweaters across a bench to dry. They watched the flag at the stern flap in the wind as the ferry pulled out from the bay, headed into the pass, watched the gulls and terns gliding behind the fishing boats headed in the same direction. She'd brought paper, Shelby, and they practiced the folds to pass the time. Made the fish, the baby starling, the teacup, and the seven-pointed star. A young girl sat across from them, next to her mother. Though Halloween had passed, the girl wore a grinning skeleton mask. Her eyes looked wide through the holes, and as

Shelby and Phillip completed each figure, each animal or structure, she slipped the mask to the top of her head, hugged the toy elephant doll she held in her hands, looked away and then back again at the folded paper set next to the socks and sweaters. Then the girl pulled the mask back down over her face.

"You're scary looking," said Phillip.

"So are you," said the girl.

The girl's mother flipped through a magazine, not taking her eyes from the pages. At one point she handed the girl a peppermint and a napkin. The other passengers, few this time of year, looked out on the water or walked out to the deck, feet spread wide with the dip and roll of the vessel. A radio hummed with static, not music but news, a buzz of quiet voices discussing stocks and markets, bills and pending deals. White spray from the water splashed against the decks and the windows.

"Would you like one of these?" said Shelby. She pointed at the folded papers.

"Depends which one," said the girl.

"You can pick it."

The girl pushed her mask up to her forehead again. She looked up at her mother for a moment and then back at the line of figures. She ignored the fish and the boot, the cube and the starling. She eyed the teacup.

"I'll take the star," she said.

"Go get it," said Shelby.

The girl slid off the bench, pressed her feet against the floor, hesitated, and then took two steps to the opposite bench. She held her elephant doll tight, then touched one of the sweaters for a moment, and then took her hand away. She clicked her tongue while deciding and took both the star and the teacup, then returned to her own side, leaning against her mother.

"I like your elephant," said Shelby.

"You can't have it."

"I didn't say I wanted it. I just like it."

The girl turned the elephant's face toward her, examined it. "I left the good one at home," she said.

In the Seattle terminal, they waited, wanting to stay warm. Outside, the rain had not let up, gave no sign that it would. They ate an apple each, shared a sandwich, wiped the peanut butter from each other's lips. Shelby hoped she might find answers to questions on the boy's lips, with her finger, wondered if he might be thinking the same thing. They said little though, were comfortable and intrigued with each other's silence. Phillip brought out a long plastic garbage bag and they tore it in half, a side sheltering each, and walked out into the rain.

They looked for street signs and examined Shelby's map in the doorway of a bookstore, walked along the dock, staring out at the large black-and-red tankers, the smaller fishing boats, the yachts in the harbor in the rain. A rope trailed after a ship, tied to the stern like a long, thick water snake. Phillip thought about Shelby's eyes, which he liked. He thought about a lot of things: his mother, who they were going to see, his roll of money in his pocket, the skeleton mask on the girl on the ferryboat. In his notebook he'd drawn similar masks, but they were the faces of aliens, not skeletons, although he saw the resemblance now. When he could afford it, he rented old movies—anything science fiction—read dime novels from the used book store on 7th Street. He watched the sky at night. What would they be like? He drew robots and three-headed creatures, hovering cubes and giant eyes. Then, reading more, he'd become serious. If they came, they'd be near to humans—would appear in that form at least. He was not completely certain, but had settled on this theory, not his own, but read in books.

He thought about the aliens a lot. Thought they might seek him out—not just him, but all the people who believed. He sketched and sketched in his notebook. His mother, when she'd lived with him, thought the drawings foolish. The faces were smooth and expressionless, the limbs he didn't know about—how many and how long—but the eyes, dark and deep, were warm in his drawings. Eyes looking for an answer, scientific but not unfeeling. He thought he might wait another year, believing. After that, he'd have to give it up. He believed, but he didn't have faith. It was a problem, he felt, that he had in many areas. Sometimes, he thought life might not be out there after all, and if it was, it might not visit him.

They found the address in a phone booth, shared a cigarette inside the glass, kept out of the rain. After, they found the barbershop on James Street, a shop away from the corner, but they could only make out shapes—people sitting, the motion of hands—through the fogged window.

Inside, they sat down in a row of chairs under a television, kept their eyes on the floor at first, watching the strands of hair turn in the puddles of water, listening to the buzz of a razor, the click of scissors.

"Be with you in a minute," said the barber.

The man's head was bald, but he had a full gray beard, thick and clipped at the sideburns and moustache, thin on the chin. He chewed on a toothpick. One of his eyes was gray also, looked damaged in the glow of the fluorescent lights. The customer had his eyes closed, seemed asleep as the barber held the hair between index and middle fingers, snipped some away. A newspaper lay open on the seat next to Shelby, but she watched the reflection of the television in the mirror behind the barber. As they waited the president walked down a ramp from a helicopter, and a crowd, at night, stood outside a building billowing smoke. Two women swam through floodwater in a red river, and an astronaut floated in zero gravity. Space was dark and open behind him. On Earth, a young boy in an orange jumpsuit was led away in shackles, hand and foot.

They listened to the slap of customers' shoes in the puddle

near the door, waited for the bell to ring in the frame. The barber toweled off his hands, set his money in a drawer.

"Which one or both?" he said.

"You know Carney Booth?" said Shelby.

The man set the towel on the chair, closed the lid over the damaged eye for a moment, looked Shelby up and down, then Phillip.

"I might," he said. "Who's asking?"

"A friend."

"There's a few types of friends out in the world. Which kind would you be?"

"My sister's his girlfriend."

The barber nodded. "Seems like he might have a few of those."

"Maybe," said Shelby. "But I got one of his favors to call in."

"What kind of favor'd you give him?"

Shelby looked over at Phillip, who kept his gaze at the floor.

"Your name's Otis," she said to the man.

"You could read that on the window outside."

"You were army buddies."

"Navy."

"Then you know him?"

"I knew a man named Carney," the man said. "I'm not sure about a favor, though. What are you asking for?"

"A lift up to Rawlins. Just take an hour, far as I can tell."

The man considered. "Two hours there, two hours back. Take up most of my day."

"We've got to be there at three, but we'll get back on our own."

The man turned his head, as if he was refiguring the conversation. "Nothing but a prison up there," he said.

"That's right."

"You visiting?"

"That's right."

"Who?" said the man.

Shelby nudged Phillip. “My mom,” the boy said.

“What’s she in for?”

Phillip said nothing, shrugged.

“Am I mumbling?” said the man.

“No sir,” said Phillip. “Drugs.”

The man picked up the towel from the chair and sat down, set his feet up on the stand.

“What’s so interesting about that floor?” he said.

Shelby glanced at Phillip but said nothing.

“Something more interesting than the person you’re talking to?”

They looked up at him, turned their eyes away for a moment, then looked again.

“You don’t like my eye,” he said.

“It’s fine,” said Shelby.

“It scares you.”

“No sir.”

“I’m old enough to know a lie when I hear it,” he said.

They looked at his eye. A gray film seemed to cover it, and beyond the film, the pupil took away the color, seemed to bleed into the white. It was neither menacing nor warm, only there, staring at them. Phillip wondered what the man could see.

“It scares me a little,” he said.

The man looked out the window, at the bell at the top of the door frame. They listened for the sound, Shelby and Phillip, aimed their own eyes back to the floor, watched the hair float in the puddle.

“You’ll get used to it,” the man said. “I have.”

They drove out the highway north, took a two-lane road from there, past the lumber mills with the saws and the stacks of cottonwood trees and the lines of trucks idling at the loading docks. Shelby sat in the backseat of the car, listened to the strum of an acoustic guitar from the tape player. Through the window, through the rain, she saw the lights of a high school, could see the heads of students in a classroom, computers against the wall, a large gymnasium next to the school. She could not make out faces, but the students seemed like they were going places, the way they held themselves. She felt far away from Bremerton, missed it, like you'd miss the humidity of summer, the bone cold of rain in a truck headed toward the coastline, missed the voices of people you liked but didn't quite trust.

She could see the eyes of the man in the rearview mirror.

"You like this music?" he said.

Shelby listened. It sounded rough, static in the background. The guitar player seemed as if he didn't know where he was headed with the riff, with the melody, seemed as if he'd stay awhile where he was.

"This is your playing."

The man set his eyes back on the road. "That's right. You didn't answer the question, though."

"I like it."

"I told you I know a lie when I hear one."

"You're not knowing one now," she said.

"I'm not sure," he said. "I'm deciding."

Phillip warmed his hands at the vents, turned his hands over and under at the hot air. He felt inside his jacket for the present he'd wrapped for his mother, felt the square of the package, the corners and the crinkle of paper.

The man shifted the toothpick in his mouth. "What's Carney up to?" he said.

"Works at the courthouse," said Shelby.

"Where?"

"Bremerton."

"Good lord," said the man. "What's he do there?"

"Janitor."

The man nodded. "That sounds right. You tell him hello for me?"

"I'll tell him."

"I could tell you some stories," said Otis.

"Is that right?"

"Yep," he said.

Shelby waited. They passed mile markers on the right, a rail bridge where a line of tankers and boxcars sat overhead, a reservoir that stretched for as far as Shelby could see. The man said nothing, told no stories.

"Can I ask you something?" Shelby said.

"All right."

"What kind of favor you owe him for?"

The man shrugged. "He got me some dope or something. Not even sure it was him. I got a vague recollection he's got something coming, but I can't name it. Let that be a lesson to both of you. Write down your favors so you'll remember."

They drove on, listening to the whirr of the wipers, the tap of rain on the windshield, the guitar on the tape deck as it cut off, flipped, played the other side. The man's guitar skill was not good, Shelby thought, but not bad either. He seemed to know when to pause, knew the space between chords, knew the right notes if not the combinations. Phillip took out a sheet of paper from his back pocket, set it flat against his knee, set it like he'd set the others, began to tear and fold.

"Borrow your toothpick?" he said to the man.

"My toothpick?"

"That's right."

The man drove on for a while, looked at Shelby in the rearview mirror, closed the lid over the damaged eye. He slipped out the pick, handed it to the boy.

Phillip folded, ripped away some paper, took out a penknife and cut slits in the folds, stuck in the toothpick. They drove on. When he was done, Phillip set the paper guitar on the dashboard, lengthwise, pointing the neck toward the man, the toothpick sitting in for the strings.

"How much longer you got in school?" said the man.

"A year for me," said Shelby. "After this one. Two for him."

"Where you headed after that?"

"Who says we're headed anywhere?"

"Everybody, as far as I hear, heads out of Bremerton."

"You been?"

"Out?" said the man. "Or Bremerton?"

"Both then."

Otis picked up the guitar from the dashboard, set it on top of the steering wheel.

"In the navy, Carney and I saw Germany and Japan, Hawaii and the tip of Greenland. We got off the ship when we could. You wonder, what you see in a port town, and what that tells of the rest of the place. I've seen thirteen countries and four continents, but I'd like to see more. Bremerton I've seen, took the ferry out. My wife and I like the water. I've seen worse and I've seen better. Have I been out? That's a good question. I've been out, but I'm not sure if I've been in."

The man turned the wheel, and the guitar slid off onto the floor. On a straightaway, he leaned forward and felt at the floorboard, found the paper and set it back on the dash. He wiped his fist at the window to clear off the mist.

"That's a fine guitar," he said.

As the rain tapered to a drizzle, the breeze from the coastline picked up, bending trees over power lines, blowing sand and black wet leaves across the road. When it was offered, Otis took an apple from the book bag and after set the core next to the guitar on the dashboard. The dull glow of the sun—still behind clouds—began its descent toward the Olympics, and shadows stretched out from barns and shacks, from the clusters of sheep and goats behind fences. Phillip creased and folded more paper, making a shark, then a lighthouse, though not a good one. He unfolded, started over, made a frog that he set on Shelby's hand.

"We got a trick on this one," she said.

"What's that?" said Otis.

Shelby pushed down on the back tip of the frog, pressed it to the edge of the seat top, let her finger go. The frog hopped forward, landing head-first between the boy and the man.

Otis looked down and studied the frog. "Y'all don't have much to do out in Bremerton, do you?" he said.

"It's for luck," said Phillip. "Frogs bring it."

"That right?"

"You got a frog in your garden, it means something good's going on."

"How about in your car?"

"Same I suppose."

The man picked up the frog and set it next to the guitar, next to the apple core.

"We're about there," the man said. "How long's this visit?"

"A couple hours," said Phillip. "We're catching a bus back. You did your favor and then some."

Ahead, they could see a stoplight and what served as a town—a market and a post office, a boarded-up restaurant named Billy's. A man passed them on the sidewalk, kept his raincoat closed against the wind. Otis slowed the car and stopped at the light.

"It isn't my business to ask, but how long's your mom in for?"

"Five years," said Phillip.

"And how much of that she done?"

"One, a little more."

"She sold?"

"We lived in a house that sold. Same thing before the judge."

"She could've pled that down," said Otis. "I know that business."

Phillip looked out at the market on the corner. "She wouldn't testify against her boyfriend, so they sent her down."

"Love?" said Otis.

Phillip considered that. "Didn't seem like it."

The man shifted into first when the light changed. "Maybe not to you," he said. "Bet they were keen on sending you to a home."

"I been to a home last year in Tacoma."

Otis looked over at Phillip. "Not even a deal for you?"

"Not from them."

"But your mom could've pulled one."

Phillip stared out the window. Up ahead, Shelby could see the towers of the prison, the wire and the fences, a concrete square, ugly and dark like the sky. She closed up her book bag and zipped her jacket.

"I think I've answered more than I had to," said Phillip.

"All right," said Otis. "I got somewhere I didn't mean to go."

The man circled the prison block, looked out through the drizzle and the gray light. He found the parking lot and the entranceway to the gate. A line of people—visitors, old men and women, lots of young children—stood under an aluminum rooftop, dressed for cold and wet. A guard in a green slicker stood behind the fence.

Phillip slipped his fingers into the door latch but didn't open. Shelby waited on him.

"Y'all can stay dry here till it's time to go."

"We've kept you long enough," said Phillip. "Thanks for the ride." They got out, stood in the drizzle as they collected their things. The air was cold and heavy, and the wind blew sand in their eyes and hair.

Otis leaned forward, pointed at the dashboard. "You forgot your little doo-dad."

"That's for you," said Phillip. "That frog'll make something good happen."

"I'll believe that when I see it," said the man.

They closed their doors and watched as the car moved past the line of people, heading toward the exit near the state road. One of the brake lights flickered like a dim red sparkler, and the windows were fogged over in the side and back. They couldn't see Otis anymore, not the eye or the gray. They stood in the drizzle with their packs, brushed the sand from their own eyes, then walked to the rooftop, waited at the back of the line.

In the greeting room, families fanned out to the line of benches, rows against the cinder-block walls and down the center. Outside, they'd stood quiet in the drizzle, listening to the raindrops ping against the aluminum rooftop. But inside there was a faint buzz of voices, eyes set on the clock on the wall. Grime and dust caked the windows. The room smelled of disinfectant and coffee. Children played with toy trucks and cars, blocks and electronic games, some on the floor, others on top of benches. A pall of smoke drifted up toward the ceiling as grandparents and a few fathers lit up cigarettes, listened for the turn of the lock at the far door, told their kids to quiet down.

Phillip took out the boxed present from his jacket, set it at the edge of their bench. Shelby was unsure of what to do. She thought about the bus station she'd seen on one of her maps, but hadn't spotted it on the way into town. She tried to keep her mind on the present, took hold of Phillip's hand and rubbed at his middle knuckle. He kept still, kept his hand in hers. Above them, the rows of lights buzzed and hummed, echoed against the high ceiling. Phillip looked lost.

"I thought you'd been before," she said.

"I never said that."

She looked down at his hand. "You want to draw something?"

"No."

"I got a notebook in the bag."

"You can take that carton out if you want."

She unzipped the bag, reached past the bread and the maps, took out the cigarettes. As the lock turned, the sound echoed above the pitch of the lights. The children stopped their play at the trucks and blocks, at the games. Men stubbed out their cigarettes. A tall guard came out the door, followed by the first of the prisoners.

Phillip and Shelby watched them come. They were each dressed in red, the women, all of them with their hair tied back or shaved short. Some were old, gray, others little older than Shelby. They walked in single file, then spread, some running, some walking to the tables. An older prisoner put her glasses on. There were hugs, a shriek of delight here or there. A few simple nods. Many kept the same distant, cold expression as they sat down with their families. Children seemed to be the center of attention. An old man set his watch, glanced at the clock. One woman in long, dark braids circled the room, examined each cluster of visitors at the benches, examined Phillip and Shelby. No one had come for her.

Phillip stood as a woman was wheeled through the door in a chair. Her skin was pale and gray, her eyes sunk in lines of wrinkles and brows, and one of her legs had been amputated at the knee. Her red pant leg was tied in a knot below. She pointed at their table, and the tall guard wheeled her over, set a brace against the rubber tire, edged back through the door, observing the other prisoners.

"Hey," said Phillip.

The woman had long, black-and-gray locks of hair pulled back behind her ears. She kept her dark eyes aimed at the table, glanced once up at Shelby.

"Hello," she said.

"This is Shelby."

The woman nodded. She looked down at her legs. "What have you brought for me?"

They listened to the buzz of voices around them. Phillip reached into his pocket, took out a chocolate bar, slid it gently across the table to the woman. She looked at it but kept her hands down at her sides, at the wheels of the chair. Her hair was slick, seemed not to have been washed in days.

"Go on," Phillip said.

When she made no further movement, he unwrapped the bar, reached to her hand, placed it between the fingers. Behind them, a child began to cry. Laughter here and there. The guards said nothing, stood together in a huddle near the door.

"How are you?" he said.

"This leg is getting me down." She took a bite of chocolate.

"I'm in school," he said. "Shelby helps me."

"He helps me too," said Shelby.

The woman nodded. "Have you found him?"

Phillip slid the cigarettes across the table. "These are for you too."

The woman picked up the carton and placed it in her lap.

"I see you took some," the woman said.

"It was a long trip."

"I asked you a question."

Phillip picked at the tabletop with his finger, drew what looked to Shelby like a face, large eyes and a thin mouth. He'd hunched his shoulders, become smaller. He circled the skull again and again. When he took his finger away, Shelby tried to find the face in the dust.

"It's hard."

"It's harder in here," said the woman. "It's been half a year and you can't do one thing I ask?"

"I made some calls. Your boyfriend was in Portland for a while. After that, I lost him."

"That does me a lot of good."

Phillip picked up the box. "I'll keep looking."

"I want a phone number."

"You'll get it."

The woman took a small bite of chocolate and looked at the

clock on the wall. Shelby couldn't guess her age. She held herself old but looked younger up close. The woman's fingernails were clipped short, pointed at the tips.

"It takes an effort to come down here from the hospital," she said. "I'm in pain a lot. Next time you come, bring some news."

"I brought you something better," said Phillip.

The woman looked at the package. "Open it then," said the woman. "My hands can't fool with that paper."

Phillip tore the wrap up the side, slipped out the cardboard box. Shelby sat with hands flat on the table, watched for some expression in the woman's face but found none. When he opened the top, he took out something wrapped in paper towels. He placed it in front of his mother.

She set her hands on the towels, pulled them away. A set of binoculars, small and black, pointed up at the ceiling.

"They're used," Phillip said. "Not too strong, but you can see out your window with them. Check out the stars at night."

"How much you pay for these?" the woman said.

"Not much."

"I don't have a window," she said. "Nobody's got a window here. What do you think this is? I only get out a few hours a day."

"You can use them then."

"Blind myself looking up at the sky? You blew your money, boy."

Phillip said nothing, kept his gaze on the binoculars, which the woman had not yet touched. He seemed to slip a little in his chair, seemed to want to disappear. Behind the woman, two of the guards broke from the huddle at the door, looked past them, spread out a bit.

"He went to a lot of trouble," said Shelby, and the woman turned her eyes toward her. "You should be more thankful."

"And you should wait for an invitation. This isn't any business of yours."

The woman's eyes were direct, seemed hateful. Shelby looked

away. In the silence between the three of them, they listened to the tables around them, the people. An argument, louder than theirs, had broken out in a corner, and the two guards circled toward the table, sized up the situation.

The woman lifted the binoculars, brought them to her eyes, looked up at the ceiling, the clock, then the guards. She turned the focus ring with her smallest finger, then pointed the lenses at Phillip. Shelby tried to see the woman's eyes through the lenses. The woman's teeth were yellow behind her lips.

"You've grown," she said.

In the cold and dark they made their way to the bus station, past the walls of the prison, the wire and the fencing, past the market and the stoplight. They turned left on Hawkins Street, moved from glow to glow beneath the streetlamps. Cars passed slowly on the rain-slick road. They seemed to be the only people on foot. Shelby watched her white breath cloud from under her hood, watched their reflections in puddles under the lamp glow. She reached out, took Phillip's arm, slowed him down. As they passed over each pool of water, she tried to bring herself and Phillip into focus, but they were moving too quickly, or Phillip would stamp his foot into the puddle. Circles spread from his boot step, blurred the reflections.

There was little left of the bus station, only a concrete shell and a pile of burned, broken furniture left against the side of a dumpster. The plot of land, what remained of the building, reminded Shelby of Bremerton. They seemed to be home again, but still far away. Out in the road, they could hear the rush of drain water in the gutters. Phillip pushed a cinder block over with his boot. They held hands and shivered in the dark.

Across the road was a car, parked facing the state road. Beyond it they could make the outline of the Olympics, could even smell the bay from where they stood. One of the backlights of the car flickered red, reflected against the water on the street.

They crossed the road, tried to see in through the fog. They hesitated, climbed into the backseat, shut the door behind them. It was eight o'clock.

Otis was leaning forward, against the wheel, flicking the back of the paper frog on the dash. The creature jumped at each flick, knocking against the windshield, falling on its side after. Otis set it back upright and flicked again. They listened to the tap against the glass.

Eventually, he turned, put his arm up on the seat next to him, held the frog between his fingertips. He looked at them with his two eyes, both big, one damaged.

"How'd it go?" he said.

They set their hands in their laps, looked there, listened to the rush of rainwater outside, felt a pain in their fingertips as their hands began to warm. The glow from the dashboard lit the car—the seats, the vinyl ceiling, the windows—in a dull green and white. Otis waited, looked at the frog, at the creases and folds.

"This guy didn't want to sit still," he said.

CONTRIBUTORS

GAIL GALLOWAY ADAMS is the author of *The Purchase of Order*, which received the 1987 Flannery O'Connor Award for Short Fiction. She is a professor emeritus at West Virginia University, where she taught creative writing for over twenty years. Adams served as fiction editor for *Arts and Letters: A Literary Journal* and for the *Potomac Review*. She has been a reader/judge for several short fiction awards series. She has recently taught at Kenyon College, West Virginia Wesleyan College, and the Wild Acres Writers Workshop. She also works privately as a short story and novel editorial consultant and lives in Tallahassee, Florida.

GEOFFREY BECKER is the author of *Black Elvis*, which received the 2008 Flannery O'Connor Award for Short Fiction. He is also the author of one previous collection, *Dangerous Men*, and the novels *Hot Springs* and *Bluestown*. His story "Black Elvis" was selected by E. L. Doctorow for *The Best American Short Stories 2000*. Becker is a professor of English at Towson University.

DANIEL CURLEY (1918–1988) was the author of *Living with Snakes*, which won the 1984 Flannery O'Connor Award for Short Fiction. He was one of the editors of *Accent* and founded and edited its offspring *Ascent* from 1974 until his death in 1988. In addition to three novels and several collections of short stories, he wrote criticism, poetry, plays, and three books for children. A posthumous collection, *The Curandero*, was published in 1991.

PHILIP F. DEAVER (1946–2018) was the author of *Silent Retreats*, which won the 1987 Flannery O'Connor Award, as well as the poetry collection *How Men Pray* and the novel *Forty Martyrs*. His short fiction was published in such literary journals as the *Florida Review*, the *Kenyon Review*, the *New England Review*, and the *Missouri Review*. It was also anthologized in *Prize Stories: The O. Henry Awards*, *Best American Short Stories*, *Best American Catholic Short Stories*, and *Bottom of the Ninth: Great Contemporary Baseball Short Stories*. Deaver taught in the English Department at Rollins College and was permanent writer in residence there. He was also on the fiction faculty in the Spalding University brief residency MFA program.

DENNIS HATHAWAY is the author of *The Consequences of Desire*, which received the 1992 Flannery O'Connor Award for Short Fiction. He grew up on an Iowa farm and now lives with his wife in Venice, California. His short stories have appeared in a number of literary magazines, including *TriQuarterly*, the *Georgia Review*, and the *Southwest Review*. He has been a journalist, building contractor, and head of the Los Angeles–based Coalition to Ban Billboard Blight. He was the founding editor of *Crania*, an online literary magazine, and taught fiction writing at the University of California, Los Angeles. He is also the author of *The Taste of Flesh*, a collection of poetry.

MARY HOOD is the author of *How Far She Went*, a winner of the 1983 Flannery O'Connor Award for Short Fiction, *Familiar Heat*, *And Venus Is Blue*, and *A Clear View of the Southern Sky*. Her work has been published in the *Georgia Review*, *North American Review*, and *Yankee*, among other publications. She was inducted into the Georgia Writers Hall of Fame in 2014.

TOM KEALEY is the author of *Thieves I've Known*, which received the 2012 Flannery O'Connor Award for Short Fiction. He is also the author of *The Creative Writing MFA Handbook*. His stories have appeared in *Best American Nonrequired Reading*, *Glimmer Train*, *Story Quarterly*, *Prairie Schooner*, and the *San Francisco Chronicle*. His nonfiction has appeared in *Poets and Writers* and *The Writer*. He received his MFA in creative writing from the University of Massachusetts Amherst, where he received the Distinguished Teaching Award. Tom is a former Stegner Fellow and has taught creative writing at Stanford University since 2003.

PETER LASALLE, 2006 Flannery O'Connor Award for Short Fiction winner for *Tell Borges If You See Him*, is the author of eight previous books, including both novels and short story collections—most recently *Sleeping Mask: Fictions* and *The City at Three P.M.: Writing, Reading, and Traveling*. His fiction and essays have been selected for several award anthologies, including *Best American Short Stories*, *Best American Mystery Sto-*

ries, *Best American Fantasy*, *Best American Travel Writing*, *Sports Best Short Stories*, *Best of the West*, and *Prize Stories: The O. Henry Awards*. He lives in Austin, Texas, where he is a member of the creative writing faculty at the University of Texas, and Narragansett, in his native Rhode Island.

E. J. LEVY is the author of *Love, in Theory*, which received the 2011 Flannery O'Connor Award for Short Fiction and the Great Lakes Colleges Association's New Writers Award. Her work has appeared in the *Paris Review*, the *Missouri Review*, the *Gettysburg Review*, the *New York Times*, and *Best American Essays* and has received a Pushcart Prize and Nelson Algren Finalist Award, among other honors. She is also the author of the memoir *Amazons: A Love Story* and editor of *Tasting Life Twice: Literary Lesbian Fiction by New American Writers*, which won the Lambda Literary Award. Levy teaches in the MFA Program at Colorado State University.

SUSAN NEVILLE is the author of six works of creative nonfiction: *Fabrication: Essays on Making Things and Making Meaning*, *Twilight in Arcadia*, *Iconography: A Writer's Meditation*, *Butler's Big Dance*, *Sailing the Inland Sea*, and *Light*. Her short story collection *The Invention of Flight* received the 1983 Flannery O'Connor Award for Short Fiction, and her collection *In the House of Blue Lights* won the Richard Sullivan Prize and was listed as a Notable Book by the *Chicago Tribune*. Her stories have appeared in many anthologies, including the Pushcart Prize anthology. Neville teaches writing at Butler University and in the Warren Wilson MFA Program for Writers.

DIANNE NELSON OBERHANSLY is the author of *A Brief History of Male Nudes in America*, which received the 1992 Flannery O'Connor Award for Short Fiction. She is also the coauthor of the novel *Downwinders: An Atomic Tale*, and her fiction has appeared in the *Iowa Review*, *Ploughshares*, and the *New England Review*.

LORI OSTLUND's first collection of stories, *The Bigness of the World*, received the 2008 Flannery O'Connor Award for Short Fiction, the California Book Award for First Fiction, and the Edmund White Debut Fiction Award. It was shortlisted for the William Saroyan International Prize for Writing, was a Lambda finalist, and was named a Notable Book by the Short Story Prize. Her stories have appeared in the *Best American Short Stories*, the *PEN/O. Henry Prize Stories*, *ZYZZYVA*, the *Georgia Review*, the

Kenyon Review, and *New England Review*, among other publications. In 2009, Lori received a Rona Jaffe Foundation Award. She is the author of the novel *After the Parade* and lives in San Francisco.

ANNE PANNING is the author of *Super America*, which received the 2006 Flannery O'Connor Award for Short Fiction, as well as another short story collection, a novel, and a memoir. She teaches creative writing at SUNY-Brockport and is codirector of the Brockport Writers Forum reading series.

MELISSA PRITCHARD is the author of twelve books, including a biography and collection of essays. Her first short story collection, *Spirit Seizures*, won the 1988 Flannery O'Connor Award for Short Fiction, the Carl Sandburg Award, and the James Phelan Award from the San Francisco Foundation, and it was named a *New York Times* Editor's Choice and Notable Book of the Year. A five-time winner of *Pushcart* and *O. Henry Prizes* and consistently cited in *Best American Short Stories*, Melissa has published fiction and non-fiction in such literary journals, anthologies, textbooks, magazines as the *Paris Review*, *Ploughshares*, *A Public Space*, *Conjunctions*, *Agni*, *Ecotone*, the *Gettysburg Review*, *O, The Oprah Magazine*, the *Nation*, the *New York Times* and the *Chicago Tribune*. A recent Marguerite and Lamar Smith Fellow at the Carson McCullers Center for Writers and Musicians in Columbus, Georgia, Melissa has recently completely a novel, *Tempest: The Extraordinary Life of Fanny Kemble*, that will be published in 2021.

MARGOT SINGER is the author of *The Pale of Settlement*, which received the 2006 Flannery O'Connor Award for Short Fiction, as well as a novel, *Underground Fugue*, winner of the 2017 Edward Lewis Wallant Award and finalist for the 2019 Sami Rohr Prize for Jewish Fiction. She is also the coeditor, with Nicole Walker, of *Bending Genre: Essays on Creative Nonfiction*. Her stories and essays have appeared in many literary magazines. She is a professor of English and creative writing at Denison University in Granville, Ohio.

SANDRA THOMPSON is a native of Chicago and a graduate of Ohio Wesleyan University and Brooklyn College, where she received her MFA. She lives in Tampa, Florida.

THE FLANNERY O'CONNOR AWARD
FOR SHORT FICTION

DAVID WALTON, *Evening Out*
LEIGH ALLISON WILSON, *From the Bottom Up*
SANDRA THOMPSON, *Close-Ups*
SUSAN NEVILLE, *The Invention of Flight*
MARY HOOD, *How Far She Went*
FRANÇOIS CAMOIN, *Why Men Are Afraid of Women*
MOLLY GILES, *Rough Translations*
DANIEL CURLEY, *Living with Snakes*
PETER MEINKE, *The Piano Tuner*
TONY ARDIZZONE, *The Evening News*
SALVATORE LA PUMA, *The Boys of Bensonhurst*
MELISSA PRITCHARD, *Spirit Seizures*
PHILIP F. DEAVER, *Silent Retreats*
GAIL GALLOWAY ADAMS, *The Purchase of Order*
CAROLE L. GLICKFELD, *Useful Gifts*
ANTONYA NELSON, *The Expendables*
NANCY ZAFRIS, *The People I Know*
DEBRA MONROE, *The Source of Trouble*
ROBERT ABEL, *Ghost Traps*
T. M. MCNALLY, *Low Flying Aircraft*
ALFRED DEPEW, *The Melancholy of Departure*
DENNIS HATHAWAY, *The Consequences of Desire*
RITA CIRESI, *Mother Rocket*
DIANNE NELSON OBERHANSLY, *A Brief History of Male Nudes in America*
CHRISTOPHER MCILROY, *All My Relations*
ALYCE MILLER, *The Nature of Longing*
CAROL LEE LORENZO, *Nervous Dancer*
C. M. MAYO, *Sky over El Nido*
WENDY BRENNER, *Large Animals in Everyday Life*
PAUL RAWLINS, *No Lie Like Love*
HARVEY GROSSINGER, *The Quarry*
HA JIN, *Under the Red Flag*
ANDY PLATTNER, *Winter Money*
FRANK SOOS, *Unified Field Theory*
MARY CLYDE, *Survival Rates*

HESTER KAPLAN, *The Edge of Marriage*
DARRELL SPENCER, *CAUTION Men in Trees*
ROBERT ANDERSON, *Ice Age*
BILL ROORBACH, *Big Bend*
DANA JOHNSON, *Break Any Woman Down*
GINA OCHSNER, *The Necessary Grace to Fall*
KELLIE WELLS, *Compression Scars*
ERIC SHADE, *Eyesores*
CATHERINE BRADY, *Curled in the Bed of Love*
ED ALLEN, *Ate It Anyway*
GARY FINCKE, *Sorry I Worried You*
BARBARA SUTTON, *The Send-Away Girl*
DAVID CROUSE, *Copy Cats*
RANDY F. NELSON, *The Imaginary Lives of Mechanical Men*
GREG DOWNS, *Spit Baths*
PETER LASALLE, *Tell Borges If You See Him: Tales of Contemporary Somnambulism*
ANNE PANNING, *Super America*
MARGOT SINGER, *The Pale of Settlement*
ANDREW PORTER, *The Theory of Light and Matter*
PETER SELGIN, *Drowning Lessons*
GEOFFREY BECKER, *Black Elvis*
LORI OSTLUND, *The Bigness of the World*
LINDA LEGARDE GROVER, *The Dance Boots*
JESSICA TREADWAY, *Please Come Back To Me*
AMINA GAUTIER, *At-Risk*
MELINDA MOUSTAKIS, *Bear Down, Bear North*
E. J. LEVY, *Love, in Theory*
HUGH SHEEHY, *The Invisibles*
JACQUELIN GORMAN, *The Viewing Room*
TOM KEALEY, *Thieves I've Known*
KARIN LIN-GREENBERG, *Faulty Predictions*
MONICA MCFAWN, *Bright Shards of Someplace Else*
TONI GRAHAM, *The Suicide Club*
SIAMAK VOSSOUGHI, *Better Than War*
LISA GRALEY, *The Current That Carries*
ANNE RAEFF, *The Jungle around Us*
BECKY MANDELBAUM, *Bad Kansas*

KIRSTEN SUNDBERG LUNSTRUM, *What We Do with the Wreckage*

COLETTE SARTOR, *Once Removed*

PATRICK EARL RYAN, *If We Were Electric*

ANNIVERSARY ANTHOLOGIES

TENTH ANNIVERSARY

The Flannery O'Connor Award: Selected Stories, EDITED BY CHARLES EAST

FIFTEENTH ANNIVERSARY

Listening to the Voices: Stories from the Flannery O'Connor Award, EDITED BY CHARLES EAST

THIRTIETH ANNIVERSARY

Stories from the Flannery O'Connor Award: A 30th Anniversary Anthology: The Early Years, EDITED BY CHARLES EAST

Stories from the Flannery O'Connor Award: A 30th Anniversary Anthology: The Recent Years, EDITED BY NANCY ZAFRIS

THEMATIC ANTHOLOGIES

Hold That Knowledge: Stories about Love from the Flannery O'Connor Award for Short Fiction, EDITED BY ETHAN LAUGHMAN

The Slow Release: Stories about Death from the Flannery O'Connor Award for Short Fiction, EDITED BY ETHAN LAUGHMAN

Rituals to Observe: Stories about Holidays from the Flannery O'Connor Award for Short Fiction, EDITED BY ETHAN LAUGHMAN

Spinning Away from the Center: Stories about Homesickness and Homecoming from the Flannery O'Connor Award for Short Fiction, EDITED BY ETHAN LAUGHMAN

Good and Balanced: Stories about Sports from the Flannery O'Connor Award for Short Fiction, EDITED BY ETHAN LAUGHMAN

Down on the Sidewalk: Stories about Children and Childhood from the Flannery O'Connor Award for Short Fiction,
EDITED BY ETHAN LAUGHMAN

A Day's Pay: Stories about Work from the Flannery O'Connor Award for Short Fiction,
EDITED BY ETHAN LAUGHMAN

A Perfect Souvenir: Stories about Travel from the Flannery O'Connor Award for Short Fiction,
EDITED BY ETHAN LAUGHMAN

CPSIA information can be obtained
at www.ICGtesting.com
Printed in the USA
LVHW092356140820
663097LV00011B/331